Praise for *Discord's Apple*

"[A] uniquely intense and edgy feel. Make sure you take a bite!"
—*RT Book Reviews*

"A most remarkable book, original and compelling with strong, sympathetic characters . . . I certainly could not stop reading it."
—Roberta Gellis, author of *Fortune's Bride*

"Myths, magic, and mayhem abound in Carrie Vaughn's *Discord's Apple*. Once you take a bite, you won't be able to put it down."
—Lori Handeland, *New York Times* bestselling author of *Apocalypse Happens*

"Carrie Vaughn masterfully weaves together comic books, Greek gods, King Arthur, and a world on the brink of nuclear war. *Discord's Apple* is phenomenal!"
—Jackie Kessler, coauthor of *Shades of Gray*

"With *Discord's Apple* Carrie Vaughn has created an engaging modern addition to the world of Greek myth. Vaughn has a powerful gift for marrying the mythic and the mundane to produce the extraordinary. Like Vaughn's Kitty Norville, Evie Walker is a thoroughly believable young woman coping with problems that range from the utterly real (her father's terminal illness) to the absolutely surreal (Homer's Odyssey has decided to come for a visit). The result is a voyage of discovery that will make the reader very glad they didn't miss the boat."

—Kelly McCullough, author of *WebMage* and *MythOS*

Discord's Apple

CARRIE VAUGHN

A TOM DOHERTY ASSOCIATES BOOK
NEW YORK

DISCORD'S APPLE

Copyright © 2010 by Carrie Vaughn, LLC

All rights reserved.

A Tor Book
Published by Tom Doherty Associates, LLC
175 Fifth Avenue
New York, NY 10010

www.tor-forge.com

Tor® is a registered trademark of Tom Doherty Associates, LLC.

ISBN 978-0-7653-6459-3

First Edition: July 2010
First Mass Market Edition: March 2011

Printed in the United States of America

0 9 8 7 6 5 4 3 2 1

To the memory of the two people
whose passings in 2002 made this story happen:

My grandfather, Robert Lee Vaughn

My great aunt, Rose Matern Pearl

ACKNOWLEDGMENTS

All these people helped in various ways to put this book in your hands: Jo Anne and Larry Vaughn, Rob and Deb Vaughn, Al and Mary Linder, Max Campanella, Michael Bateman, Stacy Hague-Hill, David Hartwell, Dan Hooker, Ashley Grayson, and Carolyn Grayson. And, tangentially, though I didn't even know it at the time: J. Michael Straczynski, Jessica Steen, Larry Hama, Peter Jackson, Anonymous 4, Edith Hamilton, and, of course, Virgil.

Discord's Apple

I

※

Finally, after driving all night, Evie arrived.

Close to town, bells and candy canes made of faded tinsel decorated the telephone poles. The same decorations had hung on the poles every year for as long as Evie could remember; they had no sparkle left. Or maybe she was too tired to notice. In the last two days, she'd only had a nap outside Albuquerque.

Hopes Fort, Colorado, was one of those small towns that dotted the Great Plains, where Main Street turned into the state highway and the post office was attached to the feed store. Hopes Fort had been dying, one boarded-up building at a time, for the last fifty years. Still, somehow the town held on, like the aged relative whose chronic illness never seemed to worsen despite all predictions to the contrary. The holiday decorations, no matter how tattered, still went up every year.

Her phone beeped, and she hooked the hands-free over her ear.

Bruce scratched at her on the other end of the connection. "Evie?"

"Bruce, speak up. The connection's funky."

"Have you seen the news?" Panic edged his voice. She'd been out of L.A. for only two days—what dire crisis could possibly have struck?

"No, I've been driving all day."

"You haven't even listened to the radio?"

"No." Rather than try to find radio reception while driving through the wilds of Arizona and New Mexico, she'd depended on her digital player.

He made a noise like a deflating balloon. "The Kremlin's been bombed. Obliterated. A Cessna filled with drums of kerosene rammed it. They're thinking it's Mongolian rebels."

She took a moment to register that he was talking about current events and not a plot point in their comic book. "Then our May storyline is out the window."

The Eagle Eye Commandos couldn't raid the building complex if it wasn't there. She should have seen this one coming.

"Yeah. Unless we can put some kind of 'how things might have been' spin on it."

"We did that when India and Pakistan dropped nukes on each other. Why don't we do Westerns like everyone else?"

"Because we got a letter from the President thanking us for our patriotic creativity."

"I didn't even vote for him."

"Then maybe it's because we sold half a million copies last year."

"Oh yeah." She pressed her head back on the headrest, stretching her arms against the steering wheel. She had to drive all the way through town to get to the farmland on the other side, where the family's house was. The town looked desolate; she hadn't seen anyone even walking around. "At least the issue hasn't gone to press yet. So. The Kremlin's been bombed. The Eagle Eyes can still raid it. They just have to search the rubble. We'll look really up to date."

It sounded silly, but then all *Eagle Eye Commandos* storylines started out silly. Working them through to the end with some degree of earnestness transformed them somehow, from adolescent military fantasies to—well, sophisticated military fantasies. They could search the rubble for . . . for hidden evidence on the whereabouts of captured American spies, which was what the original storyline had them looking for. They wouldn't have to change a thing. Except all those gorgeous panels Bruce had drawn of Red Square would have to go.

"I'm going to have to redraw the entire book, aren't I?"

"I'll e-mail you a new script in a day or two."

"Yeah. How's your dad?"

She let out a sigh. "I haven't seen him yet."

"Well, good luck."

"Thanks."

She clicked off her phone and rubbed her eyes.

The Tastee-Freez where she'd spent so much time in high school was gone, the ice cream cone sign on its pole dismantled. Nothing had moved in to replace it. The hokey ice cream stand had been the only place to hang out, unless one of your friends had a car to drive into Pueblo, an hour away. More kids must have cars these days. Or Hopes Fort had fewer kids.

Since high school, she'd only been back here for holidays, when the town was at its bleakest. No wonder it always depressed her. But maybe she wasn't being fair.

Halfway down Main Street, a cop had set up a roadblock: a single hazard barricade pulled into the middle of the pavement. The one officer manning the checkpoint climbed out of the car, which was parked on the curb, and held up his hand, directing her to slow down.

Smiling, she stopped and rolled down her window. "Well, Officer. You got me."

"Evie Walker? Hell, it's been *years*!"

He wore a starched blue uniform, but the blond crew cut and bulky shoulders were the same. Johnny Brewster had been a linebacker in high school. He'd gotten a little rounder in the middle since then.

"Who thought giving you a badge was a good idea?"

"Me and some of the guys had a little too much to drink and drew straws. I got the short one."

"Ouch."

"Can I get you to pop your trunk while we talk?"

Checkpoint searches. In Hopes Fort.

Amused, she popped the trunk lever, then climbed out of the car. She put her hands in the pockets of her green canvas army surplus jacket and leaned against the door while Johnny opened the trunk door and made a survey of the contents: two filled gas cans, blankets, a roadside emergency kit, and odd bits of travel detritus. Her suitcase and a few gallon jugs of water were in the backseat.

"Thanks," he said. "A lot of folks aren't this under-standing."

"I'm the last person to complain about security."

He looked away and muttered, "I guess so."

With better checkpoints, her mother might still be alive.

"You have a permit for the extra gas?"

She'd brought the gas because she hadn't wanted to face fuel rationing or closed gas stations on the drive across the desert. The slip of paper was in her glove box. "I didn't think security restrictions would be in effect out here."

"Rules are rules. We have to keep track of people coming in and out of town."

"So shouldn't you have roadblocks at either end of Main Street?"

He shrugged, unconcerned. "We only have enough people for one checkpoint."

"They have *real* checkpoints in L.A.," she said. And lots of them, at every major exit and interchange. It sometimes took all day to get from Pomona to Hollywood.

"I bet. They also have a reason for 'em. I don't know how you stand it." He slammed closed the trunk. "How's your dad?"

This was Hopes Fort: everybody must have known about him. "I haven't seen him yet. You probably know better than I do."

"He *says* he's fine."

That sounded like her father—always cheerful. "I should probably get out there."

Johnny pulled the barrier out of the way (L.A. had

automated titanium barriers) while she got back in the car.

"Thanks, Johnny."

For three generations, the Walker family had lived in a brick ranch house on a few acres of prairie. Evie's grandfather had grown up on the farm the land used to be part of. The farm had long since been broken up and sold, except for the token parcel and the house to which her grandparents had retired. They'd died when Evie was in college. Evie's father had lived in town and worked as a mail carrier until five years ago, when he took his own place in rural retirement.

Evie still thought of it as her grandparents' house, a place she went to for holidays and backyard adventures. Her father hadn't changed it much when he moved in—he took over the furniture, the heirlooms, the pictures on the wall, the shelves full of books. At first, Evie had had trouble thinking of her father as anything more than a house sitter there. But over the last couple years, when she noticed that his hair was gray and that he had started wearing bifocals, he reminded her more and more of her grandparents. He had stopped being a visitor and metamorphosed into the house's proper resident.

She was his only child, and the house would come to her someday. By the time she retired, there'd be nothing left of Hopes Fort and no reason to be here. Except it had been the place where her grandfather and father had grown up. She supposed that meant something.

Later in the afternoon than she'd planned, she pulled into the long driveway behind her father's twenty-year-old rusting blue pickup. Out of habit, she locked her car, even though this was possibly the one place in the universe she could comfortably leave it unlocked. The house itself was well cared for, neat if unremarkable. It had a carport at the end of the driveway rather than a garage, screened windows, a small front porch, and an expansive front yard with a lawn of dried prairie grasses. She'd driven by a dozen places just like it to get here.

A dog, a huge bristling wolfhound-looking thing, sprang from the front porch, barking loud and deep like a growling bear.

Evie almost turned and ran. Her father didn't have a dog.

The front door opened and Frank Walker appeared, looking out over the driveway. "Mab! Come, Mab, it's all right."

The dog stopped barking and trotted back to him, throwing suspicious glances over its shoulder.

He scratched the dog's ears and took hold of the ruff of fur at its neck. "Come on up, Evie. Mab just gets a little excited."

Cautiously, Evie continued to the porch. She had to lift her arm to show the animal the back of her hand—the thing's head came up to her waist. The dog sniffed her hand, then started wagging its tail. Evie hoped it didn't try jumping on her—it would be a body-slam.

"Meet Queen Mab," her father said.

"When did you get a dog?"

"She was a stray. Showed up on the porch a while back. Since I caught a couple of prowlers last month, I thought having Mab around might be a good thing."

"Prowlers? Out here?"

"Oh, prowlers, salesmen—you'd be surprised how many visitors I get."

In fact, someone was standing in the doorway behind him.

He wore a black leather duster and carried a large paper-wrapped package in both arms. Edging around Evie's father, he looked suspiciously at Evie.

Frank said to him, "If you won't be needing anything else, you'll probably want to get going before nightfall."

"Right. Thanks for your help." He nodded at Evie as he passed. "Ma'am."

He had an unplaceable accent, almost New England, almost West Texas. Wire-rimmed spectacles rode low on a long nose. He might have dressed himself out of a studio costume shop rummage sale. Playing the part of the doomed hero in a historical horror film.

The stranger walked down the gravel driveway, the light breeze licking the hem of his duster. There wasn't another car. No buses ran this way. Where did he think he was going?

"Who was that?" Evie said.

"He came for something in the storeroom."

"You're selling Grandma and Grandpa's stuff?" As far as she knew, the basement storeroom hadn't been disturbed since her grandparents' time. The place was dusty and sacred, like a museum vault. She'd never even been in it. As a kid, she hadn't been allowed in there; then she'd moved away.

"Oh, no," he said. "He just showed up and asked if I had what he needed. I did, so I gave it to him."

"What was it?"

"Nothing important."

Evie looked at her father, really looked at him. She searched for any sign of illness, any hint that gave credence to his announcement of two days ago. His phone call had sent her roaring out of Los Angeles the next morning. She didn't know what to expect, if she would find him changed beyond recognition, withered and defeated, or if he would be—like this. Like normal, like she had always seen him: a little over average height, filled out through the middle but not overweight, straight gray hair cut short, his soft face creased with age, but not ancient. He wore slacks and a button-up shirt, and went stocking-footed.

"Come in out of the cold." He held the door open for her. A lonely wicker wreath decorated it, a solitary concession to the holiday.

He might have been paler. Were his hands shaking? Was his back stooped? She couldn't tell. She went inside.

"Dad. Are you okay?"

He shrugged. That told her. If he'd been fine, or even just okay, he'd have said so.

"Should . . . should you be in the hospital or something?"

"No. I have to stay here and keep an eye on things."

"What is there to keep an eye on? No farm, no animals—" Except the dog, which was new. Her voice was beseeching. "Are you okay?"

"It's metastasized. I've decided not to undergo treatment."

He said it like he might have said it was going to snow. Simple fact, a little anticipation, but nothing to get excited about. Evie thought her rib cage might burst, the way her heart pounded. Her father stood before her; he hadn't changed. Everything had changed. *It's prostate cancer. It's serious,* he'd said when he called her. She wanted to grab his collar and shake him. But you didn't do that to your father.

So she stood there like a child and whined.

"You've given up," she said.

"I've accepted fate."

"But—" She gestured aimlessly, arguments failing in her throat. He wasn't going to argue. He was stone, not willing to be persuaded. "But you can't do that. You can't—"

"I can't what?" he said, and he had the gall to smile. "I can't die?"

She didn't believe him then. For a moment, she let herself believe that he'd been lying about the whole thing. This was a trick to get her to come early for her Christmas visit. He didn't look sick, he didn't act sick, except for a horrible calm that made his features still as ice.

Evie turned away, her eyes stinging, her face contorting with the effort not to cry.

"Shh, Evie, come here." While she didn't move toward him, she didn't resist when he pulled her into an embrace.

"You can't die without trying," she said, her voice breaking, muffled as she spoke into his shoulder.

"I'll hold on as long as I can."

He made supper for her—macaroni and cheese. He'd never been a creative cook. *Comfort food, my ass,* she thought. She didn't eat much. Her stomach clenched every time she looked at him.

They stayed up late talking. He asked her about her work, and she rambled on about the comics business, the stress of deadlines, and the frustrations of markets and distribution. When she talked, she wasn't thinking about him. She settled into the guest room with the wood-frame twin bed that she'd slept in when she visited her grandparents, the bed that had been her father's when he was young. She didn't sleep right away, but lay curled up, hugging the goose-down pillow, feeling small—ten years old again.

He hadn't asked her to come home. He'd called to tell her he was sick, and she'd just come. That was what you did. He didn't argue or try to tell her she didn't have to. Which, when she thought about it, was another sign that he really was sick. He hadn't yet said, *I'm fine, don't worry about me. Nothing to worry about.*

What neither of them hadn't explicitly said, what she hadn't understood until she was lying there in the dark, nested in the bed that made her feel like a child, in the room next to the room where her father lay dying by increments, was that she was here to help him die. She would stay until he was gone, whether it took weeks or months or—maybe?—years, and then she would be alone with the house and the dark.

She missed her mother at that moment. She missed her mother all the time, really, but the longing was the phantom ache of an amputated limb. It was part of her, and most of the time she didn't notice. But certain moments were like reaching for something with a hand that wasn't there. Evie wanted to run to her mother and cry, make her talk sense into Dad, make *her* stay with him and watch him die. But it was left to Evie to do by herself.

She wasn't ready to lose her father, too. She'd be crippled all over again.

2

"If they're going to believe that I escaped your plan to sacrifice me, I'll have to look like a prisoner," Sinon said.

"I've thought of this." Odysseus had stood so proudly before the war chieftains, not at all cowed by their wealth or power. He made no secret that he thought most of them vain and petty. He had wanted to let Helen rot in Troy and blame Menelaus for letting Paris carry her off.

Now he looked grim, preoccupied with the details of his plan. His gaze turned inward, and his face was furrowed with worry. Sinon thought, *This is what he will look like as an old man.*

Sinon had come to Troy a boy, an untried warrior wearing his first growth of beard and carrying his first spear. Under Odysseus's command, he had grown to manhood, shed his first blood, seen his own blood shed, learned of honor. And of common sense. He would follow Odysseus to the end of time itself.

"Maybe we could get Neoptolemus to have at me." Sinon grinned, meaning it as a joke.

Odysseus shook his head quickly. "I don't trust that vicious whelp to know when to stop. I had planned on doing it myself."

Of course. Odysseus planned for everything, and he hated asking other men to do the difficult work.

Sinon and Odysseus went some distance along the beach, away from camp, where they could have privacy. The camp itself was in chaos—hundreds of tents being brought down, horses being loaded onto ships, supplies packed and carried off, all by torchlight. More than that, the sound of construction—men hammering hundreds of planks of wood into place—overwhelmed even the sound of waves breaking.

This was all part of the plan.

They stopped along the river that poured from the hills above Troy to form a brackish marsh where it joined the sea. Here, the rolling waves and chatter of night insects were audible again.

An escaped prisoner would have rope burns around his wrists. Sinon stripped down to a thin tunic. Odysseus tied his hands with rope and bound his wrists to a post driven into the beach.

Pulling on leather gloves to protect his hands, Odysseus said, "I don't want to do this, Sinon."

"I know. But it must be done."

"A few choice bruises. A black eye. That's all."

Sinon nodded and squared his shoulders, bracing.

His jaw clenched, Odysseus made a fist and backhanded Sinon. His head whipped back as he fell, his arms jerking on the bindings.

Over and over, Odysseus struck him. Sinon had been hit before, he'd been wounded in battle. He knew how to block pain. Keep breathing. No matter that his ears rang and that blood clogged his nose. It would be over soon.

Sinon flinched back when Odysseus grabbed his hair to hold his head up.

"Easy, there. I'm done. Priam himself will pity you."

He tried to smile, but winced when his lip cracked. His left eye was swelling shut already. "You hit like a thunderbolt. I'm glad you're on our side."

"Gods, you're bleeding."

"I thought that was what we wanted."

"Save your breath for the Trojans, my friend. Let's have a look at your hands."

The ropes had made bleeding rashes around both his wrists. Odysseus brought a waterskin and made him drink, but they didn't wash the wounds. Let them swell, blacken, and look as grisly as possible.

The pain would put truth into his voice.

Time was passing. The ships had already set sail, carrying the bulk of the army into hiding. The horse was ready. Odysseus needed to take his place among the warriors hiding inside.

"Wait in the swamps. At dawn's first light, make for the city gates. If they suspect the horse, if they destroy it—and us—you may still live. They may still believe your story and spare you."

"No—"

"If so, you must go back to Ithaca and tell Penelope I'm sorry that I could not return."

That task, bringing news of Odysseus's death to his wife, was more daunting than lying to a city full of Trojans.

"This will work," Sinon said to his mentor.

Odysseus took Sinon's face in his hands. "I will see you again inside the walls of Troy."

"Inside the walls of Troy. Yes."

Odysseus left him.

Sinon splashed water from the river on his face to clear blood from his nose, mouth, and beard, and to keep himself awake. The bruises and cuts would heal—Odysseus had calculated the blows to look awful without causing permanent damage. Ever an optimist. His head ached, but he didn't dare lie down and sleep. Timing was everything. He had to be at the gates before the Trojans could make a decision about the horse. He had to be there to convince them. His tunic was spattered with dirt and blood. He certainly looked the part of an escaped sacrifice victim.

Just before dawn, he started the walk. He wanted to be sure he had enough time to reach the city. The gates looked far away.

Sunlight crossed the sky when he saw the finished horse for the first time.

Taller than the city gate, it stood like a war steed preparing for a charge, head held high, body stout. It was made of planks lashed together, darker wood making a harness, hooves, and glaring eyes. An immense sculpture, it appeared seamless. Sinon couldn't see a trapdoor or any sign that it was hollow at all. It stood on a wheeled platform, a tempting prize to simply roll inside the walls.

The city of Troy with its great temples and palaces, all shining marble decked with gold, occupied a set of hills and dominated the plains around it. Invincible stone walls surrounded it, and for ten years, the Achaeans had thrown themselves uselessly at those walls. The morning sun rose behind it to form a halo, and cast golden light on the prize the Trojans would never be able to resist.

By the gods, this could work.

Trojans were already gathered around the horse. They'd awakened to a sight they had not seen in ten years: the beach clear of Greek boats, the camp of the Achaean army empty. The invaders had fled. The Trojans had immediately come out to explore. As if disbelieving their eyes, they had to walk the ground to convince themselves the Greeks were really gone.

A pair of soldiers on patrol found him creeping along the outer wall. "You! Greek! Hold there!"

He waited for them to catch him. They did so as brutally as he might have expected of a people who'd been under siege, throwing him to the ground, kicking him, reopening the cuts and waking the bruises Odysseus had given him. When they drew daggers, Sinon thought they would kill him right there, ruining the plan entirely. But he begged like the piteous exile he was playing, and they put their knives away. Mindless of his wounds, they bound him and dragged him to the gates, where the lords and priests of Troy waited.

Think of the story. Tell them the story.

"We found a Greek dog skulking on the beach," one of the soldiers said, and shoved Sinon to the ground.

He struggled to his knees and got his bearings. The horse towered above, casting its morning shadow over the sand. The crowd that had gathered formed a circle around a tall man draped in a purple robe. He was old, but held himself proudly, and wore a silver band on his nearly bald head. This had to be Priam, King of the Trojans.

Sinon caught his eye. He would speak to this man alone.

He spat, scowling with hatred. "I am no Greek. Not anymore."

Priam looked down on him. "Explain yourself."

The story. The pain of betrayal. The wounds on his wrists. "They needed to make a sacrifice to bring fair winds for their journey. A human sacrifice of blood, since that was how they won fair winds for their departure. Odysseus—" He snarled when he said the name, as if it had a sour taste. "—has always hated me since I served his rival, Palomedes. He tricked the Greeks into murdering him, and now came his chance to kill me. He named me as the sacrifice. But I escaped. They had to sail with the tide and could not chase after me." He gasped, short of breath, and bowed his head. "My lord, you are my only hope of shelter now."

His guards shifted behind him, gripping weapons they didn't dare raise. They weren't happy with his story. But others of the crowd murmured, "Butchers!" and "Poor man."

Priam's frown deepened. His voice was gentle. "You have been ill-used. Do you truly hate them now?"

Sinon's face contorted with pain. "I do."

"Untie him." The guards cut the ropes. Sinon slumped, relieved. "We can give you shelter here. If you tell us what they meant to do with this." Priam gestured at the horse. "Is it truly an offering as the inscription says? Or is it another Greek trick?"

The bait was set. The trap must close. His story must be true.

He chuckled, wiping at saliva that dripped down his numb chin. "The oracles revealed that Pallas Athena was angry at the theft of the Palladium from her temple. And they thought that a good prank at the time. They built this to appease her."

"Why did they make it so large?"

He did not have to pretend to wince in pain. The cut on his lip stung. He was still kneeling in the dust, his back bowed. "Because—because they did not want you to carry it inside the city. That would turn Fortune toward you and your city and away from them. They hoped that you would destroy it, and bring Athena's anger onto yourselves."

He spoke knowingly, wryly, as if to say, *The Greeks are fools to think they could trick you so. You know the truth when you hear it.* He spoke to convince them: *I am truth. You believe they'd do this to me because you believe they're treacherous dogs. I am easy to believe.*

They nodded among themselves, whispering, glancing at the horse with covetous eyes. Sinon knelt before them, a broken man without pride, without hope, with nothing to lose by telling them the truth.

He should have been a bard.

A woman fought to the front of the crowd.

She was young and wore the white robes of a priestess. Her skin was pure, shining with beauty. Gold cords laced her black hair, binding back the thick curls.

"No! Father, no!" At last she broke free from the hands that tried to hold her back. She clutched at Priam, tugging his sleeve, clawing at his arm. "Father, it's a trick! Don't listen to him, he is lying, it's a trick, the greatest trick of all! Centuries from now, our name will mean 'trick' because of this! Generations to come will think us fools!"

Priam's daughter. Sinon thought her beautiful, even as her words chilled him.

Gently but firmly, as he might push away an insistent puppy, Priam took the woman's wrists and held her off. "What do you mean?"

"The horse is hollow and filled with Greeks! If you bring it into the city, they'll burn us to ashes! There will be nothing left!" She begged, her eyes wide and face taut with fear.

Sinon stared. His instinct was to jump to his feet and run away. It was all over, the prophetess had spoiled everything. As if she felt his gaze on her, she turned and pointed at him, her mouth open in a horrified grimace.

She knew—damn her, she knew! He could do nothing but keep his place and look confused.

Someone in the crowd laughed. "That's ridiculous!"

Priam regarded his daughter sadly. "Cassandra, is this another one of your foolish dreams?"

"It's true, it's true! Everything is true!" She stomped in place, screaming. A nearby gentlewoman grabbed her arms and held her still. Priam closed his eyes, seeming suddenly weary.

The gentlewoman said, "Her madness speaks nonsense, sire."

Cassandra screamed until the woman took her away.

Madness. They thought her mad. Sinon tried to look pitying instead of relieved.

The murmurs among the crowd had started again:

"It is a gift from the gods!" and "The war is truly ended!" And finally, "Bring the horse in! The magnificent horse must live in the city! May the blessing of Athena be upon us!"

At last Priam, either listening to the cheers or taking his own counsel, said, "Yes. Bring men to drag the horse into the city. We should have some trophy for all this hardship. And you." He knelt and touched Sinon's shoulder. "Take some rest within our walls."

"Thank you, my lord. Thank you."

The gratitude, at least, was genuine.

3

Frank dropped a spoon on the floor while lifting it from the drawer to his cereal bowl on the counter, and Evie jumped out of her chair, her heart racing.

"Dad, are you okay?" She rushed to grab the spoon and hand it to him before he could stoop to reach it.

He straightened, scowling as he took it from her. "I just dropped a spoon."

Pouting, she clenched her hands.

He said, "I'm not going to drop dead in front of you. You'll have some warning, trust me."

Turning away, she pinched the bridge of her nose to stop herself from crying again, then stalked back to the table and her own bowl of cereal.

They'd kill each other before he could die of cancer if they kept this up. "Maybe I shouldn't have come."

"No, I'm glad you're here."

It was just as well she had to rewrite the entire script for the May issue of *Eagle Eyes*. It would give her something to do instead of staring at her father, watching for symptoms.

She insisted on clearing the dishes, asking all the

while if there was anything else he needed, if there was anything else she could do to help. Did the garbage need to go out? (No.) Did the dog need walking? (Mab had a pen out back and walked herself.) Cleaning? Cooking? *Anything?*

"Evie, I've lived alone for five years. I can take care of myself."

This left her with her eyes watering, yet again.

He closed his eyes and seemed to be counting to ten. "Why don't you run to the store? I'm almost out of eggs and bread. I probably need to stock up since there's two of us."

She jumped at the chance to do something, *anything*. And to get out of the house. She hadn't even been back a day, and she was feeling claustrophobic.

He tried to give her money to pay for the groceries.

"No, I'll get it."

"Nonsense. You had to travel all this way, you're staying here as a guest—take it."

The starving-artist days when she'd struggled to make ends meet with a part-time data-entry job were still vivid in their memories. He wasn't used to her being able to pay, much less offering to do so.

"There's little enough I can do while I'm here—let me buy groceries for you."

"Evie—"

Take a deep breath, count to ten. Like father, like daughter. "You can buy next time."

After a moment, he put the bills back into his pocket. "Okay. My ration book is on top of the microwave. At least take that."

She'd have to make sure to really stock up, so that next time didn't happen for a while.

Hopes Fort had seen its heyday when her grandparents were teenagers. The sugar plant and steel mill had been in operation then. They closed down after World War II. Work dried up, and most of the agriculture became unprofitable. None of the buildings downtown had been constructed later than about 1960.

Another high school classmate who hadn't left town was a manager at the Safeway. Evie had caused a mild scandal after graduation when she went to Los Angeles for college. Most people who left town went into the military, or if they went to college at all it was to one of the state universities before moving to the Denver suburbs to raise their 2.5 kids. Everyone was convinced she'd get shot on the L.A. freeways within months. They wanted to know if she'd have to wear a bulletproof vest to go to class.

She traded a few pleasantries with the manager, who asked how Frank was doing. Evie said fine because she didn't want to explain in any more detail—and more than that, she didn't want to start crying.

The store was almost empty. Many of the shelves were also empty. Evie piled her cart with what she could, mostly canned staples and dry goods. She pushed her cart to the only open checkout lane and started unloading. Between her father's ration coupons and her own, she was able to cover the haul.

A man stepped into place behind her. She felt bad that he'd have to wait while the clerk rang up her cart. He only had a candy bar on the conveyor belt.

He stood too close to her. She inched forward, away

from him. And he inched forward, right up to her again. She tried to ignore him.

"You're Frank Walker's daughter," said a voice in her ear.

She turned around to stare straight at him. He might have been a classmate from high school; he seemed about the right age. But she didn't recognize him. He looked back expectantly. Slightly shorter than she, he had an olive complexion, tanned, with dark eyes and brown hair, thick and tousled. Clean-shaven. He wore a blue felt pea coat over a white oxford shirt, unbuttoned at the neck.

"You a friend of my dad's?"

"Not really."

"Then how do you know that?" She took careful note of his features and tried to interpret his casual smile. She wondered if her father had reported his prowler to the police, or if he had gotten a description.

"It's a small town. Not hard to find things out."

"What do you want?"

"I only wanted to meet you."

The clerk glanced up, then returned to swiping food over the sensor. Each item passed with a beep. Evie turned away from the stranger and dug in her pocket for her debit card. Strange, definitely strange. Strange the same way that guy in the duster back at the house yesterday was strange. His look was likewise unplaceable, his accent unidentifiable.

She paid as quickly as she could and started putting the bags in her cart. The man paid for his candy bar, walked past her and out of the store without a second glance. She sighed, relieved.

He was waiting for her at her car, standing by the rear bumper, hands in his pockets, watching for her. She stopped, gripped her cart hard, and considered going back into the store and calling the police.

Before she could make a decision, he came toward her and spoke. "Can I help you with your bags?"

He was short, and while she couldn't judge his build under the coat, she thought she could take him if it came to that.

"Are you stalking my dad?" she said.

"Not at all. But I am looking for something. I think it might be in your father's basement."

"That's it, I'm calling the police."

"Please don't, Evie."

Her heart pounded. He wasn't threatening her. He didn't move any closer. He spoke kindly, with psychotic calm. The neighbors would say how nice and quiet he always seemed.

"Who are you?"

"Call me Alex." He raised his hand, as if offering it to be shaken, but paused midmotion, hand outstretched, elbow bent, gaze studying her. Then he turned and walked away.

Civil defense posters decorated the outside of the supermarket. They were the same ones she saw everywhere in L.A.: the wickedly surreal poster of the bugeyed face emerging from a cloud of gas demanding, DO YOU KNOW WHERE YOUR MASK IS? and the shadowed figure stalking behind a quaint family home, labeled REPORT STRANGERS! It seemed a little laughable finding them in Hopes Fort. Nothing ever happened here, no one knew the town existed, it surely wasn't a target. But the schools still ran attack drills.

Evie knew where her gas mask was: in its bag under the front seat of the car. In L.A., she carried it everywhere in her backpack, like everyone did. Here? It would be like locking her car doors in the driveway.

But as Johnny said, the rules were still in effect, even here.

She pulled onto Main Street and stopped at the police checkpoint. Johnny wasn't there today. The deputy in charge was about twenty years older and surly.

She rolled down her window and offered her ID. "Where can I find Johnny Brewster?"

"Back at the station. Pop your trunk, please, ma'am."

"You have the phone number?"

"Yeah." The guy had to look in every single grocery bag.

"Can you give it to me?" she said after the pause made it clear he wasn't going to answer.

He looked her up and down, then glanced at the California plates on the car.

"Look," she said. "We went to high school together. I just have to ask him something."

Finally, he gave her the number and let her through the checkpoint.

She dialed the number into her mobile phone. "Johnny? It's Evie."

"Hey, what's up?"

"I just had a run-in with somebody, and I wondered if you knew him. He said his name was Alex." She told him about the encounter and gave him the stranger's description.

"That doesn't ring any bells, but I'll keep my eyes open."

"Thanks." Report Strangers! Damn straight.

Evie stayed up late that night, tucked half under the covers of the guest bed, laptop perched on her lap, amazingly enough, and delved into the adventures of the Eagle Eye Commandos.

Crammed in the back of the unit's Blackhawk, Sarge and Matchlock were arguing about weapon caliber again. (".60 all the way." "Overkill, man. That's so inelegant. You wanna do this *pretty*, don't you?") In the cockpit, Tracker and the pilot, Jeeves (as in "Home, Jeeves"), rolled their eyes. Talon—Captain Andrew Talon, hero of this outfit—reminded them that they were on a mission and asked them to be quiet. He ordered them, really, but with Talon, it never sounded like an order. It was like he was asking a favor, one gentleman to another, and you couldn't help but want to comply.

The plan was for Jeeves to drop off the others near Moscow, retreat outside of Russian radar surveillance, then return to pick them up in six hours. Sarge and Matchlock were ex–Special Forces, with specialties in covert ops, sniping, demolitions, the whole nine yards. They covered the landing and their entry into the city perfectly. Talon brought up the rear.

Tracker, the intelligence expert, moved watchfully ahead of Talon. She kept her blond hair tucked under a black bandanna and smudged her cheeks with paint. Sexy, if you liked that sort of thing. Tracker was the embodiment of some of Evie's more outlandish teenage daydreams.

They had just started on their route to the Kremlin when they heard a plane, the drone of an engine sail-

ing overhead, Dopplering to a higher pitch as its alti-
tude decreased, faster and faster. A moment later, a
massive explosion rocked the world. A pillar of flame
erupted from the aptly named Red Square; then the
shock wave hit. The four soldiers dropped to the
ground and covered their heads.

In a strange twist, the team helped with the rescue
effort, which included digging out Talon's counterpart
in the Russian version of the Eagle Eyes, the Company
of the Gray Bear. In gratitude, Agent Slovsky did more
than give them the evidence about the missing
spies—he told them the exact location in Siberia where
they were being held. Moreover, the team promised to
hand over any information they found regarding the
terrorists who had perpetrated this act. An event of this
magnitude could only bring the rival powers of the
world closer together.

All the lessons of history to the contrary. Evie's ide-
alism astonished her sometimes.

She e-mailed that much of the reworked script to
Bruce, who had probably chewed all his pencils to
pieces with worrying. While she was online, she opened
a Web browser and did a search on prostate cancer. In
fairly short order, she learned that the standard treatment for advanced stage prostate cancer was a proce-
dure called an orchiectomy. Medical castration. She
didn't get much further than that before shutting down
her machine. She just didn't want to know. She turned
off the lamp on the bedstand and hoped for sleep.

A hard wind blew, rattling the windowpanes. The
Eagle Eye storyline turned back and forth in her
head—there was always so much more than she could
get into a script: thoughts, expression, the little pieces

of the characters' backgrounds that might come into play at certain moments. She wrote novels in her head and grew frustrated that she hadn't yet found the patience to put a novel to paper.

She couldn't sleep.

She went to the kitchen to find some tea or a glass of water and passed the doorway to the basement.

When her grandparents lived in the house, the basement had been off-limits. She could play anywhere in the yard, read any of the books—fascinating fairy stories and ancient histories—on the dozens of shelves in the living room, but the basement was for grown-ups. When she was old enough to think about it, she assumed that meant power tools and cleaning solvents. By the time her father moved into the house, she was out of college and never spent more than a weekend at a time there and never took much interest in the basement.

Now she assumed that the prohibition no longer applied.

A bare bulb hanging from the ceiling lit the stairs. The basement was unfinished, framework and heating ducts exposed, a second room blocked off with bare drywall. At the foot of the stairs was a workroom with a rack of tools, a table saw, and a nebulous unfinished woodworking project propped against a set of metal shelves.

In the middle of the drywall at one end of the workroom was a closed door.

Stocking-footed, robe wrapped around her T-shirt and bare legs, she crept down the stairs to that door and opened it.

It was a storage room: shelves crammed with troves of objects, crates stacked as high as the ceiling, boxes piled to create the narrow walkways of a maze through a room whose edges were lost in darkness. The air smelled dusty, with a bite of cold seeping from the cracked concrete floor.

She looked for a light switch or a cord dangling from a ceiling bulb, but couldn't find anything. Back in the workroom, she retrieved a flashlight, then entered the storage area, feeling like she was spelunking.

She couldn't see much in the beam of light: the shadows and angles of boxes, tarps draped over a few corners, forming weird lurking shapes. She felt six years old again, on an adventure in her own house simply because she was sneaking around past midnight.

Passing the flashlight beam back and forth, she identified some items: a thick hammer, like a sledgehammer, on a short handle, the wood shiny from use; an old-fashioned broom, brush stalks wrapped around a dark staff; a cup made of chipped clay; a sheepskin folded on a shelf. In the flashlight's sickly glow, the fleece looked yellow, shiny almost. No dust dulled it, even though it must have lain there for years. She ran her hand over it. It felt soft, fresh, and sent a charge up her arm, a static shock.

All the objects looked archaic and out of place, but none of them looked old. On the next shelf over, she found a musical instrument, strings on a vertical frame. Not a harp, but a lyre. She plucked a string. It gave back a clear tone. She bet it was still in tune. The note seemed to echo. She shivered.

This was a museum. The stuff here must have been

worth a fortune. Her grandparents might have gathered such a collection over the course of their lives. But why hadn't anyone told Evie about it?

A stack of papers rested on the shelf by the door. Hoping it was some kind of inventory, something that might tell her what exactly all this was, she picked up the pages and leafed through them. The handwriting on them belonged to her mother, Emma. These were the loose-leaf pages she made her notes on. Emma Walker had been a travel writer, mostly articles for magazines. It was a hobby she'd maneuvered into a part-time career. Evie supposed she'd learned to write from her, though she'd taken the impulse in an entirely different direction.

Emma had been in Seattle doing research when she died.

The first page was a description of a garden. Evie couldn't guess where or when; it didn't have a label. It didn't matter. The pages held her mother's voice. Evie put them back on the shelf, where they looked out of place and lonely.

She left the room, closing the door softly, as if an infant slept inside. It was precious, wondrous. The hair on the back of her neck stood on end.

She made tea and sat at the kitchen table with a pen and sheet of paper to write longhand, which she hadn't done in ages. It helped sometimes, making the words physical. Not much story happened. Mostly, she made lists, character sketches, snippets of description for if, when, she ever got around to writing the novel.

She was asleep with her head on the kitchen table when her father emerged for breakfast in the morning.

"Trouble sleeping?" he said, standing on the other side of the table, amused.

Stretching the kinks out of her back and neck, she rubbed her face. "Yeah. No. I don't know, I just meant to get some tea." She didn't remember falling asleep; her body still felt like it was midnight.

"It was the wind blowing last night. Rattles the whole house. It kept me awake, too." He didn't act like it. He was already dressed for the day. He poured a glass of orange juice and drank it while he pulled his coat from the rack by the door.

She wanted to ask him about the storeroom, but realized he was getting ready to go out. "Where are you going?"

"I've got a Watch shift this morning." He was on the local Citizens' Watch, had been since her mother died. The local police didn't have enough people to staff the checkpoints and continue their usual workload. Citizens' Watch took up the slack.

"Are you sure—I mean, are you sure you should still be doing that? I didn't think you'd still—"

"I'm not dead yet," he said cheerfully.

"But what if something happens?"

"Nothing's going to happen."

"But—"

"Evie, I plan to keep things as normal as possible for as long as I can. I like the Watch. It gets me out. I've got everyone in town looking out for me. I'll be fine."

This was like when she was in high school, with her parents standing in the kitchen, listing all the reasons she shouldn't go out after the game, with all the drunks on the road, and her insisting that she'd be *fine*.

He put the empty glass in the sink. He'd reached

the door when he looked back and said, "You want to come along?"

"I should try to get some work done. I don't want to leave Bruce hanging."

"I'll see you after lunch, then."

"Dad?"

He hesitated, hand on the doorknob.

"I went downstairs last night." She let that hang for a moment, waiting for him to offer a response, wondering what he would say without her prompting him.

"Oh?" was all he said.

She wet her lips and tried again. "The storeroom—has the stuff in there ever been cataloged? Do you have any idea what all is down there? What it's worth? You could have your own antique show."

A slow smile grew on his lips, and the look in his eye told her before he even spoke that he wasn't going to answer her question.

"I'll see you this afternoon," he said, then was gone.

Figured. Though she wondered why a roomful of antiques demanded such deep dark secrecy. Had someone in their family's history been a master thief? Run a pawnshop in the last century and never bothered to sell off the assets? Was a budding museum curator? At least he hadn't gotten angry at her for invading the forbidden storeroom.

She set up her laptop in the living room, on the coffee table, and sat on the hardwood floor in her robe and stocking feet. She'd shower and change later. Who did she have to impress?

Curled up in the middle of the carpet, napping politely, Mab kept her company. When Evie got up for a glass of water or to stretch her muscles, Mab always looked at her, ears cocked, alert. When Evie relaxed, so did Mab. Evie worked up the courage to scratch the dog's ears; Mab acknowledged the attention with a couple thumps of her tail. Her father must have kept the stray dog for company.

Bruce had already e-mailed her sketches of the new pages. He must have been up all night, too. Once colored, the Cessna explosion was going to be spectacular. He had it covering a two-page spread.

So, what to write next. They had a formula that demanded a certain number of shots fired each issue, and she was in danger of running short. She needed a battle scene.

The crew barreled across the tundra in a stolen Jeep, racing against an execution order sent out for one of the men they were supposed to rescue. The Blackhawk was out of commission for now—sabotage in the fuel tank. The Russians were supposed to be helping them, but someone on the inside didn't want them to succeed. A three-way battle ensued, and no one was sure who was siding with whom.

Usually, Evie wrote things like "chase scene" and "fight," and let Bruce's capable imagination construct the details in four-color panels that splashed across entire pages.

But something about this battle tickled her story instincts. Throw out a clue, a hook that could carry the plot to the next issue. An enemy chopper ran them down. Matchlock managed to steer them into a gully and under cover, but not before Talon saw a face he swore he knew, a man he thought he had left behind to die in the arctic years before. Talon had had to make a decision—stay to save his platoon-mate, or leave and ensure the success of the mission. Talon had abandoned him. The memory still haunted him.

And there the issue ended, centered on the expression of stark disbelief on Talon's face.

Next issue: He'll want to follow the enemy chopper. He'll want to learn what had happened to his friend, how he'd survived. Tracker argues with him. Her mind is on the spy imprisoned in Siberia. On the mission. She'll go alone if she has to, she'll defy him—

Someone knocked on the door.

Evie couldn't see who it was out the kitchen window. Mab wasn't barking. She opened the door.

An old woman stood on the porch, looking at Evie with a patient, expectant expression. Mab turned a circle and wagged her tail, as if asking for praise, or forgiveness, or any acknowledgment of her canine presence.

"Can I help you?" Evie felt awkward in her unwashed, half-dressed state, not worthy to appear before this kind old woman.

"Perhaps," she said. "I'm looking for something, and I thought it might be here."

Her skin was wrinkled like old linen, and her hair was ash gray and tied in a bun at her neck. Her eyes were clear and green.

She might have been anyone, from anywhere. Someone from town, from down the street, from the next farm over, looking for a stick of butter, or wanting to borrow a hammer. But Evie's blood rushed in her ears. She felt electrified, like when she'd touched the fleece in the storeroom.

Her words seemed to come from some other lips. "What are you looking for?"

"Shoes. A pair of slippers, like you might wear with a ball gown."

Evie didn't know where the words came from. She spoke on a hunch. "Glass slippers?"

The woman smiled, lighting her face. "Yes, exactly."

"Come in." Moving softly, Evie led her to the basement. She stopped the woman outside the storeroom. "Wait here."

She didn't even need the flashlight this time. She stepped around the stacks of crates and warrens of shelves. Dozens of boxes, a hundred objects wrapped in cloth and packed away, and Evie knew where to go. Only her second time in this room, and she knew. Against the side wall was a wardrobe made of oak with beveled edges and brass knobs. Inside hung gowns—rich, amazing gowns that seemed to sparkle with their own light, shimmering and changing color when Evie tilted her head. At the bottom of the wardrobe, shoes were stacked. Iron shoes that might be put in a fire until they were red hot. A tiny pair of boots that might have fit a cat. Sandals with leather wings stitched to them. Gold slippers, silk slippers. Glass slippers to fit a pair of small feet—blown glass, etched with ribbons and lines to make them look as if they'd been sewn. Flashing, they caught the scant light, which seemed to shine deep within the glass. Evie picked them up; they were light, fragile. She couldn't imagine dancing in them.

Then, without her own volition—like a character in a story, she thought wildly—she was walking to the door. The glass slippers were drawn to the old woman. They led Evie back to her, and Evie let them guide her. She didn't have a choice.

Holding them in both hands, she presented them to the woman. With both hands, the woman took them from her.

"Oh! Not even a scratch on them. They might have been made yesterday. Better than I had hoped." She cradled them to her breast and turned a wondering gaze on Evie. "Thank you so much."

"You're welcome."

Evie saw the woman to the door. Scratching Mab's ears, she watched her walk down the driveway to the road, but turned away rather than see if the old woman was going to walk all the way to town, or if she'd simply disappear into thin air, back to where she came from. Evie didn't want to know. Her hands were shaking.

Like something from a story. A golden fleece. A pair of glass slippers. The slippers *knew* that the old woman had come for them, as if they had a sentience of their own. Did every object in the storeroom have that same sense of *knowing*?

She didn't even know how to ask that question.

When her father returned, she was sitting at the kitchen table, hands pressed flat to its surface. It was how she finally got them to stop trembling.

"Evie? What's wrong."

Carefully, she explained. "An old woman came to the door. She asked for glass slippers. I found them in the basement, so I gave them to her. Is that okay?"

He sat across from her. "That isn't the right question. Tell me: Could you have *not* given them to her?"

She shook her head. "They *wanted* to be with her." She winced, knowing how odd it sounded, knowing it made no sense, but she had no other words to say. She could still feel the shoes pulling at her grasp.

"Then it's okay." He reached across and touched her hand.

"It wasn't me, Dad. It was something else, like someone was moving my arms and making me talk—"

His lips thinned. His eyes were sad, though, making his whole expression grim, resigned. "I knew there was a reason you needed to come home. The Storeroom will be yours when I'm gone."

No. She wanted to deny it, but there was a power pressing down on him. On her. The same sense, the same charge that led her to the glass slippers prevented the word *no* from leaving her mouth. She had her own life, she didn't want this . . . this *weight*.

She didn't want her father to ever be *gone*.

"I don't understand," she said simply.

"You will, in time." He sounded like a mystic sage. A wizard, not her father. Another character from a story, and she couldn't turn the page to see what happened next.

When Irving Walker left Saint Louis with his wife, Amelia, they took only three horses—two to ride and one to pack. What the packhorse couldn't carry, they didn't bring. The folk who saw them off thought it scandalous, Irving Walker putting his wife through that, not giving her the safety of a wagon train, making her ride in the open, exposed to the elements and all the dangers inherent in the crossing of the Great Plains. But they didn't know it was Amelia's idea. Irving asked her what she needed to bring, and she showed him one bag. "That's all?" he said. "All the important things, yes." They'd have a freedom they wouldn't have with a wagon and oxen. They needed to be free, away from people and civilization. That was why they were leaving Missouri in the first place. It had gotten too crowded.

Along the Arkansas River, where the Santa Fe Trail turned south to Mexico, an enterprising businessman named George K. Hope built an adobe fort to serve as a base of operations for his trading company, made up of fur trappers, Mexican merchants, and Indian traders. Within twenty years, Hope's Fort became a *primary way station for explorers heading west, merchants serving the pipeline between the United States and Mexico, and settlers looking for their fortunes beyond the Great American Desert.*

When George Hope saw Irving and Amelia Walker approaching the fort with nothing but three horses and the packs they carried, he swore that even after all his years on the plains and all he'd seen in that time, he'd never seen anything like it.

Ten miles or so up the river, where a village had started to put down roots, Irving built a farmhouse with a massive cellar, which Amelia filled with the contents of the one bag she carried with her.

4

That night, Troy slept, drunk with wine and celebration.

Sinon climbed to the top of the wall and lit a torch, the signal for the Greek army to return. Then he went to the main square, where the horse stood. Wide streets led out from the square, giving easy access to the heart of the city and its riches. As he watched, a door on the horse's belly swung out, and Odysseus dropped to the ground.

He spent a moment stretching arms and legs, easing the cramps from sitting motionless all day. Nevertheless, he drew his sword in a heartbeat when Sinon approached.

"Easy," Sinon said, his arms raised. "I'm a friend, I think."

Odysseus's gaze widened. "Sinon, thank the gods!" They met in two strides and embraced. Odysseus stank of sweat and bodies, from being locked in close quarters with a dozen other men. But they were here, within the walls of Troy.

"You lit the torch?" Odysseus said, stepping back to grip Sinon's shoulders.

"Yes."

"Then we should open the gate. The army will be here soon." The man's eyes blazed in the dark of night. Sinon grinned, though his swollen face felt stiff.

A short hour later, Troy was on fire.

Sinon didn't fight much. He'd done his part for the final battle, had gathered enough wounds, and found that he was too weary to do more. He'd be more of a hindrance than a help, lagging behind while the army pillaged the city. Troy was rich. There'd be plunder enough for all. Right now, all the treasure he wanted was rest.

He found a vantage point at the temple of Apollo, a rotunda built on the highest hill. He hiked the steps to the portico and leaned on a column. From here, he could see most of the city. The fires started on a few roofs had swallowed entire blocks. He smelled the smoke, thick and caustic. The Trojans had been caught off guard. They ran out of burning buildings, fleeing in blind panic from bands of Greek soldiers. The Greeks, identifiable by the waving crests on their helmets, scoured the streets. Screams, shouts, the clanging of weapons and armor, drifted to him here.

The streets ran with blood. As well they should. The Trojans had been safe behind their walls for too long. Now let them suffer for their pride.

Sinon crossed his arms and mused.

Something bronze clattered on the marble floor behind him. He grabbed his sword and looked.

A woman reached for the dagger she had dropped.

Her black hair was unbound, streaming in tangles down her shoulders. She wore the white tunic of a priestess, dusted with soot and blood. She limped, and her face was bruised. She was crying, the sobs coming in dry gasps.

She held the knife like she was thinking of lunging at him, and her face twisted in anguish. "I'll kill you! I'll kill you!"

He gripped his sword, but kept it low, not to threaten but to guard, to show she couldn't reach him before he could defend himself. "I think not."

"Then there is only this," she said, and lay the point of the dagger on her own chest.

He jumped at her and knocked the weapon out of her hand before she could drive it through her ribs. Screaming, she fell away from him, pawing at him, as if his presence pained her.

She'd been raped, of course. There probably wasn't a woman in Troy who'd reach morning unscathed.

"You're Cassandra," he said, finally recognizing her.

Huddled against the next column, she steadied her breathing. "And you're the liar."

He started to argue, but he knew what he'd done. What name he'd earned for himself. Two sides to every battle. To the Greeks, he was a hero. But theirs was not the only story to tell. "Yes."

"And you want to have your piece of me as well." She spat the words.

"No," he said, and meant it. She was pitiable, trembling on the ground, hugging her tunic tight around her shoulders. She'd dropped the knife because her hands were shaking.

"You've changed the world today, Liar. Think what

you could have done if you'd told the truth. All the people who would be alive now. The city would still be alive."

They both looked over the nightmare below them, the inferno and the battles that carried on from house to house.

"And what of the Greek dead? Paris brought this on you when he took what was not his," Sinon said.

Cassandra shook her head. "It was the gods. The gods have played us. Do you see them? I do. Athena fights for Odysseus, there, guiding his spear. And there is Aphrodite, going to save her son, Aeneas. And Poseidon, shaking the walls of the palace. Do you see them?"

Sinon didn't, but her words painted a picture: giants among men, the gods and goddesses of Olympus moving people like they were game pieces.

He sat down, leaning against the column next to hers. "They say you're a seer. A prophetess, but that no one ever believes you."

"I am cursed," she said, forming a vacant, mad smile. "I *told* them the horse is hollow and filled with Greeks. They laughed. Ridiculous. And it is, of course it is! I speak, I tell, I plead, and they never listen. And they wonder that I'm mad."

He chuckled, a soft, ironic noise.

She looked sharply at him. "What?"

"And there I was, lying with every word I spoke. And they believed me."

She covered her mouth. He thought she was going to start crying again, that the gesture was to hold back tears. But the skin around her eyes crinkled, and she laughed.

"We're an awful pair," she said. She looked away, but the smile lingered.

They sat together until dawn. When the sky began to pale with the rose-colored fingers of dawn, he found the courage to say, "I could take you home with me. They—" He nodded to the smoldering city, its streets now paved with bloodied bodies, an occasional scream still tainting the air. "—they will be making slaves of all the women. I could ask for you. I know it is not—it is not what you would wish. But I would be kind. I promise, I could protect you—"

She was already shaking her head, as he expected.

"I'm bound for another. Fate has measured out my thread to a frayed end. But—thank you. It is an . . . unexpected kindness that you offer. As kindness goes in these times."

He wanted to say more. He felt like he ought to say more, to defend himself and the sacking of the city. She seemed to be mocking him.

A small group of Greeks climbed the path up the hill, flushing out the last of the stragglers. Below, on the street leading outside the city, the warriors were herding the surviving women and children. They were a weeping mass of bodies, clinging together, shuddering. Crying like sheep. No men were left alive.

Cassandra saw this scene as well. She hugged the marble column, pressing her cheek to the ridged stone. "I don't want to go."

He stood, straightening his sword belt, smoothing his tunic. "I'll go with you, if you like."

"It won't help. Nothing will help, don't you understand? I'm already dead."

He waited for the soldiers, standing by Cassandra as if he had captured her himself.

A trio of the Greeks reached the temple. One of them spoke to the others, then stepped forward alone. He still wore his helmet, masking his face and giving him an inhuman expression. His tunic, breastplate, and arms were covered with blood.

"Sinon! Sinon the Hero!"

Sinon raised his hand in greeting. He didn't know him, but he shouldn't have been surprised that this one knew his name. He supposed he was famous now—the man who cracked the walls of Troy with a lie.

Smiling broadly, the newcomer stared at Cassandra. "I hope you haven't spoiled this one too badly. King Agamemnon has asked for her. She's the most beautiful of Priam's daughters."

One couldn't tell by looking at her now. Tears and soot streaked her face, which was still contorted from crying. Her hair was tangled, her clothing soiled. But her eyes still shone with spirit. Sinon remembered her from the day before—had it only been a day?—shouting, defiant: *He is lying!*

"She's mad, you know," Sinon said.

"Hmph. So she's lost her mind. That isn't what the good king wants her for." The soldier moved to grab her.

Before he could reach her, Cassandra struggled to her feet, pulling herself up against the column. Sinon reached to help her, but she shrugged away from him. She kept her gaze on the helmeted soldier, glaring at him like she could peel back his skin with a thought.

"He is dead. Your King. Your Agamemnon. He

doesn't know it yet, but he is." Scowling, the soldier again went to take hold of her, but she evaded him, circling the pillar, keeping the stone between them. "He doesn't know what's been happening at his home, but I do, and he is already dead. We're all dead. All of us."

Then she looked at Sinon, her dark eyes lit with madness. "Except for you." Her gaze narrowed, her head tilting curiously. Wonderingly, she said, "You don't die."

She was mocking him again. Except she never lied. And she was a prophetess. But the phrase could mean anything. It could be a symbol. Men made careers interpreting the phrases of oracles. It could mean anything.

"Come on." The soldier caught her at last, his fingers digging into her arm. She didn't make a sound, didn't struggle at all. He dragged her down the steps, and Cassandra stared at Sinon until they reached the street and traveled out of sight.

Slowly, Sinon followed, descending the steps carefully, as if he walked on coals. The world had changed this night. Language itself had changed, and he didn't understand the sounds he heard on the air.

Before he could raise his foot to leave the temple stairs and start on the path down to the city walls, an arm closed around his neck in a lock. Sinon grabbed the arm, trying to pull away, but his attacker was too strong, unnaturally strong. He dragged Sinon back up the steps as easily as he might have pulled a feather. The unseen man—for he was unseen, Sinon craned his head back, rolled his eyes to try to gauge the stoutness of the arm that held him so tightly, and saw that nothing held him at all—gripped him firmly, locking him against his body. Sinon was trapped, immobile, his head tilted far back, his lungs struggling to draw breath.

A voice, taut with anger and sweet with power, said at his ear, "Hera promised Cassandra to Agamemnon. But I will be compensated for the loss of my priestess, and you have desecrated my temple with your presence. You are mine, mortal. I will have you, Liar. You will feel what is being done to the women of Troy. You are now a slave."

The arm released him, only to grab the front of his tunic and slam him to the marble floor of the portico. Sinon's head bounced, his teeth cracking. His vision flashed as pain seared his skull.

For a moment he saw the invisible one who attacked him: a man, thick golden hair crowning a beautiful, smooth-cheeked face and brushing perfect, sculpted shoulders. His glaring eyes were the pale blue of the sky.

Sinon winced. "Apollo!"

Apollo grinned and hauled him inside the temple.

5

When Evie was little, she used to think there was a rule book, some kind of golden understanding that enlightened you when you became an adult. "When I grow up" was a place, a real state of being, where one shed childhood like a worn-out carapace. Then she learned that if kids were cruel, so were adults. Not much really changed except the size and expense of the toys. There was no book, no magic moment of enlightenment, and she took a grim satisfaction in realizing that everyone spent most of their time being just as confused as she was.

But this was different. She could feel a key sitting in her hand, even though she couldn't quite grasp it. She could sense the door about to open. The door to the Storeroom, and what it meant. And unlike that great false Grail of adulthood, understanding really would come. When her father passed away.

She was an heir waiting for the seal on the will to be broken. And she didn't want anything to do with it.

Her father went out again the next day. Evie thought he looked paler. Had he taken an extra painkiller at breakfast? She didn't say anything. She didn't want to argue anymore about him going out. He could take care of himself.

She worked on the script. The team splits up. Talon can't get the image of his long-lost friend out of his mind. The others have never seen him like this— agitated, obsessed. It makes them nervous. The Captain has always been their anchor. Sarge offers to go with him while the others continue on the original mission to rescue the captured spy.

Tracker feels like she's betrayed Talon by insisting on going on without him. She feels disloyal and wonders if he'll ever forgive her. The hint of her feelings for him have been there for the last two dozen issues. Will it come out in the open soon? The tension is fierce.

So Talon and Sarge are sneaking into the stronghold of the Mongolian terrorists. The other three race deeper into Siberia—

A knock rattled the kitchen door.

Evie's heart started speeding—a Pavlovian response of anxiety. *Not again,* she thought. *Not this again, please.* She didn't want to stand and move to the door. Her hands were sweating and her limbs felt stiff.

The knock came again. It could have been just a neighbor. The postman. *Please let it just be the postman.* She went to answer.

Mab trotted to the kitchen with her. She looked at the door, her head low, brown eyes glaring. A growl rumbled deep in her throat.

This wasn't like yesterday.

Evie scratched the dog's back, and Mab wagged her tail once, but never stopped staring at the door. Evie wondered who was waiting on the porch. She opened the door a crack, in case Mab decided to launch an attack.

She was glad she was showered and dressed today. The woman standing on the porch was extraordinarily poised. Evie felt small and scruffy next to her, but at least she didn't feel half-dressed.

The visitor was tall, elegantly slender, like a 1940s starlet. She wore an expensive-looking, calf-length dark coat belted at her waist, and high heels. Her black hair was pulled to the back of her head and held in place with invisible clips, as if by magic. Her dark eyes were exotic, while her expression was indifferent.

"Can I help you?" Evie asked cautiously.

The woman smiled, barely shifting her features. "I wondered if you might have something for me."

Not again, she thought. *I don't want this—*

Evie didn't feel that tingling electric thrill that the old woman brought with her yesterday. Far from it: she felt sick to her stomach. She didn't understand enough to know what the feeling meant.

Mab growled, the rumble leaving her throat and echoing between her bared teeth.

She shook her head. "No. There's nothing here for you. I'm sorry."

The woman's manner shifted. The smile became that of a predator. The gaze became piercing. "Are you certain about that?"

"Yes. I'm sure." Mab inched toward the door. Evie put her hand on the dog's ruff. Mab didn't wear a collar. Evie didn't think she could hold her back if she decided to attack.

"One wonders if you know what you're talking about."

One does, indeed. Evie bit her lip and glared.

"Might I have a look? You keep things in the basement, don't you?" The woman stepped forward, like she was going to push open the door and invite herself inside.

Evie grabbed Mab in a bear hug just as the dog launched herself at the woman, barking fiercely enough to rattle windows.

"Ma'am, trust me," Evie said, hugging Mab's shoulders, leaning with her whole weight to keep the dog back. "We don't have anything for you."

The woman didn't seem to notice the chaos happening in front of her. She held up a gloved hand, palm facing the door. Turning her hand, she brushed with her fingers like she was stirring the air.

"I can't cross the threshold," she said. She glanced at Evie, almost as an afterthought. "But you could invite me in. Would you do that, Evie Walker?"

Evie shook her head. She hugged Mab harder; it made her feel safer. As much as she didn't know about this, she knew she didn't want this woman entering the house.

The woman's voice was patient, calm, like she would stand there all day, politely asking to be let inside, until Evie could do nothing but relent.

Mab was still barking, fearless. Mab would protect her. But the woman didn't spare a glance for the dog, and seemed unflustered by the barking.

A figure ran onto the porch and slid to a stop before banging into the wall of the house. He was young, determined, and wore a pea coat—Alex, from the grocery store. The woman turned, stepping away from him.

He lowered himself to his knees. Clasping his hands,

reaching them toward her, he spoke to the woman in a language Evie didn't recognize, much less understand.

"*Ho hupsalos—aurain kataballe, seh enoiksomai. Ouk anagignoskei hos essi.*"

The woman hesitated a moment, then approached him. Alex squeezed his eyes shut with something that looked like fear.

"*Se exoida—Apollou aysta.*" She touched his cheek, and Alex bore it as if she were a lioness breathing down his neck—silent and trembling. Her finger brushed his throat and hooked on his necklace, a bronze chain with thick links in a band around the base of his neck.

Mab had returned to growling. She stood between Evie and the door, so massive that Evie almost couldn't see outside. She couldn't remember sitting, but she was on the floor.

The stranger glanced at her, then at Alex again, then marched down the porch and across the gravel drive in her high heels without wobbling once.

Falling silent at last, Mab turned and licked Evie's face.

"I'm fine," she mumbled absently, ineffectively trying to push Mab away.

"Are you?" It was Alex, leaning against the wall on the other side of the door. They looked at each other across the threshold.

"Yeah." Mab eyed him warily, but didn't growl. Evie thought that a point in his favor. "Who was that? Who are you?"

They had known each other. She hadn't understood them, but their words had held a tone of ritual and familiarity.

He shook his head absently, more a gesture of denial than of ignorance. "I thought she was dead. Years ago. She should be dead."

"Who *is* she? What's she doing here?"

"Same as me, evidently. Looking for something."

"For what?"

"Don't know. Could be anything." He let out a tired sigh. A sheen of sweat dampened his brow.

"Who are you?"

Smiling, he looked away. "A traveler."

She didn't know whether to invite him in for coffee to coax the whole story out of him, or slap him for being so cryptic. "Why are you spying on us? You were watching the house, weren't you?"

A car pulled into the driveway, kicking up gravel. It wasn't her father's pickup, but the passenger door opened and Frank started to climb out. The driver—one of Frank's friends, Pete Losasso from the hardware store—rushed to the passenger side to help him. He took her father's arm.

Frank brushed him away, but he leaned on the door. "I'm fine." Her father's voice carried across the driveway. Then, "Thanks for the ride, Pete. I'll get the truck back tomorrow."

Pete stood by the car, watching until Frank reached the porch. He was limping.

Evie stood, keeping her hand on Mab's back. What had happened? Alex stood with her, his brow furrowed.

"He's sick, isn't he?" he asked softly.

Her father didn't seem to notice Alex until he came to lean on the railing of the porch steps. At that point, he stared hard at Alex, glanced questioningly at Evie, then turned and waved to Pete, who took the cue to drive away.

"Dad, you okay?"

He glared, a silent reprimand for even asking the question, then nodded at Alex. "Is this guy bothering you?"

"No." Far from it. She had a feeling he'd saved her from something. But she didn't tell her father about the woman, about what had brought Alex here. She didn't want him to worry.

Her father said to Alex, "I told you, there's nothing here for you."

"A man can hope." He gave Evie a look that made her blush. "I won't trouble you again, Mr. Walker." He turned his collar up, nodded a farewell to Evie, and walked off the porch, his hands shoved in his coat pockets. She almost ran after him. She had more questions, like what had *he* been looking for in the Storeroom?

She said, "So that guy's been here before?"

"Yeah. I'm pretty sure he's harmless. Just . . . desperate."

"About what?"

"Couldn't say."

"What's going on?" She was surprised at how angry she sounded. "This all has to do with the basement, and I don't understand—and don't tell me I *will*!"

"Evie, I can't explain. It's impossible to explain."

He started to climb up the stairs, wincing. Thoughts of the Storeroom and the confrontation at the door left Evie's mind entirely, and she wanted to rush to his side to help him, but she didn't dare. He'd push her away, and they'd fight.

"What's wrong?"

"Just a sore back. I'll lie down, rest a bit. It'll pass."

A factoid from her Internet research presented itself: *If the cancer has metastasized to the spine, spinal cord compression along with back pain can ensue.*

"How long has this been happening?"

"A while now." He moved slowly, taking each step like he was afraid of jostling himself.

Mab, wagging her tail madly, pushed past Evie and trotted to him, nudging him, ducking her head, whining. "Oh, hey there, I'm fine, girl. I'm fine." His voice brightened as he scratched the dog's ears. He seemed to stand a little straighter and wince a little less with Mab at his side. He could lean on her without looking like he needed help.

Thanks, Mab.

"I'll make you some tea," Evie said, turning away before he could argue.

Bruce had faced deadlines worse than this. He'd drawn a twenty-page book in two days, once. It hadn't been his best work by any stretch, and he'd slept for twelve straight hours when he finished. But it could be done.

He didn't want to have to work like that on *Eagle Eyes*. Drawing a good explosion took *time*. But at the start, he and Evie had decided to acknowledge current events in the storylines, to make the book as relevant as possible, raising it above the level of a military fetishist's dream.

Maybe that was why he was procrastinating. It wasn't like Evie hadn't done her part and not sent him enough script to work with. But he wanted more time. He wasn't going to get it. So he didn't work at all.

It certainly wasn't that he lacked for inspiration. All he had to do was look out his window.

In the years since its creation, Homeland Security had authorized local militias in every major city, then promptly lost control of many of them to local politics, gangs, and organized crime. Gang warfare and underworld conflicts now had a veneer of government approval. When the tribalistic skirmishes got out of hand, the National Guard had to come in to sort out the situation. It had happened two or three times in L.A., but never this close to home.

The Pasadena Militia had taken offense at some territorial insult offered by the Glendale Militia. The Guard instituted a security lockdown. Bruce hadn't been able to leave Glendale in two days. It wouldn't have been so bad, but his girlfriend Callie had gotten stuck outside, at her job at a Los Feliz hair salon. She was staying with her cousin, so at least she was safe. Bruce would have felt better if they'd been together, safe.

Evie, who lived a quarter mile closer to Pasadena, was lucky she got out of the city when she did. He couldn't imagine having a sick father three states away and not being able to leave the house.

His apartment was just a couple of blocks off Colorado Boulevard. He could see a sliver of the intersection and an armored troop carrier zipping by on the empty road. He wondered if he could get them to pose for a drawing. He wondered if any of them even read *Eagle Eye Commandos,* and if they'd be impressed with him.

The TV offered a counterpoint. He'd left it on all day, switching back and forth between a local news station for better coverage of the Glendale and Pasadena lockdown, and a national news network for updates on the situation in Russia. Evie was going to be pissed off. The situation there was deteriorating so rapidly, the revised script was already in danger of becoming obsolete. They kept setting storylines in Russia because it was exciting, rife with plot potential. A little too rife, unfortunately.

The news anchors' voices faded to an insect chatter in his consciousness. He sat by his apartment window and stared out. The sun was setting, turning the polluted sky a shade of neon orange he'd only ever seen in L.A.

He ought to get back to work on the book, but he kept waiting to see if the Guard turned up his street, soldiers marching with their rifles in hand.

Finally, he called Evie's mobile phone. It rang half a dozen times; then her voice mail picked up. He didn't leave a message. She probably just hadn't found the phone in time.

A minute later, his own mobile rang. He answered, "Yeah?"

"Sorry, I had to dig in my bag for the phone."

He smiled. Ah, predictability.

"What's up?" Evie said.

"What do you want, local or global?"

"Geez, global I guess, to start with."

She sounded exhausted. He resisted the urge to ask how she was doing, how her father was doing, how bad was it really. Not that she'd tell him, one way or the other.

"Let's see. Russia and India have declared war on China."

"God, that was fast," she said.

"Don't tell me you saw it coming."

"No, but I can't say I'm surprised."

"Russia's claiming the Chinese government backed the Mongolians who dropped the plane on Red Square. I think it's just an excuse, but never mind. Congress is debating about who to side with. The U.S. has got aid treaties with all of them still on the books. That's what we get for making friends with everyone, eh? We can't side with the terrorists, but we can't side against our largest trade market, can we? It's a mess."

She didn't say anything, and for a moment he wondered if they were still connected.

"Evie?"

"Hm?"

"Are you okay?"

"I'm just tired."

He didn't buy it, but let it slide. "How are we going to spin this in the story?"

"Until we know who the President and Congress are going to back, we won't know. Maybe we should get the Eagle Eyes out of Siberia and send them to . . . Peru or someplace. Are there any wars in Peru right now?"

"The way things have been going lately, it's probably sunk into the ocean." She laughed, which encouraged him to broach the difficult question. "How's your dad?"

A beat passed before she said, "You know he got a dog? This huge Irish wolfhound. She's great—I'll have to send you pictures."

The misdirection meant the situation there was bad. As terrible as it was being stranded in a security lockdown across town from Callie, he wouldn't want to trade places with Evie.

"That'd be cool," he said, not really interested in the dog but wanting to be supportive. "I should get going. We've got work to do, right?"

"Right."

Work always gave them something to hide behind.

They signed off, and Bruce didn't feel any better after the conversation than he had before it. It seemed like all their lives were blowing up at the same time.

The sunset's orange faded to brown.

The woman shed her coat and pulled off her gloves, tossing them over the back of the desk chair in the matchbox that passed for a hotel room in this village. The carpet was brown, worn; the bedspread a garish paisley in shades of red and orange; the cheap paneling was coming off the walls. The place smelled of mice. So unsuitable. In her own mind, she was still the Queen, though she hadn't worn a crown in centuries. The day would come again, and she had suffered far worse conditions than this over the years. She had spent the last three thousand years crawling out of ruin.

There was a closet near the bathroom. She knocked sharply on the closed door, three distinct raps. In response, the door slid open, pulled from the inside, and a few wisps of fog trailed from darkness. The young man who stepped out of the passage looked eighteen or nineteen, lithe and fine-boned, with tanned skin and curly brown hair. His hazel eyes flashed; his movements were quick and precise. He closed the door, then set about buttoning the cuffs of his white silk shirt.

"Finally," he said. "I was so *bored*."

"Then I'll give you work," the Queen said.

He looked up from his shirt cuffs to meet her gaze at last. His smile was crooked, disguising who-knew-what mischief. He made an ostentatious bow. "It is my fate to serve the powerful."

"As if you had no power of your own. I know differently. You're only bitter that the stories have reduced you to a friendly, harmless spirit." She pinched his chin lightly.

He grinned all the wider. "Not so bitter as I would be if the stories had reduced me to a frigid old harridan."

He was too much to bear by half. She turned away and spoke easily, as if she had not heard him. "The Marquis was correct. The trail he's been following ends here. There are only two of them, father and daughter. But I can't get inside to get at the Storeroom. Can you find a way into the house?"

"Simple. A task for children. I'll be there and back before you know I've gone."

"Not likely," she said with a purr.

"A turn of phrase, milady," he said, snapping his fingers. "Yet you will be amazed at my speed, startled at the thoroughness with which I complete my task, awed by the—"

"Robin—don't overexert yourself, hm? This is only just starting."

"I hear you and obey." He bowed and blew her a kiss, though the look in his eyes was dark, and walked out the door in a perfectly casual manner.

She went to the bathroom to draw a hot bath, sighing at the Fates that left her to make deals with one such as him. Still, she'd had worse servants, even at the height of her power. She wouldn't make an enemy of someone who could help her. So few these days had the skills she needed. A hedge-witch here, a self-styled magician there—obscure saints of obscure miracles. Under her guidance, they'd become useful. She hadn't been able to find the Walkers herself, but she had found the Marquis, and he had found someone else searching for the Storeroom, and the path became clear.

That man who'd been at the Walker house—he might be another one she could use. The daughter hadn't even seemed aware that the house was protected, but the man . . . She hadn't heard that language spoken in three thousand years. How had he survived from that time?

And how could she use him to her advantage?

Her father didn't leave the house the next day, which made Evie both relieved and worried. She didn't want him going out, to collapse somewhere and need help without anyone nearby. But how sick was he, to feel like he couldn't go out?

She tried to put her mind on her work.

Here was Tracker, sick with worry about Talon, distracted from her own task. She should have gone with him. That's when Jeeves says, "You're in love with him." It's out now. She can deny it or ignore it. She remains immobile, mired in indecision and uncertainty.

Evie stared at the screen, mired in indecision. Whenever she felt like she'd written herself into a corner, she inserted a battle. *Attacked by terrorists, chase scene here.* She'd have to answer Jeeves's statement later.

After lunch, she told her father she was going to catch up with friends. He'd spent much of the day in his armchair in the living room, reading, as if nothing were wrong. He didn't say much to her when she left. She gave him her cell phone number, told him to call her if he needed anything, *anything* at all.

Either he would or he wouldn't.

Mab was napping in the kitchen. Evie knelt by her, resting her hand on the dog's head. "Look after him, 'kay?" Mab's tail thumped the floor. Her dark eyes were liquid and earnest.

The Prairie Schooner had been Hopes Fort's only motel since the fifties. These days, it was owned by Carlos and Gracie Alvarez. Evie had gone to school with their sons.

"Hi, Mr. Alvarez," she said to the family patriarch, who sat behind the counter. It didn't matter that she was all grown up now; he'd always be Mr. Alvarez. He was a middle-aged man with a paunch and thinning hair. He hadn't changed at all in the last ten years. She seemed to remember that his sons, Stu and Harry, were living in Pueblo now.

"Well, Evie Walker, hello." He stood and offered a friendly handshake, which she bore amiably. "What brings you back to town? You need a room?"

"No, I'm seeing my dad for Christmas."

"Sure. Hey, I heard that he—I mean, if there's anything—" He let the offer end with a shrug.

He's not dead yet, she wanted to growl. Did everyone in town know? Were there signs up at the Safeway?

"Thanks. Actually, I have a question for you. Do you have a guy staying here? About this tall, dark hair, kind of tough looking." Was Alex tough looking? She seemed to remember his frame being on the thin side. But capable. Handsome even? "Wears a big felt jacket. Also a woman, maybe in her thirties, elegant, well dressed. But they're not together. Probably." This wasn't making sense.

He didn't even have to stop and think. "Nope. I've only got three rooms filled right now, the usual holiday crowd. Relatives' places are overflowing, so they come here. Two families with young kids and one older woman."

"You haven't had anyone like them in the last week or so?"

"No. 'Fraid not."

No standoffish single guys, nothing unusual. Alex would certainly stand out, if he were staying here. "Right. Thanks. So—how's business?"

He shrugged. "People don't travel much these days. But we get by."

"How are Stu and Harry?" Carlos Alvarez rambled on about them and their families—they had a rapidly growing collection of children, Evie gathered. She listened politely. If she hadn't wanted to sit through the report, she shouldn't have asked the question. Finally, she was able to work in, "Well, tell them I said hello."

"I sure will. You tell your dad to take care of himself."

If only she could.

She sat in her car for a while, watching the doors of the guest rooms lined up behind the main office. The motel was a one-story building. Red doors stood out against the white siding and the gray asphalt shingles. Except for new coats of paint, the place probably looked exactly as it had fifty years ago. Only two other cars were parked in the lot. Evie didn't know what she was waiting for. She didn't know where else to find Alex. Strangers in town stayed at the motel, right? She supposed she could go ask Johnny Brewster if the police had seen anything. Someone like Alex stood out in a place like Hopes Fort.

She put her car into reverse, looked out the back window for oncoming traffic, looked over her other shoulder, and started backing. When she checked the rearview mirror, a man stood behind the car.

Gasping, she pounded the brake. In the rearview mirror, she saw him jerk, like he'd been hit. She swore he hadn't been there when she looked a second ago.

She shifted to park, hit the emergency brake for good measure, and rushed out of the car. "Are you okay?"

He was leaning on her trunk. Smoothing the sleeves of his shirt, he straightened, smiling a little, unflustered. He was younger than she first thought, in his early twenties. Short, thin, and baby-faced, he had curly brown hair, tousled around his ears.

He said, "I should watch where I'm going, huh?"

"I'm really sorry, I thought I looked, I didn't see you there—"

"Hey, not a problem. No worries." Flashing a brilliant smile, he touched her hand.

And she thought, how strong his hands were, how

sure his touch, which felt like a spark racing up her arm, into her mind, and he was smiling for *her*.

"What's your name?" he said. "I'm new here in town, and I've been wondering where's a good place to get some dinner. Maybe you could show me."

His words tingled. He didn't let go of her hand. She shook her head. *Another* stranger in town. Looking for *her*.

"I don't think . . ."

He looked away, his tanned face blushing a little, his smile turning sly. "I know it's a little forward of me. But I'm a believer in fate, and it's just possible that I showed up here, at this exact time, and you almost ran over me for a reason."

He made such a prospect sound reasonable. Her mind fogged. He wasn't speaking to her mind; he was speaking to another place, deep in her gut, making her want to melt.

"That doesn't make sense," she said, trying to clear away the dizziness that seemed to overtake her.

"Evie! I've been looking everywhere for you!"

She looked, and there stood Alex. He took her elbow and pulled her arm out of the stranger's reach. In spite of herself, she leaned into his touch. He was solid, and didn't send shocks along her nerves.

"Hold this," Alex said, and tossed something at the stranger. It looked like a sprig of leaves, like part of a boutonniere.

Startled, the man caught it out of reflex. For a moment, he held it with both hands. Then he shouted, an indecipherable curse, and dropped it, scuttling away from it.

Alex shoved her to the car and climbed into the front seat, pulling her in with him.

"Hurry up and drive, please," he said.

Numb and bewildered, she did. The tires squealed as she jerked forward, circled around the parking lot, and lurched into the street.

The stranger glared after her, rubbing his hands together like he was brushing dirt off them.

The Queen paced back and forth along the narrow aisle between the bed and dresser, arms crossed. Robin sat at the edge of the bed, melting an ice cube over each palm in turn.

He scowled, all his humor gone. "I thought it would be easy getting to the house through the girl. I usually do so well with them. But I didn't know about *him*. Who did you say he is?"

"He was a slave. A Greek, one of Apollo's. Detritus of history, lost in time somehow. He certainly doesn't have any power. He's nothing."

She said the words and tried to believe them, but her mind reached. He may have been nothing in himself, but what had brought him here? Whom did he serve? Surely not any of her brothers and sisters, nieces and nephews. They were all dead. She'd have known if they were still alive.

"He has enough power to irritate *me*." Robin scowled at the rash on his hands. "I hate them. I hate them both."

How could someone who'd lived so long act like such a child? "Any mortal could know such a charm."

"But if he used such a charm, then he knows who I am—*what* I am. He's dangerous."

"He's guarding her. The Walker girl," she said.

"Why?"

"He could want the house for himself."

"Or the girl," Robin said with a leer.

This should have been easy. Only two mortals in a simple house stood between her and the prize. Once she'd located the Storeroom, taking what she needed should have been easy. Three thousand years gone, and Zeus was still making life difficult for her. Leave it to him to plan so far ahead, placing obstacles for her to overcome. Maybe the Greek slave was part of that plan. Or maybe the man had his own agenda afoot. In either case, he was a nuisance.

"I'll take care of him," she said. "It will take only a moment. You stay and nurse your wounds."

Robin glowered with a hint of ancient stories, of red caps and sharp teeth. "I'll be ready for him next time. No one fools me twice."

She pressed her lips into a mocking smile and opened the door.

The woman who stepped out of the motel room was old, seventy or eighty, with white hair and soft, wrinkled skin. Dressed in a respectable skirt and blouse, she was tiny, but despite her short frame and thin bones, she managed to hold herself straight and walk with slow dignity as she crossed the parking lot to the motel office.

The proprietor sat behind the desk. He greeted her as the door opened. "Hi, Mrs. Basil. Is everything okay?"

"Hello, Mr. Alvarez. I'm not really sure." Her wrinkles deepened in confusion, and she glanced over her shoulder, through the glass door to the parking lot. "I saw something rather disturbing on the street just now." She checked, and the street itself wasn't visible from the parking lot. She could tell him anything. "It may be nothing, but I thought I should tell someone."

As she expected, Alvarez frowned, interested and concerned. "What is it?"

"There was a young woman, she had brown hair in a ponytail, a green army-looking jacket—"

"Evie Walker. She was just in here."

"Yes, well, a man stopped her on the road just now." She spoke carefully, as if she were trying very hard to remember and explain clearly, evoking sympathy for her age. "He pounded on the door, then got in the car. The poor girl looked frightened, and I think—I think he was holding a gun. Does that sort of thing happen here?"

Alvarez's face paled. His hand was shaking when he picked up the phone. "I'll call the police. I'll call right now. Can you tell them what the man looked like?"

"Well, I think so. Oh, I hope she isn't in danger."

After he contacted the police, he handed the phone to her and she described the attacker in detail—short, slim, olive-skinned, in his early thirties, dark curling hair, wearing a navy blue felt coat. The police had the description and license plate number of Evie's car on record from the checkpoint on the highway. Officer Brewster was sure they'd be found quickly, and he thanked Mrs. Basil very much for her help.

She insisted she was more than happy to be of service, and hoped the girl was safe.

Evie perched at the edge of her seat, leaning on the steering wheel while she drove. She didn't know where she was going. Just away. Alex leaned against the passenger door and stared out the windshield.

After a mile, he said, "What's your first question?"

She sat back and covered her mouth to keep from laughing. Or shrieking. When she realized she'd used the hand the stranger touched, she stared at it. The car hit a pothole. She was driving too fast and eased her foot off the gas pedal.

That guy at the motel had done something to her. Absently, she wiped her hand on her jeans.

"What was that you threw at him?" she said finally.

"Rowan."

"Rowan?"

"It's a kind of tree," he said.

"Yes, I know. Why did it hurt him like that?"

"Every magician has a weakness. Rowan is useful against that one's brand of magic."

"That one . . . who was he? Magic? What do you mean, 'brand of magic'? What did he do to me? What do you mean, magic?"

"Slow down, one at a time."

She swallowed and tried to keep her mind from tumbling. "I've been looking for you."

He glanced at her. "You have?"

"You seem to know what's going on. My father won't tell me anything. I want to know what all that stuff is doing in my dad's house. And why does everyone want it?" *And why do I feel like this? Why is it speaking to me?*

"It's not that simple."

"Who was that woman who came to the door yesterday? And who was that guy in the parking lot?"

"I'm not sure you would believe me—"

She slammed the brakes, cranking the wheel to skid to the side of the road. The tires complained, and belatedly she looked in the rearview mirror to see if anyone was about to plow into her. But this was Hopes Fort, and she was out of town already, surrounded by barren winter fields. Hers was the only car on the road.

"Who are you? Why did you save me? What did you save me from?"

Alex had one hand on the dash, the other on the back of his seat, and he pushed himself against the door, away from her. His brow was lined and anxious; his lips frowned.

"I think he's working for Hera. He probably thought he could use you to get into the Storeroom. Here." He reached his closed hand over to her. Tentative, she held her palm open, and he dropped a twig, a few inches long with rows of serrated oval leaves, bright green, into her hand. "You should keep it, in case he comes back."

She rubbed the leaves between her thumb and finger. The stranger's touch had been like a cord wrapping around her body. She would have followed him anywhere. Taken him into the house, anything. And how could a twig stop that?

"Hera? That woman? The one you talked to yesterday?"

"Hera, Queen of Olympus. Yes."

"That's crazy."

He shrugged, unconcerned.

"So which god are you? Apollo?"

Laughing, he said, "I'm not nearly golden enough."

She'd meant the question as a joke. "Then who are you?"

"Nothing. No one." He looked away.

"But you understand. You know everything."

His lips parted in a silent chuckle. "I ought to, after all this time. But I don't."

This was a very elaborate prank. What would any god—or goddess—be doing in Hopes Fort, of all places? Why would any basement in Hopes Fort serve as a Storeroom for ancient lyres and golden fleece? It didn't make any sense. An old woman coming to her house looking for glass slippers didn't make any sense.

The car had stalled. Evie shoved the sprig of rowan in her coat pocket, started the car again, and put her hands on the steering wheel. She wondered how she was going to kick Alex out of her car. But she couldn't just leave him, after he'd saved her from . . . whatever he'd saved her from. And what god had *that* been? That was twice, now.

He seemed harmless enough. Or rather, he seemed harmless enough toward *her*. For the moment. But there was no mistaking, he was stalking her, following her.

Protecting her?

He finally broke the silence. "She's looking for something in the Storeroom. That's why she came to the house yesterday, that's why she came after you today. You should try to find out what. If you want to know why she's here, why these things are happening, that's the key."

"I don't even know what all's down there."

"You could look."

"It's just a basement full of junk."

He gave her a raised-eyebrow expression that clearly disbelieved her.

She tried again to make this sound rational. "The goddess Hera wants something from my father's basement."

"Obviously."

"So, does that woman *think* she's Hera, or is it just you who thinks she is?"

"You're being willfully stubborn," he said. "She is Hera. The goddess. Married to Zeus. Queen of Olympus."

"And she wants something from my father's basement." This was starting to sound like an old comedy routine. "What does she want?"

"You won't know until you have a look."

"All right." She could do that much. Just have a look around, see if something jumped out at her. Maybe this woman was a cousin nobody had told her about, and Evie would find her picture in a photo album. "But you're coming with me. You said you know her—you might recognize something that I won't."

He didn't argue, which made her wonder if this was a bad idea. She pulled back onto the highway and drove toward home. Her hands were sweaty on the plastic of the steering wheel.

He sat quietly, watching the road ahead. She tried to study him out of the corner of her eye, as if that would tell her what she needed to know about him.

"What are you looking for?" she said to break the silence. "You've been to see my dad before. He said he didn't have anything for you."

"Yes. At least he *says* there's nothing." He spoke with a tone of bitterness and frustration, like maybe he thought her father was lying.

"But what do you think is there? What do you want to find?"

He watched the yellow, wasted prairie scroll by the car window. He said, "I'm looking for something that will kill me."

Henrich Vanderen crossed the Atlantic to escape Napoléon, and to escape being drafted into the army in Prussia. Europe had suddenly become a small place, nations sprawling everywhere. Difficult for a man to be alone in, and to find a place where he would not be bothered. He spent the journey in the ship's hold, using as a pillow the one bag he brought with him, a sturdy leather satchel closed by a drawstring.

It felt a little like betrayal, leaving the land of his fathers, of countless fathers who had come before him, fading into history like ghosts. At the same time, those ghosts urged him on. He must find a safe, isolated place where he wouldn't be bothered. The ghosts knew what was important, and they passed that knowledge to him. Find a safe place, dig in deep, and remember.

In America, he could lose himself, and no one would think him odd for wanting anonymity. People who needed to find him would. They always did. He traveled to the frontier of the new country, as far as Europeans had traveled in the wild land, and carved himself a farm in Ohio. His stumbling English, broken with a German accent, was not so out of place here. And while *the forest had many eyes, which he felt watching him when he traveled, he did not feel the iron breath of armies and governments down his back. He could start a family without fear that it would be snatched from him when he closed his eyes.*

He built a cabin, and under it he dug a cellar that became a new Storeroom, housing ancient lyres, golden fleece, and glass slippers.

One morning, he opened the door of his cabin and saw a man sitting cross-legged in front of his house. He was one of the natives, with sun-reddened skin, raven-black hair, and a broad face. He wore what looked like long gaiters made of leather, and a breastplate made of porcupine quills.

When Henrich appeared, the man opened his eyes, as if he'd been asleep, sitting with his back straight and legs tucked under him. He stood gracefully, without propping himself on his hands. His hair shimmered, and Henrich saw that it wasn't simply that his hair was shining black. He'd braided raven feathers into a tail down his back.

Henrich had heard stories of bloodthirsty natives, but he wasn't afraid of this man.

The native man approached him, arms stretched before him, cupping something in his hands. He spoke with a rough voice, like the scratching cry of a bird, in a language Henrich didn't understand. But the man gestured with his hands, and the meaning was clear. Instinct made him reach and accept the gift from the stranger.

The native put an ear of maize in his hands. Henrich met his dark-eyed gaze, and the man nodded decisively. Then he vanished into the woods at the other end of the space Henrich had cleared for his holding. A raven circled overhead.

Henrich put the maize in the Storeroom, with the rest of the treasures passed on from his ancestors into his safekeeping.

6

Men could be raped. Every boy who joined an army discovered that quickly enough. Early on, Sinon had learned to fight back—and to give in, occasionally, when the situation suited him. But he could not fight a god.

When he woke up, he was no longer in the temple at Troy. He lay on a pallet in a room that overlooked a garden. It might have been another temple in another town—Apollo had many temples. Or someplace that only the god himself knew. He was naked. His wounds had been cleaned. He was sore.

He didn't remember being brought here. Apollo's attentions toward him had lasted a long time, and he had passed out. He rubbed his eyes and let out a groan. The gods were supposed to ravish feckless girls, not hardened Achaean warriors.

"Some of us like hardened Achaean warriors." Apollo stood at the archway to the next room. He wore a short tunic, belted loosely with a silk cord. Grinning, he crossed his arms. "As well as feckless girls."

Slowly, minding the tender places, Sinon sat up. He found a chain hung around his neck like a collar. Touching it, he examined its round links of bronze, and couldn't find a clasp.

"It will never come off," Apollo said. "I sealed it around your neck myself. It shows that you belong to me. It ensures that you'll be with me for a very long time."

Sinon winced, confused. Then he thought of nothing at all. He didn't want to give Apollo any more of himself if he could help it. If Apollo could take his very thoughts, he would keep his mind as still as possible. He would be empty as air.

You don't die.

He looked away, suddenly feeling very much like that boy who'd set sail for Troy, untried, filling himself with excitement that would bury the fear. Now, after all these years, the fear won out. He squeezed shut his eyes.

He was Achaean. He was part of the army that broke Troy. He was friend to Odysseus. What would Odysseus do, were he here? Think of some way to trick the god. Be so awful a slave that Apollo would be grateful to let him go.

"I know what you're thinking, boy, and it won't work. I plan to make you like it here. You'll find clothing in the chest by the bed and food on the table in the corner. Refresh yourself. If you need anything, simply think of me and I'll come." His smile was coy and arrogant. He was master here and enjoyed the games he played.

He slipped around the corner and was gone.

Sinon opened the wooden chest and found a silk

tunic, short and functional, and leather sandals. He did not touch the food. If this was anything like the stories, eating the food would trap him here, like Persephone in the Underworld.

He explored. This wasn't a temple, at least not like any kind that he knew. He went from room to room—richly furnished living quarters, sitting rooms of marble, and even libraries—looked out of a dozen porches, doors, and windows. Gardens lay in every direction—hedges, fruit trees, fountains, pools surrounded by lilies, vines, every color of flower, every scent of herb and nectar. He set out on a path that led away from the palace. When he passed the hedge that bounded the property, his steps slowed. Looking ahead, he saw more gardens and another gleaming marble palace. He looked behind, to the porch he had just left. Then he ran ahead to this new structure. He ran through the new gardens, up the steps to the porch and through the archway to a small room.

It was the room where he'd woken up. It was the same chest by the pallet. He opened it to be sure, and found clothing arranged exactly as he'd left it. The food—fruit, cheese, wine—still sat on the table in the corner.

He went back outside, tried a different path, which again circled back to Apollo's palace without ever curving. He ran, finding new paths, marking the ones he'd already tried by scattering rose petals at intersections. He must have run for miles, like Theseus in the labyrinth, searching for the one path that would take him away. But all paths returned to the palace.

Finally, he sat at the edge of a pool, letting his feet touch the murky, opaque water. He wasn't as clever as Odysseus, not by half. That story he'd told to the Trojans—that was Odysseus's story, and Odysseus would rightly get credit for it. Sinon was no hero.

Perhaps if he didn't follow a *path* ... He set off across a lawn, following no path at all. When he reached the hedge, he went *through* it, shoving into the mass of branches, not minding how the thorns clawed at him or the fine tunic he wore. He ripped his way to the other side, thinking he might actually find himself in a nonmagical garden this time.

At last, the branches gave way and he fell out of the hedge and onto a lawn. He brushed himself off, wincing at the stinging cuts on his arms.

Ahead stood a palace. The same palace he'd just left, the same garden, the same fountains. He looked behind, over the hedge to—the same palace. He was running in circles.

"It's no use. You can't leave until I say so." Phoebus Apollo stood on the nearest path, twirling a rose between his fingers. "You'll wear yourself out if you keep this up."

Sinon squared his shoulders and met the sun god's gaze. Stupid pride—he should be on his knees. That was what gods wanted, for men to fall on their knees and praise them. Maybe that was what Apollo was waiting for, and as soon as he did, Sinon could leave.

Apollo looked like a man, not even a great man. He was rather short, his build slim, however sculpted his muscles appeared. If he were a man, Sinon could cut him to pieces. He had done nothing to inspire Sinon to fall on his knees in worship.

Except move the sun across the sky each day and create divine music.

Apollo said, "Speak to me, Sinon. I want to hear your voice. The Trojans say you have a lovely voice."

If only Sinon had remained anonymous, one of the faceless Greek soldiers. He'd be sailing home with Odysseus now. Assuming someone else had been able to play his part in the scheme.

"I am not awed by you."

"I know. That's why I decided to keep you. When you realized who I was, you didn't cower, beg, or pray. No, you fought bitterly. Or tried to, which I admire. You kept your pride. You still do."

"What do you want of me?" he asked like a common prisoner of a common captor.

"Your service. I'm in need of a valet. Perhaps even a bodyguard—at least, I have the need to *pretend* I need a bodyguard." He chuckled.

"I will not serve you."

"Give it time."

"I'll drown myself in one of your ponds."

"Try it." Apollo made a gesture, and the rose in his hand became a sword. He tossed it at Sinon.

Sinon caught it by the grip and swept it in an arc to finish the motion of its flight. He hefted it, turning it to study its edge.

"Do it," Apollo said. "Kill yourself and get the impulse out of your system."

It was a trick. Sinon knew it was. The god wouldn't have brought him here to torment him, only to watch him kill himself.

He didn't want to kill himself. He never would have thought it, even if he'd been captured by the Trojans, tortured and enslaved while all his friends perished. Courage came in persevering. Odysseus taught him that. But this place was different. Did courage mean anything here?

He would not be a slave, not to the Trojans, not to a god.

He turned the sword, gripped it with both hands, set the point in the middle of his belly, just under his ribs. His heart was racing. *This isn't right.* He gave his mind over to panic and stumbled forward, driving the sword in as he did.

Pain followed the metal through his flesh. Moaning, he fell to his knees. He stayed there, holding the wound, feeling blood pour over his hands. *Now I am a slave to Hades.*

Apollo, a mocking curl to his lip, came to him, gripped the sword, and yanked it out. Sinon cried out and doubled over, holding his belly because he felt as if his guts were spilling out.

Then the pain lessened. The blood on his hands dried. His organs didn't burst onto the grass. He straightened and looked, smoothing his hands over the front of his tunic. The cloth was still ripped, but the wound in his belly was gone. Healed.

"You cannot die." Apollo used the bloody point of his sword to flick at the chain around his neck. "Another thing—in Troy they call you the Liar. I can't have that here, for I am the god of Truth. As long as you wear that chain, you cannot lie." He turned and went away.

Sinon collapsed, his breath coming in gasps, his mind flailing, refusing to understand.

I killed myself and did not die. I am neither alive nor dead now.

Time passed. Sinon lived in luxurious captivity, richly fed and clothed, lingering amid the entertainments of the Sun Palace. Apollo summoned the best musicians, dancers, and bards to perform for him. Sinon kept to the shadows, intensely jealous because the performers could leave at the end of the evening.

He ran. He jumped hedges and raced his shadow, as if still training to be a warrior. He made himself a wooden sword out of a tree branch and practiced hitting at shrubs, scattering leaves and broken branches around him on the lawn. Sweating deadened his mind and kept him from trying to be clever like Odysseus.

The sun never set on Apollo's palace. Always, it was midday—always a little too warm, too bright. Tracking one day to the next was impossible.

One day, walking in the garden, he startled a woman who was bathing in one of the pools. She gasped, covering her breasts with her arms. He quickly turned away. With his luck, the Sun God's sister had come for a visit, and he knew the stories that told what happened to men who spied Artemis at her bath.

He'd started to leave, when she called him back. "Wait a moment. You must be Sinon. The Greek."

He stopped. Her voice was bright, good-natured.

"I'd heard you were a prisoner here. Don't be shy— stay and talk with me. You were at Troy, weren't you? Will you tell me stories of the war?"

Cautiously, he approached. She modestly hid herself in the water, only her head and neck breaking the surface. She was young, with a rosy, shining face to match her voice. He couldn't guess the color of her hair, which was dark with water and slicked back.

Smiling, she nodded at the brick-lined edge of the pool. "Sit here, so I don't get a crick in my neck staring up at you."

This had to be a trick. He had seen women at the palace—nymphs and minor goddesses come to sport with Apollo and each other, indulging in the god's hospitality. None had ever spoken to him. Sinon knelt a little way from the pool's edge.

"You don't trust me," she said.

"I don't trust anything about this place."

"Wise man."

"Who are you?"

"Celeste."

"Are you a nymph? Or something else?"

"I'm . . . something," she said. Her smile filled her expression, so at ease and lovely.

"Why are you here?"

"Do you always ask so many questions?"

He looked away, blushing. But he didn't know how to act. This was all so strange.

She answered him. "Apollo brought me here."

"You're a prisoner as well," he said, perhaps too eagerly.

She shook her head. He could see her shape in the water, rippling, without detail. He could see himself reaching to touch her. It had been so long since he'd spoken to a woman. Cassandra at Troy had been the last.

Her expression turned sly, as if like a god she knew his thoughts. "Did you rape many women at Troy?"

Angrily, he said, "I raped none." He'd been so tired, twice beaten and too weak to hold a woman, much less have her. At least, that had been his excuse to himself.

She stared at him until he felt as naked as she was. Then she said, "I believe you, hero of Greece."

Water rippling around her, she came to the edge of the pool and reached a dripping hand to touch him. The coolness of her skin sent a shock up his arm. To hold her to him would still the heat flushing along his body. Graceful, slipping like a breeze, she pulled herself out of the water so she was sitting next to him, in all her soft and pale glory. Then she kissed him.

He threw himself into lovemaking, her eagerness feeding his, both of them clawing off his tunic. He told himself he should slow down, enjoy every moment of her beauty and vigor, but he was desperate for her touch, her mouth, her body. On top of her, at the edge of the pool, rushes and lilies as a backdrop, he moaned as he entered her, and the stresses of his captivity left him.

The sound of applause carried across the pool. Sinon looked. Across the way, on a stone bench, sat Apollo, clapping, watching them as if this were a play. Celeste, her head tipped back, her expression contorted with ecstasy, didn't seem to notice.

Sinon's cheeks burned red, anger filling him all over again. He pounded into her harder than he should have, and at the moment of his release—she melted. She turned to water, a flood that slipped out of his arms and back to the pool.

He was left kneeling, breathing hard, soaking wet. Apollo grinned. He'd planned the whole thing. *Damn him.*

Scowling, Sinon stood, grabbed his tunic, and marched away.

Another time, invisible hands tied him to his pallet,

face up. Then Apollo arrived and toyed with him, bringing him to the edge, evoking pleasure even as Sinon resisted. Sinon even laughed once at a ticklish jab. It was an unexpected noise. Apollo untied him and left him exhausted, humiliated, confused.

He had no way to track the time.

7

❧❧

Under the open collar of Alex's shirt, the bronze chain glinted. He'd told Evie it was a curse, keeping him alive and ageless, when all he'd ever wanted was to die. He'd offered to slit his wrists then and there to prove it to her. She insisted she believed him. One way or another, he'd bleed all over her car and she didn't need that.

It just looked like a necklace.

Evie had to turn around and go back. She'd raced from the hotel and made the quicker right-hand turn. While she could travel side streets to avoid driving past the hotel again, she still had to go through town to get back home. Through town and the police checkpoint. Evie stopped.

Three patrol cars—Hopes Fort's entire law enforcement fleet—were parked across Main Street, blocking it. At least half a dozen people were crouched behind open car doors, aiming their handguns at her as she slowed to a stop. Hopes Fort had only a handful of officers, but a number of part-time deputies served as well, in addition to the Citizens' Watch volunteers.

"I don't know what's going on," she said. Her voice felt stiff. Silent, Alex stared hard out the windshield.

Johnny Brewster stood behind the barrier of his open car door, gripping his gun in both hands. "Get out of the car! Hands up, out of the car!"

She shouldn't have hesitated. She didn't expect herself to hesitate, but she did. Maybe because Alex didn't move either. This felt odd, an out-of-place sensation—like that stranger's hand around hers. Like a door was closing to trap her in a dark room. *I'm getting paranoid.*

"What do you want to do?" Alex said.

She wanted to go home. "I think we should get out. Slowly. This is just a misunderstanding, I'll explain it to Johnny. It'll be okay." She hoped that saying it would make it true.

"Get out of the car!" Johnny was snarling, his face turning red, furious.

Evie opened her car door. Alex opened his. She climbed out and straightened, holding her hands up by her face. On the other side of the car, Alex was doing the same.

"Put your hands on the roof of the car! Stay there, don't move!"

This was like some overwrought scene out of her comic book. Tracker, undercover, meeting with a double agent, getting in trouble at some volatile border . . . she'd have to file that away for a plot twist.

She and Alex put their hands on the roof of the car. He glanced at her. His expression was stony.

This was about him. The police wanted him. What had he done? Besides stalk her family.

Four of the cops ran out to them. Three of them

went to Alex, patted him down, pulled him away from the car, and wrenched his arms back.

Johnny Brewster came to her and gripped her arm. "Evie! Are you okay?"

She straightened. "What's wrong? What happened?"

"We got a call that some guy matching his description jumped in your car and held a gun on you."

She stared. "No, there must be a mistake. He—he's a friend. Nobody pulled a gun."

One of the other cops called, "Johnny, he doesn't have a gun."

"Check the car." The guy climbed in and looked under the seat, opened the glove box. Johnny looked back at her. "Carlos Alvarez called from the Schooner. He said that you were just there, and that one of his guests saw you get carjacked."

Several points of confusion collided in her mind in a moment of understanding. The question was, how much would she have to tell Johnny to explain the situation? Alex wasn't the one trying to kidnap her. That other guy, he must have fed Carlos the story. But how did she explain that? And how did she explain Alex? On the other hand, if she wanted Johnny to haul him away, now was her chance.

"Johnny, this has been a misunderstanding. He's a friend—I'm giving him a ride." If it wasn't the truth, it wasn't exactly a lie, either. She didn't know what he was. "How likely does a carjacking sound? Does that sort of thing happen in Hopes Fort? Has anything like that *ever* happened in Hopes Fort?"

Johnny frowned, knowing she was right. He lowered his voice. "What about that stranger you called me about? Is this him?"

She'd given Johnny a description of him, hadn't she? "No. I mean, that was a mistake. I'm sorry. It's okay, Johnny, really."

He turned to the others. "He have ID on him?"

"We didn't find *anything* on him," the same cop said. "Well, a couple of twigs in his pocket."

Johnny left her to stroll over to Alex. He'd learned his swagger straight off a prime-time police drama.

"You know it's illegal to travel without proper identification?" Johnny said.

Alex looked at him. He had the cold, still look of someone about to start a fight. Johnny must have seen it, too. He held his right hand on his hip, next to his gun, daring him. The men by the cars still had their guns drawn. If Alex threw a punch, as he seemed to want to do, somebody would shoot. *Please don't. . . .*

"Here it is," Alex said at last. He pulled a wallet from an inside coat pocket and handed it to Johnny.

Johnny glared at the cop who'd searched him. "I thought you said he didn't have anything on him."

The guy held up his hands. "I didn't find anything, I swear!"

Johnny grumbled, mostly to himself, "Figures. Never patted down a guy in his life." He opened the wallet, studied it, looked back at Alex. "I'm going to check this. Don't move."

He returned to his car and began some arcane background-checking process. Alex put his hands in his coat pockets, settling in to wait. Evie watched him. He didn't seem at all concerned that he might be shot if he so much as flinched wrong. She'd lived in L.A. for ten years; you didn't mess with the cops.

Alex had this tilt to his chin, this light in his eyes, a confidence that said he could take them all on by himself. Or he believed he could. And why not? He believed he was immortal.

Finally Johnny returned and handed the wallet back to Alex. "There's nothing on you. If Evie says you're okay, I've got no reason to hold you."

"Thank you, Officer." Alex tucked the wallet away.

They both looked at Evie.

"Can we go now?" she said, more bitingly than she had intended. She felt like she'd been holding her breath.

Crossing back to her side of the car, Johnny said, "Are you *sure* you're okay?"

"I'm fine, really." She looked away so she wouldn't glare at him.

"He's a stranger. You can't blame me for being suspicious."

"It's a wonder anyone leaves home anymore."

"Will you vouch for him? I'm going to have to report this. If I have a contact for him, it won't look suspicious. *As* suspicious."

Alex looked at her across the roof of the car. She could say the word right now, and Johnny would arrest him on suspicion of—of being a stranger in a small town. She still didn't know anything about him. For all she knew, he really was a terrorist bent on the destruction of Hopes Fort.

Like anyone would notice the destruction of Hopes Fort.

"Yes. Sure."

"Okay. I'm still going to keep an eye on him."

She and Alex were allowed to return to the car. They had to wait for the police cars to pull out of the way before they could continue on.

They were well out of town, on the prairie road to the Walker house, before either of them said anything.

"That could have gone badly," she said.

"They were more scared than we were, I think."

"You weren't scared at all." He certainly acted like he was immune to bullets.

He laughed, shaking his head. The expression quickly turned somber again. "You didn't have to stand up for me back there. You could have gotten rid of me."

And she may yet regret that decision, she thought. Evie pulled into the driveway and shut off the engine. "Let me see that wallet."

She was surprised that he didn't argue. He pulled the wallet out of the same pocket and handed it to her. Inside, she found a Georgia driver's license with his photo on it, alongside the name Simon Philips. Hometown, Athens.

"Not Alex?" He only glanced at her out the corner of his eye. "Johnny's check came up clean. How'd you hide your wallet from them?"

He swiped the wallet out of her hand and deliberately opened his coat to drop it in the inside pocket. "Magic," he said. He opened the coat again. The pocket showed no obvious bulge. She resisted an urge to pat down his coat. "Also, letting people draw their own conclusions is not the same as lying."

Her sigh probably sounded excessively annoyed. She felt suddenly exhausted. Getting stopped at a police roadblock did that to a person.

Mab was on the front porch, her head lifted, watching them approach the house. She didn't leap forward, tail wagging, to greet Evie as she did with the elder Walker—Evie guessed she was still too new for the dog to feel protective. This time, Mab watched Alex.

Evie walked ahead. "Hey, Mab. Hey, girl." She hadn't been around dogs since she moved away and felt awkward talking to this one, like she was as much a stranger here as Alex. She didn't have a right to be talking to Mab this way.

Mab glanced at her, twitched her tail slightly, then turned back to Alex, riveting him with her stare.

Alex stopped. "She doesn't like me, I think."

"She just doesn't know you." As she reached the first step of the porch, she noticed just how big Mab was. She must have weighed two hundred pounds. Evie offered her hand to the beast. Mab sniffed it, flattening her ears in a contrite gesture.

When Alex put his foot on the first step, Mab growled.

Evie almost jumped back. Instead, she forced herself to scratch the silky fur on Mab's head. Mab looked back and forth between them, her brown eyes earnest, by turns beseeching when they looked at Evie, threatening when they came to Alex. He stood with his hands at his sides, his face calm.

What would he do if Mab attacked him?

Alex took a second step onto the porch. Mab's growling doubled.

Evie took the dog's head in her hands and forced her to break eye contact with Alex.

"Mab, it's okay. He's okay. Please." She felt silly pleading with a dog, when she ought to be commanding her. But somehow she couldn't talk like that to Mab, their guardian.

While Evie was holding her head, Mab managed to slink her body around so she stood between her and Alex.

This wasn't working. Evie reached across Mab's body and took Alex's hand. She maneuvered around the massive dog until she stood side by side with him.

"Mab, it's okay, he's a friend."

The dog stopped growling, but continued staring at Alex with uncertainty. He offered his hand. She smelled it—distantly, without letting her nose make contact. But her tail wagged a few weak swipes across the porch.

Evie led Alex in through the front door. Mab stayed on the porch, watching them.

"A very devoted animal," Alex said.

They were still holding hands. She dropped his quickly and took a step away, turning toward the door to the basement.

She could see part of the living room from here. Her father wasn't there. She almost called for him, then decided against it, not wanting to explain Alex and all that had happened that afternoon.

Downstairs, Evie switched on the light, found the flashlight, and opened the door to the Storeroom. She had no idea what she was looking for. She thought of the woman's dark eyes, her poise, and her desire. What could she want? Evie panned the flashlight over shelves and boxes, a rack of quivers filled with arrows, a bundle that looked like a rolled-up carpet, a Middle Eastern–style oil lamp, an obsidian knife, a dried-up ear of maize.

"This was your idea," she called back to Alex. "What am I looking for?"

From the next room, Alex said, "I'm trying to remember the mythology and what was associated with Hera, any items that were particularly hers. Or rather, something that she wanted that *wasn't* hers."

There, something tickled the back of her mind. Something the woman wanted, but not hers, or Evie could just have given it to her. She went to a chest of drawers, beside the wardrobe with all the shoes in it. The top drawer held crowns and tiaras.

Alex hadn't entered the Storeroom. He waited outside, framed by the doorway.

"Can you come here, see if any of this reminds you of anything?"

He glanced up the stairs, then back to her. "I can't go in there."

She went back to the door. "Why not?"

He was fidgeting, picking at his sleeves before shoving his hands in his pockets. His face looked tense. "I can't cross the threshold. I shouldn't even be in the house." He drew one hand from his pocket and reached, and flattened it like he had touched a physical barrier at the threshold. It was almost exactly what the woman had done at the front door. "This house—that room—you. You all exist to keep people like me out. To keep us from taking what's in there. Your dog was right to keep me away."

"But I invited you in. If I—"

"I don't think that's a good idea. I'll wait out here."
He moved to sit on the steps.

What was he feeling that she wasn't? She'd always
felt safe in the house—and they probably never had
to worry about thieves. She returned to the chest of
drawers, to follow that nagging in her mind.

The second drawer held jewelry boxes, rings, lock-
ets, pocket watches. The third drawer held papers:
old parchment, vellum, even a few fibrous sheets that
must have been papyrus. Some had maps drawn on
them, weathered pirate maps with X marks the spot;
some letters with foreign postmarks; poems written
in illegible hands in exotic languages. That drawer
was filled with whispers tugging at the edge of Evie's
hearing.

The bottom drawer held fruit. One apple there
might have been real once, but was now a shriveled,
petrified husk with a single bite taken from it. Several
apples seemed to glow, but were too light to be made
of gold. Two were made of solid gold. They rolled
heavily on the wood base of the drawer when she
opened it. When she tried to touch them, they skittered away from her, slipping against her skin, like
they didn't want to be held. She needed two hands to
catch them, trapping them and lifting them one at a
time. One was a plain gold apple. The other, she studied closer.

It seemed to be cast in solid gold, complete with
stem. It was cool against her skin, heavy in her hand.
Her thumb touched a rough spot. Turning the flashlight to it, she found a design stamped into the gold—
five shapes, figures made of the lines and squiggles of
ancient writing:

Who do you belong to?

She felt an answer; then the answer faded. *No one.* But it was here to be kept safe. That was true of everything here.

Who did you belong to? she asked, holding an image of the striking woman in her mind.

No, not her. Close, but not her.

She grasped for a deeper answer, but that was all she heard with that odd sense that felt so strong in this room.

How ridiculous was it, to be holding a conversation with a cryptic antique?

She brought the apple to the doorway, to the light from the other room, and showed it to Alex. "Do you recognize this?"

He squinted at it, moving to the doorway, drawn to it though he held himself warily, inching toward her like he didn't want to come too close.

"It's a golden apple."

"Do you know what the inscription means?"

His expression turned leery. "What makes you think I would?"

"You seem to know everything else," she said.

He stepped back. "I don't want to touch it."

She sighed, exasperated. "Then just look at it."

He held himself aloof, as far away from it as he could and still study it. His gaze passed over the inscription, back and forth, his face still, emotionless. He swallowed.

"The language is ancient Greek in its oldest form. The writing is Mycenaean. It hasn't been used in over three thousand years. It says, *kalisetei*. It means, 'For the fairest.' This—" He pointed at the apple. "—started the Trojan War."

She felt like a child who'd been given a grenade without being told what it did. "It's the language you were speaking to her. To the woman."

"Yes."

"I thought Helen started the Trojan War."

"It goes back much further than that. Out of revenge for not being invited to the marriage of King Peleus and Thetis, the goddess Discord tossed the apple into the banquet hall. Athena, Aphrodite, and Hera argued over who, being the fairest among them, should have it. They chose a mortal man, Paris, to be the judge. And, being goddesses, they bribed him with wealth, fame, power—and love. Aphrodite offered him Helen. He chose her. And for ten years, two great civilizations fought a war over that choice."

For the fairest. It had fallen out of a story and into her hand. It was just an heirloom her grandfather or someone had picked up somewhere. The marks were just a pretty pattern. That was the trick, wasn't it? How could she *know* what this was? How could he tell her this story about a thing that might as well be a movie prop, and how could she believe him?

"Hera still wants it," Alex said. "It still has power."

"Who are you?" She kept asking that. Why should he tell her now?

"Cursed."

From upstairs, Mab started barking fiercely, as if

battling demons. Evie jumped and almost dropped the apple. Alex glanced up the stairs.

Rubbing her thumb over the inscription, she returned the apple to the chest of drawers. She closed the Storeroom door firmly behind her when she left.

"Let's see what's wrong." She tugged on his sleeve, and he followed her up the stairs.

The kitchen door slammed shut.

"Don't close your door on me, Frank Walker! I know who you are and I know you have it!" A man shouted loud enough to hear in the basement, even over Queen Mab's barking.

When she got to the kitchen, her father had opened the door a crack. He must have been sleeping; he wore a bathrobe and slippers. He was hushing the dog, who was inside, whining and turning circles, her claws clicking on the linoleum.

"Mab, down! What is it you think I have?"

"Open the door. I will not stand here like a beggar or a supplicant."

Frank sighed, his shoulders slouching. He opened the door wide, cold air or no. Mab started to launch herself, lunging like she would tackle the visitor, but she stopped just inside the doorway, between Evie's father and the stranger, barking like mad.

The visitor glowered at her. "Quiet! If you please, madam!"

Mab clamped her jaws shut. She ducked and backed a step, whining noises still straining at her throat, but she wouldn't leave Frank's side.

The visitor was an older man, around her father's age, with short steel-gray hair and a trimmed beard.

He carried a walking stick, which he propped on the porch between him and the dog. He wore a tired brown tweed suit and an air of importance.

"I've come for the sword," he said.

Frank looked the man up and down. "What sword?"

"What sword?" the man said "What *sword*? The one sword, the sword of power that may be carried only by the true king. The sword that Viviane gave over to your family's keeping fifteen hundred years ago. Didn't she tell you I'd come for it one day?"

Evie stared at the tableau like she was watching a play, with Alex breathing at her shoulder.

"I don't know. My family may have kept the sword for that long, but we don't remember who gave it to us. How do I know you're the one?"

"How maddening, to be hindered by fools. Let me explain this to you: He is coming. The sword belongs to him. Not me, not you. Him. I must see that he gets it."

"Him. The true king?"

"Yes."

"I see. Wait just a minute."

He turned and started a moment, glancing with surprise at Evie and looking harder at Alex, but he nodded and moved to the basement door. The stranger started to enter the house, but her father looked back and pointed. "Evie, make sure he stays here."

The old man glared at her. She shrugged and took her place beside Mab when he tried to step inside.

"Do you know who I am, young lady?" he said.

She had a nagging suspicion she knew who he *thought* he was.

"I could turn you into a frog. A hideous, ugly frog."

He raised his hands, fingers pointed in an arcane gesture.

She crossed her arms.

"I have a feeling she's safe in this house, even from you," Alex said.

The old man stood for a moment, pointing expectantly as if waiting for something to happen. Nothing did. Evie didn't feel so much as a hair tingle at the back of her neck.

He narrowed his eyes. "Yes. I almost forgot. This house, this family. I must hand it to Viviane—she always knew what she was doing." He looked at Alex. "And who are you?"

"A traveler. Like yourself."

"Hm, not like me at all. Sapling."

Alex stifled a chuckle with a hand over his mouth.

Her father called from the basement stairs. "Evie? Take our visitor around back. I'll meet you there."

She couldn't do anything but play along. She gestured for the man to leave first, and they filed off the porch and went to the back of the house, Mab trotting close at Evie's side.

A few moments later, her father followed, carrying a sword, held upright. It was plain, nothing like the fantastic, gem-encrusted weapons with baroque hilts and engraved pommels that teenager Evie had drawn in the margins of class notes. Functional, well balanced, one that might sing if its bearer sliced the air with it.

Both Alex and the stranger turned and stared.

"By the gods," Alex breathed.

"Ah, old friend!" the stranger said, a warm smile deepening the creases on his face.

Her father stood before a lumpy boulder that lay in

the center of an otherwise flat stretch of dried-out lawn. It was as tall as his waist, as big around as an ottoman, weathered smooth and covered with gray lichens. Part of why the house had been built here was because no one had found a way to move the rock and clear the space for plowing. When Evie was little, she'd played mountain climbing on it, and pretended it was her throne. It had been one of her favorite things about going to her grandparents' house.

Using both hands, Frank reversed the sword and placed the point on the top of the boulder. Then, taking a deep breath, he pushed. The sword went through the rock like it was snow, until only a handsbreadth of blade below the hilt remained exposed.

The sword in the stone. It was real, and it was in the Walkers' backyard. Evie almost had to sit down.

The stranger drew a sharp breath. Alex's eyes lit up. He was grinning.

"There," Frank said, brushing off his hands. "It's his sword, you say. Bring him here and let him take it."

"Damn." Disbelieving, the stranger blinked. "Didn't see that coming."

Frank stared at him. "Really?"

Alex went to the stone and paced around it, circling closer like a shark to meat. "May I?" he said, pointing at the hilt and turning to Frank.

"Sure."

Alex closed his hands around the hilt and pulled. And pulled and pulled, but the sword didn't even jiggle in its nest. Laughing, he said, "This is marvelous!"

The stranger, Merlin, looked at her father. "This is fair. I can't complain. Events must run their course—I, of all people, understand that. But I will return. And I will bring the lad."

"We'll be here," her father said.

The man stalked off, disappearing around the corner of the house.

Evie reached and let her fingertips skim the smooth metal of the cross guard, then slide down the flat of the blade, at least the few inches before it sank into the stone. The steel was warm to the touch and seemed to hum. The skin on the back of her neck tingled. The sword in the stone was real, Merlin had just marched away, those glass slippers—and Hera. The goddess, Queen of Olympus, who wanted the golden apple.

Before Evie could say a word to speak any of this out loud, to make it real in her own ears, her father doubled over, grunting as he collapsed against the rock.

Evie was at his side in a moment; Alex joined her.

"Dad, what's wrong? Dad—"

"I'm—I'll be fine. Just . . . help me get inside."

"I'll call an ambulance—"

"No, no," he said, his jaw clenched, his voice taut.

"Dad—"

"Evie, do as he says," Alex said grimly. He pulled her father's left arm over his shoulder. Evie followed his lead with his right arm.

Mab whined, shoving at Evie's hip with her nose the whole slow walk to the house.

Lucinda put her hand on her pregnant belly, pushed back the cloth draped over the doorway to her hut, and found an old/young woman standing before her. She looked old, with silver hair and creased eyes, but seemed young in the way she smiled and the straight way she held herself.

"Salve," the woman said. "I've heard that this is a place where objects may be safely stored." She was holding a long slender bundle in black oilskin.

"Yes," Lucinda said, and stepped aside. "Come in. May I offer refreshment? I have bread if you like, and some wine."

"Thank you." The woman entered and settled on one of the simple wooden chairs at the table by the hearth fire. The hut also contained a rope bed, a cupboard, and a door leading down to a root cellar.

Lucinda wished suddenly for finer surroundings, for silver dishes instead of ones of wood and clay, for a tiled floor instead of dirt. The woman was so regal, she might have been noble, certainly used to the Roman ways of more civilized regions. She didn't feel ashamed for her surroundings—Anthony worked hard to keep them comfortable. But she wanted to do more.

"When is the baby due?" the woman asked.

Lucinda smiled. "Any day, I think." Or rather, she hoped. She felt as ponderous as a mountain.

She set a clay plate before the woman and placed on it a portion of bread, cheese, and a sliced apple.

"This is lovely," the woman said. "You are generous."

"I wish I had more. Some meat or fish. This must seem like peasant fare to you."

The woman closed her eyes and shook her head. "No, never think that. How many stories have you heard of the simple gifts given to witches by the roadside? The small gift, honestly given, is more valuable than the riches of kings."

Lucinda lowered her gaze, abashed at the woman's intensity.

The woman's eyes creased, searching her. "You seem young to be the Keeper of this place."

"My father died suddenly." He'd fallen while searching for a lost sheep. The shock and pain of all his knowledge, the weight of all his responsibility crashing into her still ached.

"And you are his heir?"

She nodded.

"Then I will give you this." The woman pulled the cloth away to reveal a sword. She pulled the weapon from its scabbard and laid it on the table.

It was a beautiful piece, well wrought and shining, simple and functional. It seemed to catch the light from the fire, take it into itself and glow. The grip was *stained dark, where a hand had carried it for many years. Lucinda started to touch it, but hesitated, as if something held her back.*

"His name is Excalibur," said the woman, who ran a finger tenderly along the pommel. "He belongs to a king, who will return to claim him one day."

"When?"

The woman's gray eyes glinted. "I do not know. It could be many years."

"It—he—is very powerful, isn't he?"

"Yes. Can you keep him safe?"

With a conviction that wasn't her own, but had followed her family for generations, she said, "Yes."

Lucinda took hold of Excalibur and replaced it in its scabbard. "Good-bye," the woman whispered as Lucinda went down into the cellar. She put the sword on a shelf cut into the earth, among the other boxes and sacks stored there. She felt its power, a tingle in her arm. But it slept peacefully in the place she had given it.

He must be a great king, to wield such a sword.

When she emerged aboveground, the old woman stood by the doorway.

"I took the bread and cheese—I hope you don't mind," she said. "I'm afraid I must travel now. I can't stay."

"All right."

"Will you let me bless your child?"

A flush spread across Lucinda's cheek. "Yes, please. I would be honored."

And so the woman placed her hands on Lucinda's rounded belly, where the heir of the family grew, and whispered words of strength and courage.

Then she turned away. With every step she took across the field—Lucinda's cottage was far from any villages—she seemed more bent, more aged, and when Lucinda lost sight of her, she was like the witches of the stories.

Which she was, Lucinda supposed.

8

Apollo woke Sinon. When he spoke, his tone was serious, incongruous with the god's usual demeanor. "If you keep quiet and act the part, you will see a thing few mortals have witnessed. A Council of the Gods."

Sinon sat up, holding the coverlet around himself.

"Oh, look—is that a flash of curiosity in your eyes? Athena has called us to discuss your friend Odysseus. I would have you there to consult, since you know him. You can come as my servant if you promise to behave yourself. No tricks, no petty rebellions. I assure you, many of my colleagues are not as good-humored as I am. They'll toss you off Olympus if they find you the least bit offensive. Do you promise?"

He nodded quickly. News of Odysseus! And to see Olympus.

"I must hear the words. Say it."

"I promise."

Apollo straightened, his arrogant smile returning. "Good."

Phoebus Apollo dressed in gold, shimmering like the

sun, and wore a circlet that gleamed with its own intense light. He garbed Sinon in a white silk chiton pinned with gold brooches, leaving much of his muscular chest and arms exposed. His beard was closely trimmed, his hair tied back with a gold ribbon. Apollo brought him to a doorway. Sinon had always thought it led to a closet, but Apollo slid back the screen, and beyond the door lay nothing, a shadow, featureless space.

"You will stand behind my chair and keep my goblet filled. Deliver messages if I need you to. Keep your head bowed, and keep your thoughts to yourself. Think of wool or fog if you must think of something. They won't be able to read you so easily. Do not speak unless I give you permission, not even if Zeus himself asks you a question."

"Zeus will be there?" Sinon blinked, feeling suddenly ill.

Apollo smirked. "Of course. Now remember, *behave* yourself."

They stepped through the doorway. For a lurching moment, Sinon thought he had stepped off a cliff: his stomach turned, his mind felt dizzy, his feet tumbled over his head— But he took a second step and felt stone under his feet. He opened his eyes.

The stories told of a lofty palace, vast spaces capable of holding the heavens and filled with the blinding light of the gods, overwhelming to the eyes of mortals, inducing awe and madness.

In fact, Sinon walked on the stone base of a great bowl that had been cut out of the side of a hill. Tiers made of cracked and weathered stone, shining in the sun, had been built up one side, forming a hundred rows of benches that curved around and looked down upon the central floor. Every seat had a vantage, and the depression trapped sound. Footsteps echoed. A grove of trees closed in the other half of the circle. Sinon couldn't see beyond to look for landmarks on the chance he might recognize the place. The sky above was blue, flecked with clouds, and he smelled the ocean on a slight breeze.

"What is this place?" Sinon asked breathlessly.

"An amphitheater. Athena's design. In another five hundred years, I imagine they'll be littered all over Greece."

Without a second glance, Apollo strode forward into the plaza. Sinon followed, trying to show indifference.

On the central floor—the stage—a dozen chairs, gleaming white, made of ivory perhaps, sat in a circle. Beside each chair was a small table with a silver goblet and pitcher, and a tray of delicacies. Several people, dressed much like Sinon was, their gazes downcast, went from table to table, filling pitchers and trays with wine and food. Others stood by the chairs, meek and unmoving. Servants. Slaves. All mortal, Sinon thought.

He watched the people who weren't servants. They stood apart, in twos or threes, studying each other across the room, talking quietly. They were regal, garbed in the richest fabric and jewels, their hair oiled and perfectly arranged, tied with strings of pearls and lapis. The men were broad of shoulder, proud of mien; the women slim, curved, gleaming with marble beauty. Imperious. The gods and goddesses of Olympus.

Their gazes turned to Apollo when he and Sinon came into view. Sinon hung back, not wishing to draw attention to himself—willing, for once, to defer to

Apollo. Apollo nodded to the others, who nodded in return. Sinon felt some of their gazes pass over him, a pricking as his hair stood on end.

Think of nothing. Wool. Fog.

"Greetings, Brother. It's been ages since I've seen you." A woman in a short tunic belted with silver, wearing silver-laced sandals bounded up to Apollo like a young girl, or a deer. Where Apollo was light, she was dark, black hair tied with silver chains, her skin olive, her eyes intense.

"Greetings, Sister. It has been far too long." Apollo touched her face and leaned in to kiss her cheek lightly. His smile seemed genuine. "Tell me, what's the mood?"

"Everyone's still cranky about Troy." She rolled her eyes. "*That's* why we should put men and women on different continents and have visiting days only once a year. Men and women together cause such problems."

"That would not please some of our brethren as much as it would please you," Apollo said.

Artemis pointedly looked Sinon up and down, studying him. Sinon kept his gaze on his toes. "He's new, isn't he? Very nice."

"Yes. Thank you."

Sinon was afraid he was blushing. He lifted his gaze enough to see Artemis wink at him before she went away. He let out a sigh.

Apollo glanced at him and chuckled. "My twin sister. Lovely, isn't she? Don't get any ideas. She'd eat you alive."

Sinon snorted. "I'm only thinking about wool and fog, my lord, as you commanded."

Apollo laughed.

One of the chairs was larger than the others. It had

thick armrests and shimmering upholstery, and stood on a dais. An old man with gray hair and beard, a stern gaze, and heavy shoulders emerged from the grove of trees and moved to the chair. He drew attention to himself—he was like the North Star pulling lodestones, the way everyone fell silent and looked at him. He stepped up on the dais and rested on his throne.

This was Zeus.

Sinon had an urge to prostrate himself before that throne, to pray as he never had in his life, not even in battle. He clenched his fists.

Apollo turned to him and whispered, "You'd bow to Zeus but not to me?"

Sinon nodded. His voice shook. "He's Zeus. The Father."

"Yes, he is."

When Zeus sat, the others took the signal to make their way to their own chairs. The servants disappeared, except for the personal slaves of each of the gods, who lurked unobtrusively behind the chairs. Most of the gods had servants. A pair of girls waited on Artemis. Aphrodite had an army of maidens. (Sinon knew she was Aphrodite—he could barely look at her, she shone so brightly.) Hermes, the man with wings on his sandals, didn't have any. Nor did Zeus himself.

Sinon tried to name them all: Hephaestus, who slumped in his chair over a twisted leg; Athena, the regal woman with the gray eyes and piercing gaze; Ares, who snarled at everyone around him.

The minor deities sat on the stone benches carved into the hill, around the outside of the circle. One of the chairs of the inner circle was empty.

The goddess who sat closest to Zeus was not the

most beautiful, but she was striking. Sinon looked past her once, but found himself drawn back to her, until he could look at no one else. There was a gravity to her, much like the aura of authority that clung to Zeus. Her dark curling hair was piled on her head in a queenly fashion, respectable, admirable. Her gown was elegant, her jewels tasteful. This, then, was Hera.

Zeus spoke. Sinon expected his voice to break the silence like thunder. Instead, it was calm. It held the weight of authority without the storm.

"Athena, speak your grievance."

Athena stood. She was tall—taller than Sinon. He remembered she was a warrior goddess. She looked like she feared nothing.

"I come to plead on behalf of Odysseus the Ithacan. For ten long years, he has been the plaything of our anger, our rivalries. We should have been done with such pettiness at Troy. Instead, our bickering continues, scattering the Greeks across the oceans. Ten years have passed since Odysseus left Troy. It is time for him to return home. I would enlist your help to make this so."

Ten years.

He had been enslaved to Apollo for ten years. But he didn't feel any different than he had that night in Agamemnon's tent, when they planned the horse—

He crouched and whispered in Apollo's ear. "Ten years? It's been ten years?"

Apollo said, "Yes. And every one of Odysseus's men has died on the journey home. I saved your life, enslaving you. Now be quiet."

Athena continued. "He is being held captive by the nymph Calypso. My King Zeus, one word from you, and she would release him. He could go home, after all this time."

Odysseus, also held captive. And all his men dead. Sinon nearly wept for his friend. Odysseus would have taken to heart every one of those deaths.

Hera leaned forward, smiling sweetly. "I observe that you petition us now, when Poseidon is absent." She nodded at the empty chair.

"An astute observation, my lady. It's no secret, he hates Odysseus and would never consent to easing his path home. But he cannot oppose a decision that we all agree to. So I ask for aid now."

Ares stood. "He is a *Greek*. I oppose them on principle."

Athena raised an eyebrow, looking like she was exercising patience. "That was a long time ago. Troy is gone now."

"Because of Odysseus. Why should I help him?"

"You don't have to help him. Just don't hinder him any longer."

A pleasant soft-featured woman with hair the color of wheat—Demeter?—leaned forward. "Is he in any danger? Is Calypso mistreating him?"

"Only by keeping him prisoner."

"Then why not let him be? Why interfere?"

"Because he longs for home more than anything. Have pity on him!" Athena said, pleading with a closed fist.

Aphrodite laughed, a sound like bells. "It's true, isn't it? You *do* love him! The one man you've ever encountered who might actually be cleverer than you!"

Athena scowled.

Ares said, "Abandon him, Athena. He's just a mortal. Let him free himself, if he wants. I'm betting he'll just give up and live out his days in Calypso's arms."

Athena's lips thinned. "A bet? How much?"

"My finest war stallion."

Athena gave a full-blown smile. "Anyone else? I'll wager a golden lyre that he fights for freedom until he reaches his home."

Hermes hopped up so he crouched on the seat of his chair. "A bottle of wine from each of the four corners of the world says that he reaches home."

Aphrodite: "A casket of pearls that he surrenders." She and Ares exchanged a glance.

Apollo gestured for Sinon, who crouched by his master's chair. "It's terrible. Half of us admire Odysseus's persistence. The other half want to see how much he'll take before he gives up. What do you say? What will Odysseus do?"

"He will not give up. He'll die trying to return home."

"You know him better than the gods, who can read his thoughts? The thoughts of Odysseus are racked with despair these days."

"I fought beside him, my lord. He does not give in to despair."

Apollo said, "If I take Odysseus's part, if I ensure that he is able to return to his home and wife, will you come willingly to my bed?"

Sinon would have thrown himself off a cliff to help Odysseus. What Apollo asked—it was little enough. "Yes."

Voices volleyed around the theater. "I say he fights." Another said, "I say he doesn't!"

"Enough!" Zeus stood. Now his voice thundered, echoing against the stony hillside. Everyone fell silent. The slaves cowered behind their masters' chairs. Sinon was on his knees, head bowed. "I will not stay silent while you gamble on the lives of mortals. They are not our playthings, however much some of you might treat them as such. We destroyed one of the greatest human cities because of our rivalries. Isn't that enough?"

Apollo stood slowly, as if he had come to a momentous decision. "You are right, Father, of course. Our sister Athena is right. You should send Odysseus home."

Athena bowed to Apollo, but her gaze was narrowed, her brow creased with curiosity.

Zeus said, "And you take this position because—?"

"Because it wins us nothing to keep him away from home. I'm sure he prays to the gods daily for release. Why not answer his prayer and win a bit of faith?" He returned to his seat and rested his hand on his chin.

Ares gripped his armrests. "I want to see if I win my bet!"

"Ares, be quiet," Zeus said. "Hermes!"

The messenger god sprang from his seat and, moving so quickly he was a blur of light, crossed to Zeus's dais and bowed. "Go to Calypso and tell her she must set Odysseus on the path home. No arguments."

"At once, Father." In another flash of light, a breath of wind blowing with his passage, he was gone.

Athena bowed. "Thank you, Father."

Zeus waved her away. "You should all know that as many mortals hate us as worship us. They know it was the jealousy of vain goddesses that destroyed Troy and ruined the kingdoms of Greece. A time will come when they find they do not need us. And if they do not love us, what will they do with us then? I'm tired of listening to you lot. Leave me now."

Thus the council ended. The gods and goddesses rose, bowed to the King on his throne, and began to disperse.

Apollo said quietly to Sinon, "Do you see the woman there in the white veil and sea-green gown? She is Ino, one of the sea goddesses. Go tell her I wish to speak with her."

Sinon blinked. "You want me to *tell* a goddess?"

"I want you to deliver a message. Now, go."

The woman he had pointed out was leaving the stone benches, her two handmaidens accompanying her. Sinon had to slip around them, nearly leaping into the goddess's path. Haughty, she stared at him through the misty fabric of her veil, which rippled in the sea air. One of the handmaidens lifted her gaze, her eyes widening.

He recalled everything he had ever learned of manners and fine speech. He bowed deeply. "Great lady, my master, Phoebus Apollo of the Sun, wishes to speak words with you, if you would deign to linger for but a moment."

She might not even have been breathing, she stood so still, reacted so little. Then the veil rustled as she spoke. "Call him here. I will wait."

Sinon bowed yet again, then ran to tell Apollo. "She's waiting for you."

"Good."

Sinon followed the Sun God. Apollo stood before

Ino and merely inclined his head. "My lady. Thank you for staying."

"Your servant asked so nicely, how could I refuse?" She spared him a glance, the tiniest shifting of her head. Sinon wished he could see her without the veil.

Wool, fog.

"I need to ask a favor of you. Poseidon will hear of this. He will be angry. Watch over this Odysseus for me. See that he reaches the shore."

"You'll owe me a favor, Phoebus Apollo."

"I believe that is how such arrangements work. You will have my thanks, at such time as you feel the need to call upon it."

They nodded politely to each other, and Apollo stepped aside to let her pass. The handmaiden who'd looked up before glanced over her shoulder at Sinon. She had red hair and green eyes that made his heart clench.

Apollo said, "Poseidon will send Odysseus storms. Ino will protect him. Satisfied?"

"Yes." He looked away, feeling suddenly tired. He would never see Odysseus home and happy. But he would know his friend was safe.

"Quick now, stand behind me and look submissive."

Sinon looked up—Athena stood before them. She studied every inch of him, and he knew that she saw inside him, saw everything about him, knew who he was and what he had done.

If she knew what he'd done for Odysseus, would she care?

"Can I help you, Sister?" Apollo said.

She turned her cold gaze to the god. "I only wanted

to discover what you're getting by taking my side. Now I know." She smiled at Sinon and walked away.

"Come on," Apollo said, tipping his head as he turned to indicate that Sinon should follow.

Sinon didn't see the doorway that exited Olympus. He followed Apollo to the edge of the stone theater and found himself back in the Sun Palace. After the sun and breeze of the theater, the light and air here seemed harsh and artificial.

Apollo said, "So. What did you think of the Gods of Olympus?"

Olympus hadn't been what he expected. Sinon chuckled while he decided how best to say what he wished. The Council of the Gods had reminded him of the meeting in Agamemnon's tent as they planned the destruction of Troy. Powerful, arrogant men trying to compromise. No one willing to let go of his pride. Achilles sulking because of a perceived insult.

Ten years ago.

He said, "You're human. As human as I am. At least, you used to be."

"Very good. As clever as Odysseus. We were mortal magicians who became powerful enough to make ourselves gods. And the only things that amuse us anymore are the lives of mortals. It's ironic, don't you think?"

Sinon crossed his arms and stalked toward the god— the man. Apollo was shorter than Sinon. The Sun God grinned up at him, smug and playful. Like the whole thing was a joke he enjoyed telling again and again. The gods and their human passions. So much became clear.

He stopped just short of touching Apollo, so they could feel the heat of each other's skin.

"You're a fucking bastard," Sinon said, and kissed Apollo on the mouth.

Apollo held his face and pressed himself against Sinon. Pausing to take a breath, he said, "Yes. Yes, I am."

9

By the time Evie and Alex carried Frank to the kitchen door, he could stand again and pulled away from them.

"It's just a pain I get sometimes." His mouth was locked in a grimace, his voice harsh.

"How often is sometimes? How long has this been happening?" Evie demanded.

"Never mind."

"Dad—" Over and over again, Evie made the word a plea. *Tell me what's happening, tell me what's wrong, I don't understand.*

"I just need to rest."

He kept saying that.

Alex let him go as they entered the kitchen, but Evie clung to his arm. She trailed beside him, helpless.

Finally, in the living room, her father stopped and took hold of her shoulders. "Evie. I'm going to go to my room, take some painkillers, and lie down. I'll call you if I need anything."

She didn't believe him. His voice never sounded like that, on the edge of breaking, harsh with stifled emotion. He would suffer in silence until he curled up and disappeared into the pain.

"Promise?" she said, her voice small.

Nodding, he gave her arms a final squeeze. He let go, went into his room, limping, and closed the door.

"I should help him," she murmured. "I don't know how to help him."

"I'll leave," Alex said softly, and turned.

"No." She winced and looked away, floundering for words, wondering what she was doing. "I mean, you don't have to. Do you have a place to stay? Mr. Alvarez said you weren't at the motel."

He shrugged. "I've been here and there. I'll find a place. I always do. But if you think you could use a friend just now . . ."

If she asked him to stay and he did, she might find out more about him, she rationalized. Once again she asked herself, If the sword was Excalibur, and the woman was Hera . . . who was *he*?

"I could use the company." That sounded a little more honest.

"All right."

They stared at each other across the living room for a moment. Evie, tense and shaken, rubbed her hands and tried to keep her shoulders from bunching. Mab had settled down between the bedroom doors, lying with her head resting on her paws, looking dejected.

"You hungry?" Evie said abruptly, making a dash for the kitchen. "I'll make sandwiches."

"Can I help?"

"No, just sit down, make yourself at home."

She got as far as getting the bread out when her mobile phone rang. She ran to the living room, grabbed the phone off the coffee table, glanced apologetically at Alex, and answered the phone as she returned to the kitchen.

"Hi, Bruce."

"Have you had a chance to watch the news yet, or should I just tell you how world politics are fucking with our storyline?"

She didn't mean for her sigh to sound as forlorn as it probably did. "Things have been a little crazy here. I still haven't seen the news."

Bruce waited a second before asking, "How's your dad?"

She almost used her father's line: *Fine, okay.* Just like Frank's daughter. But Bruce was her friend—she should have been talking to him all along. She should have called him, instead of him calling her all the time.

"Not good. He isn't getting treatment, he's in pain, and there's nothing I can do. He won't talk, he's pretending like nothing's wrong—" Her voice cracked, and she shut her mouth to keep from breaking into a full-blown sob.

"Evie, I'm sorry. If there's anything—"

"I know, I know. Thanks, Bruce. I think I just need to keep working. Keep busy."

"Are you sure?"

"Yeah. So tell me, what's the President done now?"

"Well. Russia came up with proof that China's been funding the rebels. So the E.U. is siding with Russia and India. The U.S. is still waffling. Britain is waffling, and the E.U. is threatening sanctions on them for siding with the U.S."

"And we've got a whole storyline with the U.S. and Russia being friends. That'll never fly."

"This whole mess is playing like someone's idea of a fucked-up war game. It's just so unreasonable."

"Is it ever reasonable?" Evie said. She knew what he meant, though. She couldn't help but conjure this image of stern generals and power-mad heads of states standing around tables with tactical displays, shuffling around troops and weapons, with no thought to the people on the ground—the real lives their decisions impacted. "Do we wait and see what happens?"

Bruce said, "We could be waiting for ages. I say we just keep going with what we have—the new stuff that you just sent—and play it by ear."

"Do you want me to keep e-mailing scripts?"

"You know—I haven't been working much. You can if you want. Definitely keep writing. Write anything. We'll do something with it, at some point." He sounded tired.

"How are things there?"

"Citywide curfew, but that's nothing new. Callie finally got out of West Hollywood. It's not too bad."

"Hang in there."

"You, too. Call me if you need anything."

She needed to reverse time and live in last month, before her life had run away from her.

She made ham-and-cheese sandwiches, but her heart and appetite weren't really in it. Eating would give her and Alex something to do while they stared at each other. She brought two plates with the sandwiches into the living room.

She had her work spread all over the coffee table: her laptop, powered down; pages of handwritten notes she'd collected when ideas hit her late at night, in bed, in the car, and the like; and a few back issues of *Eagle Eye Commandos* she used as reference.

Alex, sitting on the armchair, was reading one of these.

The faces staring back at her on the front cover belonged to Tracker and Talon. He was about to fall off a cliff; she was holding on to him, grimacing. *Eagle Eye Commandos* number 42. She wanted to snatch it out of his hands and hide it away, apologize for it. It wasn't that she wasn't proud of her work. It was— well, sometimes she felt guilty for being proud of it. It wasn't exactly high literature.

"What do you think?" she asked, trying to sound nonchalant.

He smirked. "I like how the flying bullets leave trails."

She set down the plates, slumped onto the sofa, and smirked right back at him.

He said, "You write as E. L. Walker. Why don't you use your full name?"

"Thirteen-year-old boys wouldn't take the book seriously if they knew a girl wrote it."

"But—" He opened to a page featuring Tracker. At Evie's insistence, Bruce didn't draw her in the stereotypical comic book manner of portraying women in skintight clothing, antigravity breasts and all. She wore functional black fatigues, had a reasonably normal athletic figure, and most of the time—splicing wire in the middle of a jungle, for example—looked downright scruffy. "—this is you, isn't it? This isn't about thirteen-year-old boys' fantasies. It's about thirteen-year-old girls' fantasies."

In another life, a parallel universe, Evie had enlisted in the military. Army, Air Force, whatever. She didn't know what she would have done as a private or an airman. Administration, probably. Mostly, she'd wanted to have a bit of an adventure—basic training, for instance—and it seemed an easy way to go about it. Never mind that adventures weren't supposed to be easy. College and independence diverted her. To this day, she wondered if she could have hacked it, and wondered if she should have tried, just to see.

When she didn't answer, he turned back to the book, flipping pages without reading. "The presence of a nominally talented, self-sufficient woman hasn't seemed to hinder sales."

Alex was right. Evie never wanted Tracker to be a sex symbol. She wanted her to be a role model.

She stared at the page, her words in the speech balloons, and smiled fondly. "If just one girl out there picks up the book, and it makes her think she can do anything, I'd be happy."

Evie looked at the old covers. Tracker featured on all of them. One of the ongoing storylines focused on her, her coming-of-age, her increasing confidence in herself and her abilities. Through all the other storylines—Talon's insubordination, the unit's rebelliousness, the fight against terrorism—Tracker's personal development played a part. Often, the progress was uncertain—two steps forward, one step back as some tragedy undermined her faith in herself. At this rate, the storyline could go on forever, with Tracker never developing much beyond where she was now.

No, Evie ought to do something about that. Tracker needed to become independent. She needed to become a leader. Talon's equal, not his hero-worshipping subordinate.

"Is Bruce your boyfriend?"

"Hm?" Evie glanced up. Alex had a sandwich in hand, but he hadn't taken a bite. He looked at her questioningly.

"The phone call. I was just curious."

Evie rubbed her forehead. Not that it was any of his business. "No, he's my partner. The artist." She pointed at the comics.

"Ah, of course. That Bruce."

"He's called me almost every day. The book deals so much in current events, we try to tie in as much as we can. But things have gotten volatile. It's impossible to predict what might happen anymore. We've had a couple of major storylines yanked out from under us in the last year. He's mad at me because I haven't been watching the news."

"You've been busy."

"Yeah," she said with a painful chuckle. That was without telling Bruce about hypothetical Greek goddesses showing up on the doorstep, the basement full of mythical artifacts, or the strange man in the pea coat.

There'd been so much news to keep up with over the last few days. All of it bad, the conflicts so much greater than the Third World clashes that had preoccupied current events over the last half a century or so. No one had to wonder if Russia had nuclear weapons or not.

"It's so surreal," she said. She shook her head, rearranging her thoughts. "Bruce was saying that this is playing like some messed-up war game. It's like there are people—the people in power—moving pieces around on a game board. It makes you wonder how much of history is just people in power manipulating a game."

Alex said softly, "That isn't far from wrong."

She stared at him. "How do you know?"

He shrugged and wouldn't meet her gaze.

"Then what about Discord? What about that apple? What does it do?"

"One shudders to think," he said.

Mab raised her head, her tail thumping the floor as it wagged. A moment later, her father's door opened, and Frank himself appeared in the doorway. His hand clutched his side, but nonchalantly, as if he had put it there and forgotten it.

His brow lined quizzically, he said, "I forgot to ask: What are you doing here?"

Alex hesitated a moment, a stricken look briefly crossing his features before he lifted the sandwich and said, "Having lunch."

Evie stood. "Dad—you don't look good."

He waved her away. "I'm fine. Is he bothering you?"

"No." She debated about what to tell him. She didn't want him to worry. He shouldn't have to worry about anything but getting well. Or rather, not dying. But she could deny that anything was wrong, and he wouldn't believe her, any more than she believed it when he insisted he was fine. So she didn't say anything.

"Everything's okay?"

"Yeah." She nodded earnestly.

He didn't believe it. He looked back and forth between them, his narrowed gaze accusing them of conspiracy. He finally pointed at Alex. "Don't think you can use her to get at the Storeroom."

"Wouldn't dream of it, sir," Alex said.

Her father studied them further, then said, "Call me if you need anything. Keep an eye on things, Mab."

He scratched the wolfhound's ears. She placed herself alertly at the corner of the room, staring at Evie. He disappeared back behind his door, still limping, hiding a wince.

Alex said, "You haven't told him about Hera."

"I don't want him to worry." She curled up on the sofa, half a sandwich in hand, picking at the bread crusts. She squeezed her eyes shut against tears. Her father wasn't worried. Not once had he shown any fear or worry, any of her own emotions that she wanted to see mirrored in him. He was taking it all so calmly, as she couldn't imagine doing. She said, half to herself, "I think he wants to die."

Alex's brow was lined. "Why would he? I can understand the impulse, but why would *he* want to?"

"To be with my mother." He waited for her to continue, which she did, almost unwillingly, as if a different voice spoke her thoughts. "She died in the Seattle bombing. I keep thinking about her now. It happened so quickly. I talked to her the night before, and the next day she's just gone, nothing left. And now Dad—and I can't decide which is worse. The slow death or the sudden. I have a chance to say good-bye to him. But I have to watch him—I can already see him getting more sick, and I've only been here a few days. With Mom, at least it was over. I could just move on. But I don't know which is worse."

Just move on. That was a lie. It had been five years. She started writing *Eagle Eye Commandos* right after the Seattle bombing. She created characters who could do what she couldn't—take revenge—and who could stop the tragedies that no one in reality seemed able to prevent.

Would Emma Walker be proud that Evie had found a way to profit from her grief and anger over that day? Evie covered her mouth to make herself stop talking.

Alex sat at the edge of the armchair, leaning forward, elbows propped on his knees. He must not have been any more hungry than she, because he hadn't eaten any of the sandwich. He'd stayed when she asked, but he didn't seem comfortable. A god, a magician—someone like Hera or Merlin—ought to appear a little more sure of himself.

She was about to once again ask him who he was, when he hopped to his feet and said, "Do you drink? Is there anything alcoholic around here?"

Bewildered, she said, "Yeah, I think there's beer in the fridge."

"Right." He dropped the sandwich back on the plate and marched to the kitchen. Mab rose and trotted after him, ears pricked and alert. She didn't growl or look menacing—just had to keep an eye on him, like her father said.

Alex moved purposefully, opening the refrigerator, searching, finding his quarry in short order, and returning with two handfuls of bottles, four in all, and a church key. He cleared some of the comics away to make space for them on the coffee table.

"Most people would have used the comics as coasters," Evie said, smiling crookedly. He was successfully distracting her, and she was surprised to find herself pleased at being distracted.

"Who knows, they might be worth millions someday. But not with water rings on them." He snapped the cap off one of the bottles. It breathed a puff of fog when he offered it to her. "Come on, drink up. It'll make you feel better."

She took it, and he opened a bottle for himself. "Thanks."

"Cheers." He lifted his bottle; she lifted hers. She didn't know what they were toasting: comic books, friendly dogs—Mab had parked herself at the other end of the coffee table—fridges conveniently stocked with beer. Helplessness.

It didn't matter. He was right. She needed to feel something besides sickening anxiety, and the cold liquid pouring into her belly and alcoholic warmth seeping into her blood was an alternative.

He leaned back into the armchair. *Now* she should ask him who he really was. Or maybe he'd be more likely to give her a straight answer once he finished the beer. He might have been trying to get *her* drunk so he could convince her to sneak him into the Storeroom. She leaned back with a sigh and closed her eyes, holding the chilled bottle against her cheek.

"Do you know who that was who came by just now? Do you realize who that was?" he said with too much enthusiasm.

She'd almost forgotten: the strange old man, the sword in the stone in the backyard. The image of her father collapsing erased everything that came before it. The afternoon had shrunk to that moment.

"Yeah," she said. "It was Merlin. Merlin, Excalibur—oh my God." It sounded so foolish when she said it out loud.

Alex's eyes lit with an aura of adoration. "The stories about him—he's one of the greatest magicians who ever lived. One of the maddest. But the things he could do—"

He was carrying on, and she barely comprehended what he was saying. He spoke like an authority on the subject. Magicians, magic—those words didn't mean anything to her. Magic happened in stories, or onstage in Vegas. Not in her family's backyard.

Except she'd seen it, and she believed.

"Real magic?"

He sat back, a distant smile fading on his lips. "I once saw a woman turn to water. She spilled right out of my arms and flowed away. There used to be sirens whose voices lured sailors to their deaths. I saw a bag that, no matter how much you put into it, would always hold more. I've seen men who couldn't be killed." His voice was haunting, melodious, drawing her into his trance. "Throughout all of history there have been people who could work miracles: saints, mystics, wizards, prophets. And gods. The world used to be filled with gods. Really, they were just people wielding very great magic. The rest of the world couldn't help but worship them."

The dozens of books of folklore on the shelves expanded in Evie's mind, and the world suddenly became a darker, fiercer place. She'd dreamed of being in stories when she was young. She'd made stories her life, writing comic books. But did she really want to *live* in those worlds?

What was she supposed to do, stay here for the rest of her life looking after the Storeroom? Didn't she have a choice?

When her father called to tell her he was sick, she didn't have to come back. She could have stayed in L.A. and checked up on him over the phone. He had plenty of friends here; he didn't need her. But he was family. It's what you did. It's what it all came down to.

She was tied to this place, even as her world fell apart around her. Discord everywhere.

"What does it mean," she said, "if Merlin's come here for Excalibur? If he says he's going to bring *him*—the one who can pull it from the stone." *Arthur,* a voice in her hindbrain said. *Say it.* "What does it mean if—Arthur—is returning?" When Britain has need of its King again . . .

After the Norman invasion, the Wars of the Roses, Cromwell, Napoléon and the Blitz, how bad would things have to get to bring about the return of Arthur? How bad were they already?

Alex tapped the neck of the bottle against his chin and stared into space. "I wonder if Excalibur could kill me."

She huffed a frustrated breath and thought of flinging her bottle at him, but it was still half-full, and she didn't feel nearly tipsy enough yet. This would be easier to take if she were tipsy. Him wanting to die didn't make any more sense than the rest of it. He was young, in his thirties, strong and intelligent. Not sick like her father. That was what made the situation so horrible—she could almost understand Frank's wanting to die, wanting to be done with it as quickly as possible without resorting to suicide. It was only her selfishness that wanted him to continue living, no matter what treatment was required, what sacrifices he'd have to make. But Alex—anyone else would relish the invincibility he claimed he had. She supposed that depended on what curses went along with it.

It wasn't fair that someone who wanted to die should be invincible, while her father was in the next room dying by inches. It wasn't fair.

Thoughtful, she straightened, considering. "Why do you want to die?"

"It's the only thing left. I'm tired of living."

She wished she'd met him at another time or place, at a bar in L.A. or one of the parties her creative friends were always throwing. She could imagine him as an actor—if he'd get rid of the bulky pea coat and put on a tight T-shirt. He carried himself like he was well built inside his clothing. She wondered if that gleam in his eye would carry onto film. He held her gaze, and her stomach lurched. If she'd met him under *normal* circumstances, she might actually have *liked* him.

Maybe she already did. When he said he wanted to die, she wanted to argue with him.

She said, "Who are you? Don't dodge this time."

He stared at her for a long time, and she was content to watch him think in silence. Then he stood and went to the bookshelves. After a moment of searching, he chose a volume and handed it to her.

Virgil's *Aeneid*. Pausing to give Mab a scratch behind her ears on the way out, he left the room without a word. The kitchen door opened and closed, and Evie and Mab were alone.

What about that apple.

Robin huddled on the windowsill outside the living room of the Walker house, tiny and invisible. He had the means to evade the watchdog—he could have run the beast on a merry chase if he'd wanted, but that would only have served to raise suspicions that something was amiss. And he still wouldn't have been able to get inside the house. He didn't know how that slave fellow had managed it, except that he'd somehow befriended the girl. As Robin would have done, if he hadn't interfered.

Never mind. He had news, which was what he'd come spying for. Frank was sick, perhaps even dying. And the Walkers had the apple. If only he could find a chink in the house's armor. Break through and hold them all in his power.

When he tried to slip under the window or through the crack between the door and the frame, he came against a wall, invisible, impenetrable. On bird's wings, he circled the house three times, skittered to the eaves and over the roof, searching out ventilation slots and testing the chimney. The house had a barrier, a magical shield that guarded the threshold against any who were not welcomed inside. He might have been able to dig under it, but then simple concrete would keep him out.

The easiest way to get inside would be to convince one of the Walkers to invite him in. Otherwise, the shield would have to be dismantled. He tried attacking it, slashing a magicked dagger across the enchantment like he might cut through it. He tried to slide under it, to find an edge that he could squeak around. But the protection was complete.

It didn't lash out at him. Passive only, it merely kept him out. It didn't drive him away. He could stay perched on the windowsill all night if he wanted, and the dog wouldn't even find him. But he'd accomplish nothing that way.

The house belonged to the Walkers. If the magic was tied to them somehow, and not to the house itself, perhaps if *they* were got rid of . . . Perhaps then the house would open itself like a blossom to the bee.

On his final circuit, Robin paused to look at Excalibur, driven into the stone. It shone, bright silver against dull granite, winking along the few inches of exposed blade, though the sky was overcast. He'd arrived just in time to see Merlin stalk off in a huff. Robin barely had time to make himself like air and was lucky the old wizard hadn't caught a whiff of his magic. Not many in this modern day would recognize Robin, but Merlin would. Merlin most likely wouldn't be pleased to find Robin hanging about, known troublemaker that he was.

That was also a bit of news. Merlin was active again, after all these centuries, and the sword Excalibur was waiting to be claimed. Other forces were at play, beside those Hera was dabbling in. And Robin— shrewd Robin, knavish Robin—must ensure he found himself on the winning side when the dust settled.

Robin stayed until the Greek slave left the Walker house. He followed the man into town, treading soft as thistledown, quiet as midnight. His powers hadn't diminished over the years, but he'd so seldom had a chance to use them for good purpose. He hadn't found a cause to serve or a great power to attach himself to in centuries, since back in the Old Country. Then she found him. She was ambitious. She had use for him. And she made such grand promises. It hardly mattered if she could keep them or not. The ride would be entertaining in the meantime.

The Greek wandered, apparently aimlessly, for an hour or so. He seemed to be making a circuit of the town. He kept to the outskirts, the backstreets, where the hyperactive authorities weren't likely to see him and take note.

Toward nightfall, he reached an empty house at the end of a street overgrown with weeds. The place was boarded up, with a faded FOR RENT sign tucked in the door. It might have been empty for years. The man started to open the back door—the lock was broken, but rigged in such a way that it still appeared secure when the door was in place. He gave a little jerk, and it popped open.

Once he had it open a crack, he looked behind. "You can stop following me now."

Robin winked to visibility, keeping his expression a bored mask to disguise his annoyance at being discovered. Was the man a magician as well? Hera had called him a slave, but perhaps he was hiding something. Oh, he was definitely hiding something. Robin had only to discover what. Peel the man like a grape, and wouldn't that be fun?

Robin leaned his back against the wall and crossed his arms. The light was fading; the Greek was little more than a shadow, but Robin's night vision was excellent. He doubted the Greek could study him half as well.

"Good evening, sir," Robin said.

Unflustered, the Greek let his arms hang relaxed at his side. More than familiar with magic, he was comfortable with it. But if he were a magician himself, surely Hera would know that about him.

"What do you want?" he said.

"Information. I want to learn more about you," Robin said lightly.

He chuckled. "I'm sure you've already learned enough."

"Never," Robin said, grinning.

"You're not one of the old gods." It was a statement of fact, not a question.

"And would you recognize one of the old gods if you met one?"

"I think I would."

He sounded so sure of himself. "I learned my trade from some of the old ones. Hermes, Loki, a bit from Coyote, Hanuman—but I am a simple sprite, nothing more."

"Then you're a troublemaker. But—you're old enough to know Hermes?"

No, he wasn't—merely a devotee of the old one's art. But he didn't have to give that away. Robin shrugged. "I'm old enough. Now, my turn for a question: What are you?"

His smile was grim. "Cursed."

"And your interest in the Walker house is—?"

He leaned against the doorframe and crossed his

arms, matching Robin's pose. "Who says my interest is in the house?"

That puzzled Robin for a moment. His own quest had been so focused on the artifact, had he failed to see what else was happening? Laughable, to assume everyone would have the same goal as himself.

Thoughtful, Robin said, "Ah, I see. Or you could be throwing me off the scent. Attempting to confuse me. Deflecting attention from what you really want."

"Or not."

"What would you do to keep her safe?"

At last, Robin put him on the defensive. His shoulders clenched, though his face betrayed no emotion. Before he could answer, Robin said, "My mistress wishes to meet you. She believes you could both benefit from an alliance. Will you come with me to meet her?"

He thought for a moment the Greek slave was going to refuse. The hesitation could only mean that he was considering refusing. Finally, though, he nodded, and followed Robin into the twilight.

The second book of Virgil's *Aeneid* told the story of Troy's last day in vivid, terrifying detail. The rest of the epic was filled with tragedies, battles, lists of ancestors, warriors, wandering travels, catalogs of the dead, and destiny. But none of it held the shock and immediacy of the telling of the fall of Troy. The guy could have written for comic books, the way he painted the scenes and depicted characters with four-color fervor from one episode to the next. Evie could see it all, was scripting it in her mind even as she read. *How about it, Bruce—we revive* Classics Illustrated. . . .

Something in the story held Alex's secret. That thought nagged her through her reading, which lasted after nightfall, and long after she should have been hungry. She didn't forget to worry about her father. Every half hour, or sooner, she looked toward his bedroom. She could go check on him, but didn't want to wake him if he slept. So she looked at Queen Mab, who was curled up, napping. If something were wrong with her father, Evie felt sure Mab would know.

She found pen and paper and made a list, marking every time she encountered a likely character in the story. There were so many. She trusted the story, pretending it was real and not made up for dramatic effect. If a character died, she crossed the name off the list. If the character died in another story—Agamemnon, for example—she crossed him off the list.

That still left her with a dauntingly long list of characters with polysyllabic names and a tendency to get into trouble.

The Walker library had a wide selection of mythological references, dictionaries, encyclopedias, and the like. Had someone—her father, her grandfather?—tried to identify the objects in the basement? Could the golden fleece be *that* Golden Fleece? And the shoes, the apples, the enchanted ball gowns, the harps, the spears— Some of the books were very old.

She looked up names in the mythological encyclopedias. She crossed off more of them if she found they'd met untimely ends elsewhere. Many names still remained. Could Alex be Odysseus? He seemed to fade out of the stories, the *Odyssey* ending with the start of another adventure. She rather hoped he got to live to a ripe and happy old age, with everything he'd had to put up with. Evie thought she'd like to meet Odysseus, out of any of the names on the list.

As if he'd been a real person and not a story.

Merlin said the true king would come to retrieve the sword from the stone, in their backyard. Merlin, as if he was a real person who'd yelled at her father through the closed door.

Alex could be anyone. Or none of them. He was playing mind games with her. She put the books away, crumpled her list, and threw it on the floor. She ate one of the wilted sandwiches, thought about going to bed, but decided she wasn't tired.

She powered up her laptop.

Write anything. How long had it been since she'd done that? No scripts, no deadlines, no proposals for new projects to pay the rent.

Maybe she should try that novel.

Tracker's story was still unfinished, still tickling her mind, not leaving room for new ideas. She picked up the thread again. Tracker, Jeeves, and Matchlock were traveling across Siberia in search of American spies to rescue. Jeeves had just guessed her secret—she was in love with their commander. Rather cliché, that, looking back on it. Evie could put a twist in it somehow. Then they were attacked. Which was a cop-out, really.

But she could explain it away. The Russians were suspicious of the Americans, had been following them, wanted to stop them, and hired mercenaries to make the attack look like the work of terrorists. Tracker was separated from Jeeves and Matchlock.

The Jeep swerved to avoid an incoming missile—the bastards had rocket launchers. Sheltered by the sparse foliage that dotted the edge of the tundra, she saw another one taking aim. She didn't think about it. She jumped, handgun ready, rolled to a stop more expertly than she had any right to hope for, and fired.

She wasn't a sniper. At this distance, with this much adrenaline in her system, she shouldn't have hit him. But she did, and he slumped, his weapon falling. Jeeves, Matchlock, and the Jeep were safe.

Rising from her crouch, she looked ahead. The Jeep had swerved to a stop. A dozen soldiers carrying automatic rifles surrounded it. Jeeves and Matchlock held their hands up. Tracker caught her breath and flattened to the ground. She waited for the sound of gunfire that would tell her that her friends had been murdered where they stood. But the sound never came. Instead, the soldiers hauled them out of the Jeep. A thumping noise in the air signaled the arrival of a helicopter. The mercenaries loaded Jeeves and Matchlock into it, climbed in themselves, and flew away.

She didn't have much cover here—a few tufts of scrub, a snowdrift. But they never looked for her.

In a way, writing prose was like relearning how to walk. She had to think about complete sentences. Describe instead of label. She didn't have Bruce to draw the pictures for her. Like Tracker, she was alone.

She had a dilemma: Did she continue with the mission, or did she go after Jeeves and Matchlock? Her instincts told her it wasn't really a dilemma. They could hold out for now. If the soldiers wanted them dead, they would have killed them immediately. She had no idea where the mercenaries were taking them. The helicopter had flown west, and Russia was a very big place.

The bunker at the edge of the defunct gulag, where the prisoner was being held, was ten miles away. She could reach it before nightfall if she managed a good pace. Never mind that she had only her gun and a short-range radio with her. The bunker would have food and water, and the equipment to contact Talon.

She could do this without Talon. If she ignored the pang in her belly the thought of him gave her. He'd tell her she was crazy, trying this on her own.

No, he wouldn't, a voice inside her argued. *He has faith in you.*

She checked the body of the mercenary she'd shot, verified he was dead, and looted a pack of food rations and a canteen off him. The canteen held vodka. No good for survival—maybe she could use it to inure herself to a lingering death, if she became hopelessly lost or injured. She shook her head, chastising herself for such defeatist thinking. Maybe she could use the vodka as a bribe.

Then, loosening the collar of her coat and hardening her will, she set off at a jog across the wasteland.

Robin Goodfellow was matchless as a spy. But soon, Hera would need an army. She gathered the start of one in a bar outside town.

The bartender, his eyes a bit glazed, his movements meticulous, as if he wasn't quite sure what he was doing, or someone else was guiding his motions, stood at the bar and finished pouring a glass of wine. He set the bottle aside, his face slack. The next day, he'd remember nothing, he'd be convinced that his bar stood empty all night, and know nothing about the four people gathered here. The place was frequented by bikers and truckers. Transients. She couldn't have her people trooping in and out of her hotel room, so she gathered them here. They might have been holding an informal meeting of some innocent town club.

Smiling indulgently at the entranced bartender, she picked up the glass, took a sip, and went to the round table in the center of the room where the others waited for her, pretending to nurse their own drinks.

They were frustratingly young to her eyes. The oldest among them had only two thousand years behind him. The youngest, forty. One learned so little within the span of a natural life. Despite their youth, their inexperience, they were used to wielding power, and the world was not so rich in magic as it once was. These people would have to do.

She had drawn them here with a promise of more power than they could find or make in their individual spheres of influence. She had explained that through her, and only through her, they could combine their strength and reach for the divine. Because they were who they were, could do what they did, and knew something of power, however limited their understanding of it was, they believed her, and they answered her call.

Now she had to prove that their faith in her was not misplaced.

"I want to own this town," she said.

"What will that gain us?" The Curandera was older than she looked, a mother and healer, a bringer of rain and storms, a speaker of the languages of the earth and sky. Still in her first lifetime, she was the youngest of them, but because her knowledge of magic had been passed down to her, from mother to daughter, for a thousand years, she was powerful.

"Here lies a power that can dictate the fate of nations," said the Marquis. He was in his third or fourth lifetime, a British nobleman from the last century steeped in the culture of empire and one of the few successful practitioners in the revival of what he called ceremonial magic. He could bind, curse, break, mold, and summon. If only Hera could teach him how to do all this without his props, tools, symbols, and erroneous scholarship. He looked uncomfortable in a suit and tie, his brown hair tied in a short tail at his neck, as if the modern clothing were a costume. He ought to be wearing a frock coat and powdered wig.

"What power?" said the Curandera.

"How much do you know about chemistry?" Hera asked. "What happens to an unstable compound, where the molecular bonds are weak, or require too much energy to maintain? It breaks down. A reaction occurs until the molecules form more stable compounds. Do you see what is happening in the world? The political situation is unstable. The artificial borders, the nations constructed out of blood and misguided diplomacy are falling apart. The world is an unstable compound, and it must break down if it is to form a more stable unit. I plan to guide that reaction. I have access to the catalyst that will ignite the final decomposition."

"That's ambitious. Thinking you can mold the world, and that it will be better because you're involved?" said the Curandera. Her eyes shone, and Hera knew the thought that inspired the brightness: the idea of a female divinity remaking the world, of a matriarchy restored.

"Yes," she said simply. "It certainly couldn't be much worse."

The Curandera smiled.

The fourth of their party sat a little ways off from the table, out of the light coming through the room's only window. He was young looking, handsome in a tie and dark jacket, his short hair combed back. The Wanderer was the oldest of them, apart from Hera herself. Through sheer experience, he had gained insight. He could see patterns of the past and how they would play into the future. He could look at a man sitting perfectly still with a blank expression, and predict what that man was thinking or might do next. He had become, by the stubborn nature of his existence, a seer.

"It isn't worse," he said. He spoke slowly, with a quiet certainty that the others would wait to listen to him. "No worse than it's ever been. Perhaps better in some ways. Always, there has been chaos. The world has broken and re-formed many times—I have seen it many, many times. It does so against the will of people, and without our guidance."

Hera said, "How many times have you wanted to take control—you can see what must be done, your wisdom tells you when you see madness, when the world is run by fools. Even you, Wanderer, don't remember. There was a time when the world was not ruled by shortsighted mortal whim. I remember."

"Can you bring that time again?" he said flatly, like he didn't believe her.

If she had been able to act even a few hundred years ago, she would have gathered a very different-looking army: witches, mediums, saints, prophets. People who knew magic for what it was, people who feared the dark it could do, but worshipped its strength, whether they called it God or nature or alchemy. These people before her—they felt the power, they touched it, they identified some destiny in their skills, the strength of their knowledge of what lay underneath the surface of emotions like love and hate. But they didn't call it magic. Even the Marquis preferred to think of the power as a science that could be codified.

"I can," she said.

"Then I will follow you, for it has been two thousand years since I have seen one with such a power."

She nodded respectfully, though the Wanderer might have caught the flicker in her expression, the surge of anticipation at once again having followers and servants. He tasted his martini and watched her over the rim of his glass.

Soon, she would be able to break this world over her knee.

The door slammed open and Robin burst into the room. She'd told him to knock first. She'd have to do something about his irreverence. The imp claimed to admire Hermes, but Hermes had never been so impertinent.

Entering behind him, slouching in a felt coat, was the Greek slave who'd been at the Walker house.

Hera gave him a welcoming smile. "Good evening. Please come in and make yourself comfortable."

Walking slowly, cautiously, the Greek approached. He pulled a chair away from a different table than the others and sat. He eyed the others carefully, as if memorizing their features.

Robin stood apart, arms crossed and grinning, like he'd brought home the golden fleece all by himself.

She continued. "How much of our little endeavor did Robin explain to you?"

The Greek glanced at Robin and shrugged deeper into his coat. "Is that his name?"

"I'll take that to mean none, then. Would you like something to drink?"

He shook his head. Not one for social niceties, it seemed. But then, she couldn't blame him for being wary. He'd had experience with the old gods. What exactly had Apollo done to the lad to terrify him so?

She stepped before him. "I'm prepared to make a deal with you. I need access to the Storeroom in the Walker house."

"What makes you think I have it?" he said with a half grin.

"One step at a time. I'm a patient woman."

"I can imagine. It's taken you a long time to get here."

He may not have had any power of his own, but she'd do well not to underestimate him. He was old, and age alone would give him a great deal of knowledge, perhaps even wisdom. "You as well. We might be able to help each other. What do you want from the Storeroom? What are you looking for?"

"Hasn't your spy told you?"

Hera made a noncommittal sigh. "The only reason any of us—people like us—are interested in the Walker house is the Storeroom. I believe you're trying to get into it through the girl. I would only like to propose that when you reach your goal, you keep my interests in mind. I could make it worth your while."

"How?"

Here came the problem in dealing with immortals: What could she offer to someone who'd been alive for so long? What experience could she give him that he didn't already have, what wealth that he hadn't already collected and squandered a dozen times over? Immortals were so jaded.

"Name a price," she said, shrugging.

"I want to hear what you're offering."

What had he been, before he wore Apollo's chain? What had he become, after Apollo was gone? If nothing else, he was pleasant on the eyes. One could never have too many nice-looking men around.

"I can offer you power," she said. "I'm rebuilding a pantheon. I'll need help to see it established."

"You're offering divinity?" he said.

"Is that what you want?"

He kept his expression still. His gaze revealed nothing, not desire, fear, shock, nothing. But it was so clear. She could give him what he hadn't found in over three thousand years of life. Power. Godhood. He was a servant, like Robin. He needed only a worthy master to guide him. She could use him like a tool, and make him grateful for it.

"That isn't what he wants," the Wanderer said. He'd been staring at the Greek, studying him with his focused intensity. Looking inside him. To his credit, the Greek didn't flinch.

"What does he want?" Hera said, not taking her gaze from the Greek.

"Ask him about the chain he wears around his neck."

Hera lifted her brow. "Well?"

The Greek grimaced and said, "I want it off."

Ah, three thousand years, his master dead, and he was still a slave.

"Then I will find a way to remove it. If you will help me."

The Greek had just exposed a great deal about himself, so she didn't fault him for his stony reaction. He'd locked himself behind an emotionless wall—which he was wise to do, in a room filled with so much power.

He said, "You have a plan."

"There is a golden apple. It was mine by rights when it first came into being, but it was stolen from me. I would have it now. Since the Walkers won't give it to me, I must take it."

He nodded slowly, with understanding. "Discord's apple. The Judgment of Paris."

"You know the story. Good."

"I fought in the war over Helen, my lady. Of course I know the story."

She regarded him with renewed curiosity. Who *was* he?

"Can you find a way for me to get into the Storeroom, or bring me the apple yourself?"

"I don't know."

"See that you do, and you will be rewarded."

"My lady, can I ask you a question?"

"You may."

"How did you survive?"

"Pardon me?"

"When Zeus set the trap at Olympus, how did you survive?"

She considered. He knew too much. Even if he was Apollo's slave, Apollo hadn't known anything. The stupid boy had fallen straight into Zeus's trap, along with the rest of the family. In the stories, the gods had lived on forever. Only disbelief caused them to fade into myth. No one ever learned of the destruction of Olympus. She would have to watch this one closely indeed.

"I nearly didn't. But you must understand, Zeus was my husband. He didn't think I knew what he had planned, but I did. I had a plan of my own, and though his power nearly found me out, it didn't."

His gaze became unfocused and thoughtful.

"Does that agree with what you know?" she said.

"Yes. Yes, it does. Thank you. I should be going, I think. I have work to do."

He stood, turned up his collar, and let himself out the door.

The Wanderer said, "He's hiding something."

"Of course he is," Hera said curtly.

"He never exactly agreed to help you, you know," the Wanderer added.

"Did he *really* fight at Troy?" asked the Marquis.

"I believe he did."

The nobleman continued. "There's something else

you should know. He's the one I followed. He's the one who led us to the Storeroom. I suspect he possesses a great deal of knowledge we could use."

Hera tapped a finger on the rim of her wineglass. "Robin, you must keep a close watch on him."

"Absolutely I must."

Vita chopped vegetables while Sylvia, six years old, stirred the soup, or tried to. Vita hoped it didn't burn too badly, but she didn't have the heart to shoo her daughter away.

"When was the Trojan War, Mother?"

"Oh, hundreds of years ago."

"Then how do people know what happened?"

"They tell stories. That's why stories are so important. They help people remember."

"Why didn't anyone believe Cassandra? I would have believed her."

"No, you wouldn't have. Apollo made it so no one believed her."

"Why?"

"Cassandra made him angry, so he cursed her."

"Why?"

"Because that's what gods do."

"Is that why we pray to them? So they won't curse us?"

Oh, the blasphemy, Vita thought, biting back a smile. "Yes, my dear. That's exactly it."

Lucius came in then, and Sylvia screamed a welcome to him, ran, and hugged him. He snatched her up and spun her around until her brown hair tangled in front of her face, then he held her upside down while she screamed some more, and he leaned over to kiss Vita on the cheek.

"Supper soon? I'm famished," he said. It was planting season. He'd been in the fields since dawn.

"Yes."

"The Mouse been helping you?"

"She's been very helpful."

Finally, Lucius set Sylvia down. She collapsed in a heap, laughing and gasping for air.

"Mother's telling me about the Trojan War," Sylvia said once she had breath enough to speak.

"Oh?" Lucius eyed Vita.

"Everyone's telling stories out of Virgil's new epic. She overhears. Why don't you tell your father one of the stories?"

While Vita finished seasoning the soup, Sylvia launched into a dramatic reenactment of the fall of Troy, showing how the Greek soldiers must have had to scrunch up to hide inside the hollow horse, wriggling across the floor like the snakes from Tenedos as they attacked Laocoön, slashing the air like a warrior with a sword. Lucius pretended to be slain, then laughed, and Vita laughed, too.

In a moment of calm, Lucius said, "Who's your favorite? Which of the people in the story do you like best?"

Vita was sure Sylvia was going to say Cassandra, but she said, "Sinon."

Lucius sounded confused. "What? But he was a

terrible liar. A spy. Deceitful. There's nothing in him to admire."

"But to the Greeks he was brave. Wasn't he?"

"Humph. I suppose he was. But we're not supposed to admire the Greeks."

"Then why do we tell their stories?"

Lucius could answer that one on his own. Vita wiped her hands on a cloth. "I need to get some wine from the cellar. I'll be back in a moment."

"I'll go! I'll go!" Sylvia dashed ahead, as if to race there first, but Vita managed to snatch her around the middle and hold her back. Oof, she's getting too big for this.

"No," Vita said. "You're not allowed down there, you know that."

"You never let me see down there."

"You'll be allowed there when you're older."

Lucius stood to take Sylvia from her, distracting her with more questions about Trojans and Greeks. His gaze met Vita's, and she saw her own suddenly somber expression mirrored on his face. He also did not go into the cellar. When her mother died, she told him why he couldn't. The unspoken second part of what she had said to Sylvia hung between them.

You'll be allowed there when you're older, when I am dead.

10

Crouched in a wrestling stance, Sinon and his opponent, both naked, circled each other in the middle of a tiled courtyard at the Sun Palace. The man did not appear to be much taller or heavier, but he glared with such ferocity—eyes burning, face scowling—that Sinon felt afraid. It was the fear he used to feel before a battle, the *what if* questions that nagged and threatened to turn a warrior into a coward.

The chain felt heavy on Sinon's neck. He pushed the fear away, ignored it, pretended that it didn't exist, because the gods could sense his emotions. Ares, his opponent, would be joyous to know he was afraid.

Sinon couldn't hope to beat the God of War at wrestling. But he could try.

Ares, brown skin glowing in the sunlight shining on him, rounded his shoulders, flexing the muscles of his arms. The movement was meant to put Sinon off guard. Ares pretended that he was still preparing. But Sinon saw the muscles of his legs tense and was ready when Ares leaped at him, arms cocked, ready to scoop him up and throw him to the floor. He dodged sideways, evading Ares's grasp, and spun to knock the god on his back, making him sprawl on the rush mat where they fought. Sinon backed away and waited in his defensive posture for the next round.

Apollo laughed and applauded. "You see? He's been with us long enough that he knows our tricks. Not such an easy victory."

A dozen other gods and goddesses watched the bout, lounging on chairs and cushions, eating, drinking, talking, laughing. Apollo often entertained his brethren in the palace. He plied them with drink and learned what gossip he could. It was also a way to display his own power, his own prizes—such as Achaean warriors made into slaves.

The God of War didn't believe that the slave serving wine had once been a warrior. He challenged the Sun God to prove it. So here they were.

Ares raised himself to a crouch, panting through bared teeth like a beast. He charged again. His attacks were single-minded, uncreative. Again, Sinon jumped out of his way, over the god's reach. As he did, he curled his arm around Ares's neck and pulled hard, flipping him flat to the mat once again.

Gods are only men with power, Sinon told himself. Odysseus never bowed to Agamemnon, despite all his power. As long as Sinon could stay out of the man's reach, he could hold his own. He had to hold his own only until Apollo grew bored and called a halt to the match.

But really, what was he worried about? That Ares might kill him? He smiled a little at the ridiculousness of it all.

Ares caught the expression, and it must have enraged

him, because he snarled. This time when he flexed his muscles, he seemed to expand, growing a foot, two, three, and gaining a hundred pounds of mass. His hand could now reach around Sinon's middle.

Sinon's eyes widened in panic. He scrambled away. No one could fault him for turning tail and running. Despite his massive form, Ares moved with the speed of a hawk, his arm flying to swipe at Sinon. He struck, and Sinon rolled across the mat and into the base of a set of marble stairs. He saw stars for a moment and shook the dizziness away. Ares didn't rest, but came at him, arms reaching.

Scurrying on all fours, Sinon raced forward, between the giant's legs. He spun at the last moment and slammed into the backs of his knees. As he hoped, the knees buckled and Ares fell, but once again Sinon underestimated the giant's speed. On his knees, Ares turned and grabbed Sinon. His breath slammed out of his lungs as Ares lifted him.

So much for not getting caught.

Ares squeezed, his fingers twisting Sinon's body. Sinon winced, unable to struggle free of the tightening pressure. Then a crack echoed, and his body turned into searing fire. That was his back breaking.

Ares dropped him. He rolled and lay still, every nerve in his body writhing with pins and needles of pain. In a few moments the pain went away, replaced by a hot, thick rush, like boiling honey flowing down his back as the bones of his spine healed. He lay there a moment, trying to still his breathing, not sure if he could stand. But he could, and he did, as if it hadn't happened.

He gazed over a silent courtyard and tried to wear

a mask of indifference, as if none of it mattered. But he could feel how pale and cold his face was, and his hands were shaking.

"I won," Ares said. With a discharge of light, he returned to his original size.

"But you had to cheat to do it," Apollo said. "I think I've proved my point."

"I'll fight you next!" Ares pointed at the Sun God.

"Ares!" A luminous woman reclining on a bench called to the god. "Come here, darling. You're ruining the mood." Aphrodite reached a perfect, graceful arm to him. No one could refuse such a command, not even a god. Ares bowed to her and returned to his place at her feet.

Apollo stood at the top of the steps, appearing cheerful again. "Find your pitcher, Sinon, and serve my guests."

"Yes, my lord," he whispered, his voice still shaking. He climbed the steps to where he had left the gold pitcher of wine. He moved slowly, letting his strength return. He hoped his hands stopped trembling soon.

When he was next to Apollo, the god whispered to him. "I'm sorry for that. I'll make it up to you."

That meant a visit from the nereid in the pool, or a journey away from the Palace—to the coast, perhaps, or to a forest where they could hunt. Or a full day on his own, with no duties to perform and no harassments from any gods.

Sinon closed his eyes and nodded, unable to speak. If he opened his mouth, he'd yell, and if he yelled at Apollo in front of the others, the Sun God would never leave him in peace.

The festive mood returned soon enough.

"Wherever did you find him?" Aphrodite said, watching Sinon.

"He's a souvenir I took from Troy. A genuine Achaean warrior. In fact, he's the fellow who talked the Trojans into bringing that wretched horse into the city. You wouldn't think him capable of possessing the wit to pull off a trick like that, just looking at him, would you?"

"Indeed. Looks *and* wit. I might find a way to buy him from you." Aphrodite sipped thoughtfully from a goblet. As Sinon felt her studying him, a chill ran along his skin. He kept his eyes downcast to hide his frustration, his resignation. He waited by a column, naked and decorative, until the next guest needed a goblet filled.

"He's not for sale."

She licked wine-dampened lips. "Oh, everything's for sale."

"Why do we do it?" This came from Hermes, who made an unlikely perch on a giant urn, balancing bird-like on the rim.

"Do what?" said Apollo.

"Keep souvenirs of that war? Nobody was happy with how it turned out. It's been over for—for I don't know how many years—"

How many years? Sinon desperately hoped he'd give a number, to mark the time. But he didn't.

"—and we still find little else to talk about. I've never seen this family so passionate about anything. The reminders of it are everywhere." He glanced at Sinon, who tried not to notice. "Why is that, do you think?"

Apollo huffed. "Who knows? It's not like we couldn't

orchestrate the destruction of a civilization anytime we wanted."

Conversations stilled as the gathering paused to listen. Another said, "That's not it. This one got away from us—the mortals kept doing things we didn't plan for."

A woman in the back said, "That's true. They fascinate us so, don't they?"

"Tell me, did that fellow Odysseus ever make it home?"

"Yes," said Hermes, and Sinon let out a sigh. "He had quite a bit of housekeeping to do. Apparently his wife was getting ready to remarry—"

"No, she was trying *not* to remarry, but they all thought Odysseus was dead and every bachelor in Ithaca wanted to get ahold of the lands."

"Why didn't the son do something about it?"

"Well, I don't know—"

"Athena says the son is as clever as the father."

"She's biased. The son is probably hers—"

Sinon wanted to leave, to get a breath of air or smash the pitcher against a convenient wall. But if he moved, Apollo would draw attention to him, find a new sport to throw him into, for the amusement of his guests. Sinon would hear more news only if he kept quiet.

Hermes said, "I suppose I could hop over there quickly and see—"

"Not necessary."

Apollo sat up and pointed at Aphrodite. "Speaking of souvenirs, what did you do with that apple you were all so desperate for? I can't *believe* you all fell for that trick."

"I still have it." Apollo raised an inquisitive brow, Hermes leaned forward on his perch, and Aphrodite pouted. "I'm not going to tell you *where*. Her Most Imperiousness is still after it."

That was Hera. The other gods and goddesses rarely called her by name. No one seemed to like her much.

"Really?" Apollo said, drawling. "That's rather pathetic, isn't it?"

"Oh yes. Just last week she disguised one of her little minions as a monkey and sent him into my palace, trying to find it. I sent him back to her as a slug."

"She can't even do her own dirty work. She isn't really that powerful, is she?"

Hermes jumped from his perch and retrieved his goblet from the floor. He raised it at Sinon, who approached, head bowed. Odysseus would be appalled to see him like this, subservient and uncomplaining.

"Don't make that mistake," Hermes said as Sinon poured. "Her true strength isn't in her own power. Her strength is her ability to influence others and use their power."

Now everyone needed more wine, and once again Sinon circulated, filling the goblets raised to him. The pitcher never ran out of wine.

"She doesn't influence any of *us*."

"You'd think she'd let it go. It's just an apple. Aphrodite bribed her out of it fair and square."

A soft-spoken goddess who sat by the reflecting pool at the edge of the courtyard, touching her fingers to the water, looked up and raised her voice. "She used to be stronger. She used to be Queen in her own right. That was when mothers and priestesses were more important than warriors. Most of you are too young to remember a time when she was not always jealous."

She had long golden hair, the color of barley at harvest, and far-seeing eyes the blue of a summer sky. She frowned, creasing her face, making her seem old, which meant that the winter season was upon the earth. She was Demeter.

None of the others could say anything trite after this. They could not mock her sadness or her memories. While they might have blamed her for bringing a somber mood to their festivities, no one did. For her beauty and thoughtfulness, she was welcome everywhere.

Apollo brought out his lyre and played a light tune, and the deities seemed content to sit back and drink their wine.

Sinon went to Demeter and got down on one knee to pour her wine. Out of them all, she understood sadness.

II

Dad?" Evie tapped on his bedroom door. She'd wanted to check on him last night, but had hesitated at the late hour. If he was resting, she didn't want to disturb him. And if he wasn't okay . . . surely he'd have said something. He had a telephone. He could call 911.

"Dad?" She knocked louder. "I made coffee, you want some? Dad?" Her heart thudded. How long should she wait before she burst in? What if he was hurt? Unconscious? She closed her eyes and rested her forehead on the wall. "Dad?"

"Huh? Evie? What's wrong?" His voice came muffled, slurred, as if struggling to wakefulness.

She exhaled a relieved breath. "Nothing, I just wanted to see"—*if you're all right*—"if I could get you some coffee or something."

"Come in so I can hear you."

Carefully, she pushed open the door.

Her father was propped on a mound of pillows. His half-lidded gaze shifted slowly to track her progress.

She found a chair in the corner and brought it near his bed.

"Can I bring you breakfast?" she said, whispering, as if her voice would rattle him. She couldn't remember the last time she'd seen him eat anything.

"Not hungry. Appetite's shot to hell." He shook his head and shifted against the pillows. He wore a T-shirt and held the bed's comforter flat across his waist. He looked as sick as Evie could have imagined him looking: pale to a shade of grayness, his voice muffled, his manner vacant. For a moment, she wished she'd stayed in L.A. Then he took a deep breath, gathering the energy to focus on her and speak clearly. "Is that Alex character gone?"

"Yeah."

He frowned, an expression she remembered from her high school days.

"Don't look at me like that, he didn't stay the night or anything. He's totally not my type."

He chuckled, tipping his head back and closing his eyes. "Whatever you say."

"I've been trying to find out who he is. He never has a straight answer. When I asked last night, he gave me a copy of the *Aeneid* and walked out."

"The *Aeneid*? If he's in there, do you know how old that would make him?"

He spoke as if there were nothing strange about it. She could tell him about Hera and he wouldn't be surprised.

She did some quick math, back to when the Trojan War was thought to have taken place. "Thirty-two hundred years or so."

"Hm. I don't think I've ever met anyone that old."

So—whom had he met that made a character from the *Aeneid* showing up seem not out of the ordinary?

She managed to convince herself that he wasn't going to die in the next few moments. Sitting back in her chair, she looked around. The room was an amalgam: the furniture—the four-poster bed, oak dresser, beat-up vanity table—had been here in her grandparents' time. The faded floral comforter had been her parents' as long as she could remember, and his wallet and watch were sitting on the dresser, where he always kept them.

On the nightstand by the bed was a lamp with a half-dozen orange pill bottles clustered around its base. She wondered how many of them were painkillers. His breathing was slow, deep, like he was on the verge of falling asleep. Like he'd been drugged. She should go away and let him sleep.

She was about to stand when he spoke.

He took a long time, saying the words slowly and methodically; she waited motionless and patient. "When I was growing up here, I think my father went into the Storeroom once, to get something for someone who came to the door. Twelve-league boots. The guy was on a quest. I don't remember what for anymore. In the last month, I've had a dozen people come asking for what belongs to them, and that doesn't count the ones who've come who don't have a right to anything. It's like—the Storeroom is dispersing. Magic's going back into the world."

It was hard to believe in magic in a world where things like the Seattle bombing happened. Then again, maybe magic was the only way to stop things like Seattle happening.

"Dad—why did you put Mom's papers in the Storeroom?"

"Wanted to save them," he said. His eyes opened to slits, and a different self seemed to look out of them. "Do you know who that was, asking for the sword?"

She nodded, and he nodded back.

"Do you know what it means, if Merlin and Arthur have come back?"

She shook her head, but the movement changed. Again, she nodded, because somehow she knew. "The stories," she said.

He winced, stiffening, clutching the edge of the comforter. "Joints," he muttered. "Hips. Back. Everything."

She almost reached for him. Her muscles ached to do so. But there was nothing she could do. In another heartbeat, his face relaxed, and the spell went away.

"When Britain needs its King again," he said, "he'll come. Something's going to happen, Evie."

"I know," she said, thinking of Hera, of the apple that started a war that changed the world. What would happen if the apple went back into the world?

A calm smile softened his face. "I know you do."

She knew, the same way she knew to find the glass slippers and that nothing in the basement would kill Alex. The same way she knew she couldn't let Hera into the house.

For each thing she knew, for every new insight she learned about the Storeroom and everything inside it, her father slid a little closer to death.

Evie waited for someone to knock at the door. Someone would. She'd done nothing but answer the door since she got here. Well, that wasn't true. It only seemed like it. But if she worried about the door and who'd be at it next, she wasn't worrying about her father. He'd fallen asleep in the middle of a sentence, speculating about what Arthur would be like and when he would return, speaking with an awe-inspiring certainty that it would happen, that it wasn't just a story.

She left him alone, went to the living room to lie on the sofa, and sobbed into a pillow so she wouldn't wake him up. Mab came and put her chin on Evie's leg, gazing at her with sad brown eyes. Evie wondered where she'd come from, if she was another piece of the magic that protected the house and bound her and her father to it. Another magical artifact, emerging when she was needed.

She wondered if Alex would come back. She still couldn't guess who he was, but she kept returning to the descriptions of the fall of Troy in the *Aeneid*. He might have been part of Aeneas's crew, which sailed to Italy and founded Rome. But he'd said the language on the apple was Greek. She'd even found a book on the shelves, a coffee table book with lots of photos and illustrations, and a chart showing the script from the apple: Linear B, the language of Mycenae from around the time of the Trojan War.

Virgil provided a solution to what Evie had always thought was a supreme failure of logic in the story: Why had the Trojans been so eager to bring such a bizarre and suspicious object as the horse into the city?

The answer: The Greeks must have left behind a spy to convince the Trojans that the horse would bring them luck. Odysseus, master of the plan of the horse, chose his friend Sinon, a persuasive and credible speaker.

Evie could see them: they must have known that if Sinon failed to tell his story convincingly, the Trojans would kill him along with all those within the horse. It was not just his own life he was offering to sacrifice. He must have known that the lives of all his friends and comrades rested on his words. He would have been honored and flattered that Odysseus had asked him. He would have been afraid. But Odysseus's hand on his shoulder, his intense gaze, would have made him confident. Odysseus would have given Sinon the bruises and chafed wrists that lent proof to his tale. It was hard, beating his friend, but he would not have given the task to another. For his part, Sinon would have thrown himself into the role. So much depended on it.

At least that was how Evie would write it, if she were telling the story.

While many tales traced the fates of the heroes of the Trojan War, she couldn't find out what happened to Sinon. Not in any of the stories, not so much as a line from a poem that said he was among the company that traveled home with Odysseus and was caught up in those adventures. She would have expected to find him there, if he had survived the sacking of the city. His name faded from the record. He might even have been a pure invention of Virgil's, an ultimate example of Greek treachery, a well-wrought piece of propaganda. He could have been killed—but surely the story would have said so.

Or he could have dropped out of history. The gods who backed Troy must have been furious with him. Any one of them could have laid a curse on him. If they were anything like Hera . . . Evie's skin prickled, thinking of what they could do to him.

Sinon, then. The Liar. Why didn't that make her feel any better about Alex?

She thought about going to look for him. Hopes Fort wasn't that big. He might even have been hanging around the house still, watching, as he'd been doing all week. She could go into the yard and yell *Sinon* and see if he answered. But she didn't leave the house, because she wanted to stay near in case her father needed her.

She didn't have to stay and do nothing. She had work. She'd left Tracker in a fix. She pulled her laptop to her and returned to the story.

Tracker, alone on the tundra, hoped she would be able to keep her bearings. She felt right on the edge of losing herself. And if something happened out here, the chances of the others rescuing her were slim.

Now how was she going to get out of *this* fix? Talon could sweep in and rescue her. It wouldn't be any more unlikely than a dozen other storylines she'd done. It would return the characters back to the main plot. But this was supposed to be Tracker's story. This was Tracker's chance to shine.

She couldn't spend the whole time wallowing in self-doubt, either. So all Evie had to do was get her to the bunker at the gulag, then see what happened next. Her hands paused over the keys. She looked over the back of the sofa to the kitchen door, waiting for someone to knock.

Her father emerged around suppertime, moving slowly but appearing alert. Evie rushed to help him, and of all the wonders, he let her. She heated up soup for him. He ate half a bowl and a few crackers, and seemed pleased with the accomplishment. They spoke little, commenting on the weather, passing on the gossip from town.

"Did anyone stop by?" he said.

"No."

He limped back to bed, stopping on the way to scratch Mab's back. Evie was proud of herself for not asking, yet again, if he needed help, if he was all right. She just had to hope she could get to him in time if he stumbled.

She returned to the sofa in the living room and tried to write. How long could she keep Tracker wandering on the tundra? Because when she reached her destination, Evie would have to figure out how she was going to beat up the bad guys and rescue the prisoner. All by herself.

Both she and her laptop fell asleep after midnight.

In the morning, her mobile phone and the house's landline rang at the same time. Evie started awake, remembered where she was, and sat frozen while she decided which one to answer first. In the end she answered her mobile, which was closer and didn't require a mad dash to the kitchen. Then the house phone stopped ringing.

"They've done it," Bruce said as greeting. "They've fucking done it."

Bruce kept harping on about the world, the news,

everything, when her own world had shrunk to this house and her father. She ought to care—the world situation was going to hell. Even without watching the news, she could sense the tension in Bruce's voice. She ought to care. But she only felt tired.

"Who's done what?"

"Congress voted to back China. Who'd have guessed? Ten years ago, China was the fucking ninth level of hell, and now we're *allies*? It's unreal."

She winced. "Wasn't China backing terrorists? The Mongolians? We're not supposed to be backing a country that backs terrorists."

"An economic market of a billion and a half consumers can't be wrong, I guess."

"You know my mom died in the Seattle bombing."

"Yeah, I know, Evie." Background static on the connection filled the pause. "You're not the only one who feels that way. Protests are going on in Seattle and New York. They're about to turn them into riots. The National Guard's being called up."

"Shit." The architects of history, the generals and game-players, were at it again.

Another pause. Then, "How are we going to spin this in the book?"

She shook her head. "I don't know who the bad guys are anymore, Bruce. We could miss the deadline. Delay the publication, see how this is going to play out. Or we could zap the team to another planet and pretend like none of this is happening."

"I think I'd like to get zapped along with them. Paula isn't going to be happy." Paula was their editor, the one responsible for harnessing their creative energy and packaging it into the final product.

Evie gave a huff. "What good is being the creators of the country's bestselling comic title if we don't get any clout? Paula can deal with it."

"Roger, Captain. You sound like crap, by the way."

"I fell asleep on the sofa."

"Right. What was the last thing you wrote before you fell asleep?"

The file was still on-screen, autosaved and everything. She read him back the last few lines. The last few interesting ones, anyway. What she'd produced last night looked abysmal by the light of day.

"Shit," he said. "Tracker goes rogue. I like it. This could work."

"It wasn't really what I intended."

"Hey, don't argue. Just run with it."

"Right."

"Go take a shower. Get some coffee. Take care of yourself, okay?"

"You, too, Bruce. Hey, Bruce?"

"Yeah?"

"Does it even matter anymore?"

"What do you mean?"

"The comic. Why are we even talking about it? The world's going to hell, my father's dying—why am I still sitting down at my laptop?"

She could hear his breathing over the connection. He was tired; he'd been making himself sound cheerfully irate to hide it.

Then he said, "What choice do we have? It's what we do. Otherwise we'd have to curl up in a ball and go crazy."

She chuckled. Keep on going. It was all they could do.

"Thanks for calling."

"I'm just worried about you."

As she clicked off, her father came into the room, freshly showered, hair still damp, tucking his shirt into his jeans. He grabbed his coat off the chair he'd put it on, like he was actually planning on going somewhere.

"Dad?" She rose and followed him to the kitchen. Mab trotted along with them.

"That was Johnny on the phone. They've called up the whole Citizens' Watch. He's going to come pick me up." His car was still out from when he'd collapsed on patrol.

"You can't go out!" And how dare Johnny give him a ride in his condition.

"Why not?"

"You—you're sick." Did she really have to remind him that he'd spent yesterday in bed, doped up on drugs?

"Homeland Security's instituted a lockdown and curfew. Johnny doesn't have enough people to patrol. He needs me."

A security curfew in Hopes Fort was ridiculous—no one ever stayed out late anyway. "Dad—nothing's going to happen here. Those rules are for places like L.A. and—and Seattle."

His lips thinned, like he was holding back words, or his temper. She should have said New York, or Chicago, or Atlanta. Anywhere but Seattle. The word was like saying *failure*.

Then he said, "It's the principle of the matter, Evie. I have to do my part. I can't go to L.A. or Seattle to help. So I do what I can here. Even if it isn't much. Even if it doesn't mean anything."

He'd joined the Watch five years ago, right after Emma died. It was how he coped. Evie had the comic; he had this.

She couldn't say anything to stop him. She'd cornered herself by bringing up Seattle, and gave up her right to continue arguing.

"Dad—I think you should go to the hospital. After yesterday—I could drive you, just to get checked out—"

"What's the point? They'll tell me it's hopeless. That there's nothing they can do to save me, but they can give me something for the pain, and they'll pump me full of morphine and leave me in a bed to fade away. I can die on my own, I don't need their help." His hand on the doorknob, Mab sitting nearby and looking earnestly up at him, he said, "Watch over the Storeroom."

Stifled tears tightened her voice. "I don't care about that."

"You will." He scratched Mab's ears. "Help Evie watch the Storeroom, girl."

He closed the door behind him. Through the kitchen window, Evie watched him walk to the end of the driveway just as Johnny drove up in his police sedan. She thought her father was still limping. With his hands shoved in his coat pockets, his shoulders stiff against the chill air, it was hard to tell.

Robin Goodfellow crouched in the scrub by a fence post and watched the artist at work. The Curandera stood on the side of the highway running east out of town. The wind tangled her graying black hair; she wore a turquoise-and-silver pendant, which she gripped in her hand.

A person could go east from here, and keep going east for a thousand miles without the scenery changing much: flat winter fields covered in dry, bent stalks; a few fence posts strung with barbed wire; and sky, so much wide-open sky, a person could lose himself, wander in circles, and feel so small, he'd disappear from the universe.

The earth in this part of the world only slept. Long ago, when the mountains that made the spine of the continent were built, fires and earthquakes ravaged the land. People forgot what violence was necessary to create the beauty that decorated the postcards. That had happened so long ago, people had no need to remember. They did not care that the land was not still; it only slept.

The Curandera knelt, rubbed her hands together, then pressed them flat to the dirt. She beat the earth, making a slapping noise that carried. Again, and the slap became a thud. Then a groan that vibrated through the ground. Robin stood nervously, feeling the movement of the earth.

What Hera had said of the woman: for generations, the women of her family had been granted the power to speak to the sky, the sun, and the earth. They could feel its moods, sense waters building in the heavens, bring rain with a prayer, heal the sick, kill with a thought, speak to creatures who were not human. She could feel the veins and muscles of the earth, and the joints that moved it.

The ground lurched.

The earthquake started in earnest, and Robin clung to the fence post like it was a plywood raft put to sea. The Curandera remained on her knees, unwavering. Each time she touched the earth, another tremor racked the land, as if her slight arms were epic jackhammers.

A grumbling crack appeared across the highway. Farther along, another split broke through the asphalt. Grinding, tearing, the road came apart, one section rising while another fell, crevices growing between shattered slabs of pavement.

She raised her arms high, and the earthquake stopped.

Dust settled. Dislodged pebbles clattered and came to rest. A thick silence soon covered the world.

The Curandera knelt in a miniature canyon of her own making. For at least a mile, the road was devastated, pieces lying on top of each other, separated by gaps, like a strip of tile that some madman had taken a hammer to.

Robin leaned gasping against the fence post. "Bravo," he said at last.

She gazed across the wasted land as calmly as she had before the earthquake. "The highway west of town is the same."

"So the town's cut off?"

"Mostly. Some people do still remember how to travel on foot."

"But no one will be driving for quite some time."

He approached the Curandera and offered her his arm to escort her back to town. She turned her shoulder to him and walked alone.

Nothing ever happened in Hopes Fort. At least nothing interesting. Evie had ardently believed that her entire childhood. She clung to that belief now. Her father would be fine. Johnny would keep an eye on him and bring him home—or better, to a hospital—the minute he looked ill. Okay, the minute he *acted* ill. He looked plenty ill already.

She slumped back on the sofa. Her laptop stared at her. All she could do was write. Didn't seem very useful or heroic. The comic's production schedule seemed less relevant than ever. But what would she do if she didn't write? When she was starting out, when she wasn't sure she was ever going to be able to make a living at it, she used to play that game with herself: What would she do if she failed? Go into advertising? Open a bookstore? She'd thought up a dozen half-assed plans, including marrying a millionaire. Plenty of those hanging around L.A. Dogged persistence won out in the end. But she imagined a dozen alternate time lines, where she led lives that didn't involve writing.

If she didn't write, she'd sit here staring at the walls until she went crazy. She couldn't leave town. And Dad said to watch the Storeroom.

Exhaustion never entered into Tracker's consideration of her current situation. It simply wasn't an option. When the bunker of the gulag finally appeared—a mound in the distance on the flat, frozen waste—she dropped to her knees and crawled, offering as low a profile as she could. She kept her gun in her hand. It was just like Basic all over again. Hell, it was almost fun. If only she knew that Jeeves and Matchlock were all right, and Sarge and Talon. She shouldn't have had to do this alone.

Their information said the agent would be in the first bunker. The rest of the complex was underground, and had caved in years ago, when the last of the political dissidents were released and turned their frustrations on the structure itself.

She lay flat on the ground for two hours watching the concrete hut. No doors opened; no shapes appeared at any windows. She flexed the muscles of her limbs to keep them from cramping. Annoyed, she thought there should have been someone around: guards, a change in duty shifts, something.

She wasn't well camouflaged—her dark fatigues were meant for nighttime operations, and the land here was bright, the overcast sky stinging with light, the ground textured with pools of crusted snow and lichen-covered rock. But there didn't seem to be anyone around for miles. The bunker was still, silent. Quietly, she approached: a few steps and pause, a few more steps, looking in every direction, over her shoulders, up at the sky. She was used to having someone watch her back.

Soon, she crouched under the window of the bunker. Her gun felt clumsy in her gloved hand. Maybe she wouldn't need it. Slowly, she rose until she could peer over the sill, into the room.

The room was empty.

But a trapdoor in the floor was open.

She closed her eyes and breathed a curse. Either the spy wasn't here at all—or their information about the complex was wrong, and she wouldn't be able to just run in and run back out again.

The door was unlocked. She opened it just enough to slip inside, then swept the room, sighting down her gun.

The place was dusty, decrepit. A broken chair slumped in a corner; scraps and trash littered the floor. A table stood against a far wall. On it was a short-wave radio set. Tracker's hopes rose for a second, until she saw that it was smashed.

Footprints in the dusty floor led to the stairs under the trapdoor.

If she went down there, she'd be stuck. Only one exit, no light—something wasn't right here. But if she could learn something to take back to the others and figure out what was really going on, the risk might be worth it.

She started down the stairs.

This tunnel, at least, hadn't collapsed. When she reached the bottom of the stairs, a light became visible ahead, coming from a room. Shadows flickered, as if someone moved in front of a lamp.

Tracker pressed herself to the wall and continued forward. She heard subdued voices speaking English.

"Comrade, thank you. I look forward to a long and profitable relationship."

"Absolutely." That voice was American. "You'll have those weapons shipments, and I trust you'll use them only on targets designated by our colleague here?"

A third voice, with a clipped accent: "It would be tragic if this war were to fall out of our control."

Tracker came close enough to the door to lean around and look.

She saw the man in fatigues first. He was facing her, and her eyes widened. It was him, the agent she was supposed to rescue. She recognized him from his dossier photo.

He was shaking hands with a man in a Russian military uniform. The third man wore Chinese insignia on his uniform.

"I can guarantee we'll have American troops in place by the end of the year. With our peacekeeping efforts, we should be able to keep this thing going for years."

"And our governments will continue to leave us in control," said the Chinese officer.

They were making a deal. They wanted a world war. Whatever negotiation was being settled here would keep these men, the old military elite, in power indefinitely. Gods moving their pawns across the world.

Tracker thought of a dozen melodramatic options: stand and challenge them, demand explanation, face them down like she was in some Hollywood spy thriller. Get them to reveal their nefarious plan. Unlikely.

She should just shoot them all before they even knew she was here. But she wondered if there wasn't some logical explanation for this meeting: the Russians and the Chinese were on the edge of war, the Americans had already picked sides—and the American agent hadn't said anything about peace.

Then the choice was out of her hands.

"Tracker? You can come out of the dark now."

The American had spotted her. She didn't move from her shelter behind the doorframe. The military officers touched their guns, resting in belt holsters. The agent was smiling, though, regarding her as he would a wayward child.

"Where are your friends?" he said. "What good is my trap if I don't catch you all?"

Goddamn it, she'd walked right into it. She exhaled a silent breath. The unholy trio probably had a back entrance staked out and a way to collapse the tunnel on top of her. She revealed herself, leaning partway around the doorframe.

"Gentlemen," said the agent to his colleagues. "Meet Tracker, the intelligence expert for the Eagle Eye Commandos."

The two officers flinched, their eyes widening. Was her reputation really that scary? Probably not hers personally.

The agent turned back to her. "So. Where are they?"

"I don't know."

"They wouldn't have sent you here by yourself."

She kept her mouth shut on that one. Instead she asked, "When did you turn traitor?"

"I haven't," he said, his smile unwavering.

She winced, her brow furrowing with confusion. He chuckled, just like the villain in a spy film. "I'm here with the full authority of the U.S. government."

"Planning a war?"

"You don't think wars just happen, do you?"

"And what do you want with us?" she said, her voice hushed.

"We've decided that you've become a liability.

You and your team are out of control. And what the
U.S. can't control—it destroys."

She shot him.

A knock came at the door, and Evie almost fell off
the sofa. She muttered and took a deep breath to still
her racing heart, then gathered herself to answer the
call. She almost hoped it was Alex, wanting to know if
she'd guessed yet. But it was probably seven dwarves
looking for a glass coffin.

Mab was in the kitchen, trembling like she wanted
to bark. Wagging her tail, she looked up at Evie. So it
wasn't the bad guys. She opened the door a crack. Two
men stood on the porch. One was the brusque old
man from the other day. Merlin.

The other man was in his thirties, fresh and rugged
looking, like he spent a lot of time outdoors. Sandy
blond hair swept back from his square-jawed face to
touch the collar of his brown leather jacket. Jeans, a
gray T-shirt, and work boots completed his outfit. He
wore a trimmed beard, and laugh lines marked the
corners of his eyes. He stood straight and tall, and
smiled at her. He had blue eyes.

He looked like he should have been in a country
music video, or starring in soaps, or modeling Harley-
Davidsons. He *couldn't* be—he just couldn't be.

Mab sat nearby, her tail brushing the floor. Evie
opened the door wider. "Hello?"

The younger man said, "Hello. I've come to see
about a sword. Merlin here says it's stuck in a rock
round back." He had an accent like a mild version of
a Celtic brogue. "I thought we should ask before we
went tromping round your property."

Evie leaned against the doorframe, her knees weak. She wondered if she should bow. She wondered what sort of vacuous expression she was giving him. He was looking back expectantly, like he was used to dealing with bewildered women.

Mab took the opportunity to push around Evie and throw herself at the stranger, tail-wagging, bouncing in place. Arthur caught her before she could rear up and topple him over, as she seemed intent on doing. He kept her gently but firmly grounded.

"Well—hello, there! Aren't you a fine beast?" He scratched her ears with both hands, sliding down her back to thump her sides, and Mab whined ecstatically.

"She likes you," Evie said, her voice gone vague. Arthur beamed in reply.

"Um, Miss Walker, if you don't mind?" Merlin jerked his head to gesture around to the back of the house.

"Yeah. Um. This way." Shaking her head to dispel her foggy wonderment, she stepped off the porch. She was aware of the two men following her, Merlin trodding almost on her heels, and Arthur still playing with Mab, who bounded alongside like she'd found her soul mate.

Arthur. If she'd seen him hanging around a construction site or a biker bar, she wouldn't have given him a second glance. Until he smiled and looked at her with those eyes.

They rounded the far corner of the house, and she stepped aside. "Here it is."

Merlin had seen it before, but still he stopped to gape.

Arthur stepped past him, his face drawn with a sad,

heartbroken look, like he was approaching the dead body of a long-lost friend. History shone through his eyes, memories, intense and desolate. He looked to be in his thirties, but he was older, much older, as if he had been reborn a hundred times and retained the memories of each of those lives.

Evie wished her father were here to see this.

He reached the stone and took hold of the sword's grip. Squeezing, he took a deep breath and pulled. The sword came out as smoothly as if from a scabbard, with the barest slipping noise.

The blade gleamed when he held it aloft; he turned it, studying it with a haunted gaze. Evie resisted an impulse to drop to her knees—Arthur, the true king, the rightful bearer of Excalibur stood before her.

Arthur turned the sword so it pointed to the ground. He knelt with the point resting on earth, his hands laced together over the grip and cross guard. He bowed his head low and his lips moved, undoubtedly in prayer.

Evie's heartbeat rattled, anxious that she was watching something private, that she had no business intruding. She and Merlin stood side by side.

"How did you know to come here?" she said, her voice hoarse. "How did you find us?" Hopes Fort was halfway around the world from Britain.

He nodded at the praying Arthur and said, "Faith."

"And why—why now?"

"Because there is need."

"What need?"

"At the end of one age, the shattering of the old era, someone has to stand by to pick up the pieces and build the new one." He said this with the same straightforward tone, no matter how Evie gaped at him.

The ground began to tremble. Mab whined and turned circles, then stopped to look across the prairie at nothing. The trembling increased in violence, shaking Evie to her bones. She swore she could hear the house's foundations rattling.

After living in Southern California, she knew what an earthquake felt like. She sat down before she fell, grabbed Mab, and hugged her. Already off balance, the dog toppled into her lap. Merlin stuck out his arms for balance. Arthur, still kneeling, held his sword ready and looked for an enemy.

Then it ended.

A temblor like this wasn't particularly frightening—it might even have been as high as a 6 on the Richter scale. Except this was Colorado. Colorado had baby earthquakes, imperceptible, every decade or so. What was a magnitude-6 earthquake doing in Hopes Fort?

She ran to the house, Mab loping alongside her. Merlin and Arthur followed. She dashed into the kitchen, vaguely aware that there could be aftershocks and she should stay outside. But she had to find out if her father was okay.

The house phone was dead. The lines must have been down. She tried the light switch, and the electricity was gone as well. Hopes Fort was probably going to be a disaster area. No one around here knew what to do with a quake like that.

In a moment of irrational panic, she remembered her laptop and the thousand words or so she'd produced that morning. Her heart sinking, she checked the living room next, dreading what she'd find on the screen.

The battery had saved her. Her work was intact,

and knowing full well she was luckier than she had any right to be, she saved the file and shut down the machine. Now to check on her father.

Merlin and Arthur stood in the kitchen. The sword seemed to fill the room.

She retrieved her mobile phone and dialed Johnny Brewster's number.

"We're sorry, your call cannot be completed—"

She clicked off the phone with a huff and started pacing.

"What's happening?" Arthur said.

"Phone lines are down. Electricity's out. I'm worried about my dad." She wondered if she'd have to explain telephones and electricity to the ancient warrior, but he didn't seem confused.

"My lady, if my sword may be of any use to you, command me."

She felt dizzy, lurching with a moment of displacement. Despite the leather coat and blue jeans, he was a knight. He held his sword like he knew how to use it, his stance was ready. He had said "my lady" like he meant it. The late nights reading Tolkien and dreaming of kings, her thirteen-year-old's daydreams, came rushing back.

"Thank you," she said. "I think what I really need to do is find my dad, to make sure he's all right. I'm sure you all have . . . better things to do. Than hang around here, I mean."

Merlin crossed his arms. "Do you think it coincidence that such a tremor shook the earth at the very moment he—" He gestured significantly at Arthur. "—claimed his birthright? I believe our destiny lies here."

Evie considered, and for some reason thought of Hera on her doorstep. If she had to blame the earthquake on anyone, it would be her. "Yeah, actually, I think it is a coincidence. Sorry." Merlin scowled. Evie found her car keys and headed for the door.

Mab bounced in place beside her, bumping her nose against Evie's hip, whining, and shoving all the way to the door. With her bulk, the wolfhound significantly impeded her progress. "Mab, get out of my way! Back off!"

Mab dashed ahead and planted herself in front of the kitchen door. She wasn't so impolite as to growl, but Evie thought she looked like she wanted to. Her ears were flat, her gaze threatening. Mab didn't want her to leave.

Gently, Arthur said, "Wouldn't he come home, if something were wrong? Wouldn't someone contact you? Perhaps you should wait."

What a sane and reasonable suggestion. She rubbed her face and slumped against the wall. Mab wagged her tail apologetically.

"We could look for him, if you like."

"No, we can't," Merlin said. "Mr. Walker can take care of himself, I'm sure."

His face alight and eager, Arthur was almost bouncing. "It's a scouting mission, Merlin. I won't have a chance to do anything like this once the troubles start."

"We don't know this town, we don't know what's out there—there may be more earthquakes. Besides, you have a destiny."

"And what am I supposed to do—camp out here

until that destiny sneaks up on me and pounces? I'd rather be *doing* something."

Merlin glared at the warrior for all the world like a parent with a hyperactive child. He straightened, and said with utmost patience, "What does Miss Walker say?"

Arthur turned that brilliant, boyish expression on her. She couldn't help but smile back. She was beginning to understand what it meant to have a destiny sneak up on you and pounce.

"I'd really appreciate it if you could find out if he's okay."

Arthur lifted a brow and grinned at Merlin, as if saying, *You see?*

Merlin grumbled under his breath for a moment. "A scouting mission, eh?"

"A short one."

Exhaling a long-suffering breath, the old man said, "All right."

Evie swore Arthur did a little celebratory arm-jerk, like a teenager who'd gotten the car for the night.

She found the belt and scabbard for Excalibur in the Storeroom. Arthur wouldn't be parted from the sword, no matter how strange he'd look striding down Main Street with the weapon slung on his person. "I'll tell them I'm in a play," he said, as if he'd had to deal with the problem before.

She saw them off from the front porch.

"We'll return as soon as we have news," Arthur said. He bowed, a gracious gesture that made Evie's heart flutter. *Where was this guy when I was in high school and giddy?*

The earthquake was the signal to move.

It quickly put the town in an uproar. People weren't used to this sort of thing here. Once the phones cut out and the power lines went down, chaos took over. The Curandera had promised only that the main roads leading into town would be impassable. The rest worked nicely, however. No one could reach the town by any other method, either.

Robin watched the park in front of Town Hall from an unobtrusive doorway.

The police officer with Frank Walker dropped the old man off at the police station, to assist with the Red Cross. Frank complained, argued, and harangued the younger man, who had thought he was being sly about putting Frank in the least-strenuous job possible. Frank, it seemed, was doing his best to deny his illness. The officer—his name was Johnny—kept trying to tell Frank how much he was needed at the station. It turned out, when people started gathering at the station because the power was out and their phones were dead, Frank really was needed to help settle them down, while the uniformed officers patrolled the town to assess the damage.

A line had formed in front of Frank, who stood on the dried-up lawn in front of the police station direct-ing people to the Red Cross shelter, which had already been set up in a tent in the town park; they were dis-tributing coffee and fielding calls on a satellite phone. He held a clipboard, where he wrote down specific problems: buildings that had collapsed or looked like they were going to, gas or water lines that might have ruptured. Mostly he assured people, in a steady, confident voice, that everything was under control. Didn't matter if they really were; he only had to tell people they were. The usual government statement.

Robin cut to the front of the line.

"I *really* need someone to help me," Robin said, gripping Frank's elbow.

Frank tried to gently brush him away. "Sir, if you'll just get in line with the others—"

"I think my wife is in labor." It was the most persuasive thing Robin could think to say.

It worked. Frank's eyes got wide. He gave the clipboard to the next person in line and put his hand on Robin's back, urging him forward.

Robin led him around the corner, down a side lane, to the back of the building, where the Wanderer's rented sedan was waiting. The Wanderer stood at the open back door.

"This way, right here!" Robin said when the old man seemed to lag. He pointed at the car. He didn't keep up the act; he couldn't help but grin. Frank suspected. Brow furrowed, he looked at Robin, the Wanderer, the car, and back to Robin, as if he knew who they were.

Before he could bolt, the Wanderer said, "Mr. Walker, we really need you to get in."

His voice sent a chill down even Robin's spine. Frank turned pale. Robin couldn't exactly say what the Wanderer was or what power he wielded. Mostly it was his attitude, the implications behind his stone-like gaze, his unflappable manner. It was like the man had looked into hell and would be more than happy to tell you what he had seen there. And he would do so in that flat, emotionless tone of voice.

He didn't need to carry a weapon or make threats to get people to do what he wanted. Robin took Frank's arm and guided him into the car, closing the door behind him.

Robin got in on the other side. The Wanderer climbed into the driver's seat and moved the car into the street.

Evie tried calling Bruce on the cell phone and couldn't get a signal. Hardly surprising and just as well. What could she say to him?

Hey, Bruce, you won't believe who just showed up on my doorstep.

He'd only chew her out for not getting any pictures of the sword.

There weren't any aftershocks.

Arthur said he'd rather be doing something, and Evie understood the urge. All she could do right now was write.

She'd left Tracker totally in the air. The laptop battery was charged up. She'd write as long as she had the juice. So where was she?

She shot him.

She didn't wait for him to draw first. She'd been watching his hands at the edges of her vision; she knew he was holding a gun. Before the words had left his mouth, she leveled and fired.

Twice more she fired, and the Russian and Chinese officers lay on the floor, writhing on top of the American agent's body. The whole sequence took only a couple of seconds, because she'd been planning it since she first heard their voices.

The agent had studied her dossier, she assumed. Her dossier said that she never shot first.

Three more times she fired, three shots to three heads, killing them.

She leaned back against the wall and loaded a fresh magazine, waiting for guards to come barreling down the hallway at her. On the verge of hyperventilating, she swallowed back gasps. The room remained silent.

This was probably exactly what the agent was talking about, when he said the Eagle Eyes were out of control. She searched the bodies, not believing for a minute that they'd have any hard record of their multinational negotiations and war-brokering. But the U.S. agent had a data stick in his breast pocket. She took it. What the hell.

Apparently, they hadn't brought any guards with them. No witnesses that way. A pickup was probably scheduled for them later. She wondered what the agent had expected he was going to do with the Eagle Eyes when they showed up. Was he arrogant enough to think he could have killed them all? He might have been able to—they expected him to be on their side.

She found that the first room in the bunker was rigged to collapse, low-level explosives planted on key support beams. That was how he'd planned on getting rid of them.

Back outside, staring at the expanse of tundra, the

hopelessness of her situation hit her. She had no way to call for help. She had no place to go. Her own government had betrayed her. And her friends.

She had to find them. She had to give Talon the flash drive. He'd know what to do. He was the only one she trusted now.

She had to be out of sight when the pickup for the others came. She turned west and started walking.

The trick to writing suspense was to fling the characters into increasingly impossible situations and then find plausible ways to get them out. And hope the situation you created wasn't too impossible.

She ate the last bit of rations—a smashed-up energy bar—she had stashed in her fatigues. Washed it down with a swig of vodka, which wasn't the smartest thing she'd done all day, but it was all she had. If she found a snow patch, she'd melt as much of it as she could to rehydrate. She didn't like the way her vision was blurring.

The rhythmic, air-pounding *whump* of a low-flying helicopter sounded at the edges of her hearing. She reacted slowly. She wanted help; her hindbrain cried out that this was someone come to rescue her.

Or it could be the pickup for the meeting. Her paranoia won, and she dodged for cover.

Forests spotted the area, and she'd been heading for one of these. She ran now as the helicopter came into view to her left, a black spot growing larger and taking on form. She hesitated, looking for markings, until she realized that even if she saw an American flag on its tail, she couldn't trust it. So she kept running, into the trees, past the trees, in case they'd seen her. Just reaching cover wouldn't be enough.

The ground dropped away and she screamed.

She fell and kept falling. She hadn't simply tripped and hit the ground. A ravine had opened in the middle of the forest, a sinkhole or fault or something that meant she was now hurtling twenty feet down to another part of the forest. She curled up and tried to go limp.

Her leg caught under her, twisted wrong, and she knew what it meant. She heard the crack before she felt the pain. When she finally stopped, she lay there for a long time, flat on her back, staring up at the sky. As soon as she tried to move, she would hurt.

But she had to move. She had to find Talon.

When she sat up, pain squealed through her right leg. Tracker clamped her mouth shut and swallowed back nausea. She was dehydrated; she couldn't afford to throw up. A few deep breaths. A self-indulgent moan. Time to keep working.

Training had taught her, drilling into her over and over again what to do in a situation like this, how to survive, how to splint bones, how to keep warm. But training was nothing like reality. She couldn't tie a splint tight enough. She couldn't inflict that much pain on herself.

She gave up trying to climb out of the ravine—it hurt too much even to stand. She could rest here until morning, then make her way along the bottom. She would still be traveling west.

At least she hadn't cried yet. Every muscle ached, from clenching against the pain.

Night was falling. She was about to get even

colder. She managed to find a sheltered place, where the wind howled above her, instead of at her.

She was going to die alone in this place.

The memory stick was intact in her vest pocket. One misstep, and all her work and training came to nothing.

Captain Talon wouldn't reprimand her. He wouldn't even be angry. If she managed to get out of this and find him, he'd smile, tell her she did a good job, that she was a good soldier. His voice would be steady, kind. And all the more cruel because she didn't deserve his kindness.

One more time, because as long as she kept trying, she was moving and wouldn't freeze, she hoisted herself to her feet.

Hera, sitting in the passenger side of the front seat of the car, pulled off her sunglasses and considered Frank in the back. He stared straight ahead. Beside him, Robin was grinning, lounged back with his legs straight, seeming to enjoy himself.

"Mr. Walker, so good to meet you," Hera said.

"What's this about?" Not even pretending to be friendly. What was it about these Walkers?

"I only wondered if I could persuade you to part with a little something in your Storeroom."

"You should have come to the house."

"I did. Your daughter wasn't very helpful."

His look turned even colder, settling into the game of cloak and dagger he probably thought they were playing. The girl evidently hadn't told him about her.

"Then there's nothing there for you," Frank said.

"I don't care if you think I should have it or not. I'll take it, one way or the other." She turned to the Wanderer. "Take us to the cemetery."

They pulled onto the state highway. Two turns later brought them to an isolated part of the town, a wind-swept corner of dried-up yellow prairie. Weathered headstones and monuments lined up in rows. A few larger mausoleums stood guard around the far edge. The place was peaceful and unnoticed. They could be a family out to visit a dearly departed loved one, to lay a few flowers on a grave.

The Wanderer turned the car around a miniature cul-de-sac, then pulled over on the straightaway and shut off the engine. No one moved. They had only to wait now, entertaining each other as best they could.

The Wanderer looked at Frank in the rearview mirror. "You hide it pretty well, but you're scared, aren't you?"

Frank glanced up, meeting his gaze in the mirror, revealing nothing. "I'm not scared of you."

"Not of me. Of dying. You're terrified of dying."

"You can't threaten me."

Hera watched the exchange with interest, smiling a little at the Wanderer's insight, and at Frank's show of bravado. She said, "But I can threaten your daughter. I have someone at the house now. Evie Walker will learn that we have you. She's a very devoted daughter, isn't she?"

Frank settled back into the seat, glowering.

It was only a matter of time before Evie Walker arrived, more than willing to hand over the apple in exchange for her father's safe return.

Her laptop battery had some life to it yet, and at some point, the wireless network had been restored. She had Web access again.

She checked the major news sites for information about the earthquake and had trouble finding anything—the story rated only a sidebar blurb, far down on the list of headlines. Russia had suffered another wave of terrorist attacks: train lines, government buildings, shipyards. The Middle East had flared up again, with every separatist ethnic group taking a stand. India was massing its army, and Pakistan had responded in kind.

The difference between American and foreign news Web sites was astonishing. The foreign sites showed graphic photos, featured angry interviews, and talked about the failure of the world powers to act. The U.S. sites mentioned only that an emergency meeting of the U.N. General Assembly was in session.

She wrote.

Some time later—a minute, an hour—Tracker heard another helicopter. Or the same one, circling in a search pattern. Using a broken tree limb as a crutch, she hobbled about ten feet from where she'd landed after her fall.

She had decided that she would signal the next aircraft that came by. She needed help, and if it had to be from someone who was going to take her prisoner, so be it. Even U.S. agents sent to kill her would need her alive for a time, if they thought she could help them find the rest of her team. She couldn't drag a broken leg across Siberia.

Or maybe, just maybe, Talon and Sarge had found Jeeves and Matchlock and they were out looking for her.

She tore a strip of cloth from her shirt, soaked it in vodka from the dead mercenary's canteen, and stuffed the alcoholic cloth into the mouth of the canteen, leaving a tail hanging out. She had a lighter in her kit and lit the end of the cloth, let it flare into a good blaze, then heaved it over the edge of the ravine. She sighed with relief when it cleared the edge and didn't come bouncing back at her.

The vodka lit with a roar. Fire spilled out and caught on the surrounding trees. All in all, a nice little signal fire. She hobbled far enough away that she wouldn't be engulfed by the blaze in the next few minutes.

The thumping beat of the helicopter motor became louder as it approached to investigate. Tracker had only to wait to see who found her.

It didn't take long. Not as long as she would have liked. She wanted to scuttle to some high ground, some vantage where she could hide if she didn't like the look of whoever found her. But in seconds, the tops of the trees were swaying with the wind of the descending helicopter. She couldn't see it; it must have found a clearing nearby. The troops inside must have hit the ground before the craft had even landed, because she heard voices calling. What language . . . what language . . . she strained to understand.

The first one came over the rise, circling around

the flaming patch where her fireball had ignited. She was on her feet—her foot—leaning on a tree, waiting, dizzy, unable to catch her breath. Another figure followed the first. Both were dressed in olive fatigues, wore knit masks and sunglasses.

She should have recognized them, she so wanted to recognize them.

They saw her then, aimed their rifles at her, and shouted something. The words were muffled.

When she saw the American flag on one uniform, she fainted.

Someone knocked at the door just then, of course. Evie saved the file before racing to the kitchen, Mab loping at her heels. Maybe Johnny, realizing how sick Frank was, had finally brought him home. Though with the quake, the police probably needed all the help they could get from the Citizens' Watch. Why did Dad always have to be helpful? Or maybe Arthur had come back to tell her that he'd seen her father and everything was fine. Of course everything was fine. What could happen? Besides earthquakes, goddesses, and the prophesied return of mythical monarchs.

She opened the kitchen door, standing in the way to keep Mab from rushing out.

Alex looked back at her. "Are you all right?" he said, gasping like he'd been running. "The earthquake—I ran over—I was worried."

She wasn't sure what to say. His question seemed so odd—his concern seemed odd. Why was he worried about her? What did he want from her?

"You're Sinon," she said.

A smile broke, pleasantly softening his face. "I knew you'd figure it out. Can I come in?"

She stayed fast in the doorway. Beside her, Mab wasn't wagging her tail.

"I don't think I can trust you."

While Alex's—Sinon's—smile didn't fade, it took on an edge, a different gleam to his eye. "Because I lied my way past the walls of Troy?"

She flushed, a wave of dizziness burning along her skin. She hadn't wanted to believe. How much easier it was to think he was just a clever, witty man.

"You were terrorists. The Trojan Horse—it was the Bronze Age version of a car bomb—"

"That's only because you read Virgil's side of it. We waged honest war for ten years. Then we became desperate. No one can blame us for what we did. We paid for our victory."

He seemed so calm. But then he'd had to deal with it for three thousand years. How could he not be calm? "You were a spy. What would you do to get into the Storeroom?"

"Nothing," he said gently. "I'll stay away, if you want me to."

"Will you tell me something?"

"Anything." His earnestness made her nervous.

"Are you working for Hera?"

"Why would you think that?"

"Because I don't know anything about you, because you were following me. You're spying on the house, you know more about what's happening here than I do, you could read the writing on the apple. You act like you know her—what are you *doing* here? Why aren't you *dead*?" She ran out of breath before she could ask him what the Trojan War had been like.

Standing there, slouched in his jacket, he didn't look like a Greek warrior. She tried to imagine him in one of those crested helms from the pottery glazes.

Then she blurted, "Was Helen really the most beautiful woman in the world?"

He looked away, bit his lip, then said, "Yes. I saw her once, standing on the wall of Troy. It wasn't just her looks, but the way she moved. Every turn of her head was grace itself. Nothing wasted. Remember, though, she was a demigoddess. Zeus's daughter. Comparing apples and oranges, putting her up against mortal women."

Evie shook her head, amazed, awed, befuddled. She didn't believe it, looking at him, his creased expression like he was getting ready to laugh at a joke at her expense. He seemed—normal. Pleasant. Not mythological at all, not like Hera, who'd shaken Evie to her bones.

Yet that haunted voice that kept drawing her to the Storeroom murmured, *He's old, this one. Very old.*

She sighed. "All the things you've seen. All the things you must have forgotten—how can you stand it?"

"I don't have a choice. I—I have this vision, that a billion years from now the world ends, swallowed up at last by a bloated sun or crumbled to ash. And I'm still here. I live through it, floating in space with nothing to do and no place to go. The lone repository of human history, and a mediocre one at that. Maybe some god out there will have pity on me and take me in—but I think they've all gone away. I can't blame them. But I don't have their power, so I'm stuck here with whatever fate hands me."

"Have you thought about going insane?" It would seem like a reasonable thing to do, given his circumstances.

"Did once. Got boring, so I snapped out of it."

She looked hard at him, wanting to be kind. "I can't think of anything in the Storeroom that will help you. I'm sorry."

"Listen," he said, running his hand through his hair. "Hera's planning something. She's a bitter old bitch. But I can get close to her, find out what she's planning—"

"Can I trust you?"

"Yes."

"Did you say the same thing to her?"

He closed his mouth on whatever obvious answer he'd been ready to give.

Someone was walking up the driveway. Evie stared at the figure over Alex's shoulder. He caught her gaze and turned to look.

She wondered who it would be this time: Jack come to fetch some golden eggs, a Persian merchant searching for a rolled-up piece of flying carpet, a Viking unfrozen from the permafrost wanting Thor's hammer. Her gut sank, and she waited for the instinct that would drag her unerringly to the basement.

Mab pricked her ears forward and growled.

The figure, a woman of average height, in early middle age, slim, and with thick black hair hanging loose down her back, walked up the driveway.

"Shit," Alex muttered, turning up the collar of his

coat and slumping against the wall as if he were an unconcerned vagrant.

The woman was cinnamon-skinned, with Latina features. Mab's growling doubled in ferocity, lips pulled back from her teeth. The strange woman stared at her, made a motion with her hand—and Mab fell quiet, frozen in her place.

"Evie Walker?" she said.

Evie nodded.

"I've come to deliver a message. Hera has your father. She'll trade him for the apple. Will you trade?"

Evie's muscles flinched in panic. *Yes, yes!* The words were on her tongue, but she couldn't say them. Instead, she said weakly, "Gave up trying to bust in?"

The woman's expression was cold and superior. "She found a better way. What's your answer?"

"I—I need—" *Yes, anything, don't hurt him!* "I need to think about it."

"Come to the cemetery this afternoon. Bring the apple. Come alone." She cast a fleeting glance at Alex as she turned to walk down the driveway.

Mab collapsed with a heartbreaking whine; Evie knelt beside her and helped her to her feet. The dog didn't seem hurt physically. But her eyes showed fear, and her tail was locked between her legs. Evie hugged her close.

Evie's voice cracked when she said, "Who was that?"

"She's working for Hera."

"What will Hera do to my father?"

"I don't know."

"I have to give it to her. I don't care, I have to—"

"Evie, think for a moment." Alex took hold of her shoulders; Evie gasped, surprised, trembling. "Think what it is—the apple of Discord. Hera will use it to start wars. She could destroy the world with it."

"The world's already at war. And I don't care, it doesn't matter—"

"Would your father want you to give it to her?"

"I don't care!" He was in her face, urging her, and she didn't want to listen. There had to be another way, had to be something she could do. "Arthur—I have to find Arthur, he can help. If we can get him back without giving her the apple, Arthur and Merlin will know how—"

"Arthur's been here? King Arthur? Did he take the sword?"

Evie nodded, and Alex breathed, "Excalibur." Then he said, "He's still here in Hopes Fort? We'll find him. You're right. He'll help."

Nodding absently, Evie agreed, and wondered which part of Hera's plan she was falling into.

A group of six army helicopters flew by, passing over the house and heading south. They pounded the air with their rotors.

Marcus screamed and dropped the axe he'd been using to chop firewood. Terrible visions struck his mind all at once, like lightning. The sky was clear, the sun warm. No storms raged; no lightning flashed. All was peaceful, except for the throbbing in his mind. Stories. Hundreds of tales, voices telling them all at once, in languages he didn't recognize, cadences that were foreign. Gods, beasts, golden fleece, enchanted swords, all stored inside a well-worn leather bag—

All stored in the cellar under the villa. He'd never gone down there, but somehow he knew. He could picture shelves of artifacts, racks of swords, golden apples and winged slippers, icons of the gods—all under his family's small house?

He ran to the house, then to the stone steps that led down to the roughly carved-out cellar. His father didn't permit any of the family to enter here. Even at their most mischievous, his children obeyed him. Somehow, the place repelled curiosity. Not anymore. He pushed back the sheepskin that hung from the lintel at the bot-

tom of the stairs, marking the cellar entrance. Even in
the dim light, he could see it was just as he had imagined, the wondrous objects of a thousand tales spread
before him.

His heart and lungs raced, unwilling to accept the
magnitude of what he saw. This was larger than him,
and he wasn't ready for what his being here meant.
What is this?

This is the Storeroom, the vision that had struck
him from within said. *You are its heir.*

"But my father—"

You are its heir.

Marcus's knees gave way. He sat on the dirt floor
and tried to catch his breath. He was sixteen. Only
sixteen. Nearly a man, yes, but—he wasn't ready. He'd
inherited the knowledge all in a terrible flash, a burst
like death. Even at the first, he'd understood what it
meant. That was why he'd screamed.

He wanted to give it all back.

Part of him believed it was a mistake. The gods
had visited a fit upon him, a false vision. He climbed
the stairs slowly. He had to know. He'd see his father
striding through the door, and Marcus would demand from him some explanation for what was happening to him, and what the cellar Storeroom really
meant.

Pale, shaking, he reached the house's main room
just as someone rushed through the archway. Not his
father, but his younger brother Tonius.

The boy was flushed and shouting. "Marcus, please,
hurry. Father's fallen, out in the field. He isn't breathing, he won't wake up, you must come help him—"

Marcus closed his eyes and wept. Bitterly, he wished his father had died slowly, of creeping old age, as fathers were supposed to. If Marcus had to carry this burden at all, he'd rather have taken it on in small parcels, so that he might not notice the growing weight of it.

12

A voice woke Sinon. "Come to me. I need you."
It wasn't a sound, but a thought in his mind, put there by Apollo. A holy summons.

Sinon rolled onto his back, folded his hands under his head, and stared at the ceiling, painted gray in the light filtering through the curtains hung around his pallet. It was never night in the Palace of the Sun, and he couldn't sleep without the curtains. He sighed. *We won the war,* he thought. *What trick of the gods made me a slave, then? I should have fought harder for my freedom.*

It was a useless thought, which he nonetheless considered often.

He rose, dressed, and went to Apollo's bedchamber.

One might have expected the place to be sumptuous, decadent. In fact, it was the opposite, simple and comfortable. This wasn't where he entertained or impressed. This was where he lived. A table held cups and a pitcher, a pair of chests sat against a wall for storage, a wide pallet occupied a corner. The drapes over the windows were closed. A lamp by the bed cast a little light.

Apollo stood from the bed. "Pour me some wine."

Sinon did so, bringing Apollo the cup.

Apollo took it and drained it in one go, then tossed the cup away. The bronze goblet clattered on the stone. "Tell me, Sinon. Do you like me?"

Sinon couldn't lie. If he tried, his jaw froze. The *no* that he wanted to spit died on his tongue.

"I don't know, my lord."

"How can you not know?"

"You—you're very difficult, my lord."

Apollo grinned slyly. "But I'm not entirely unlikable?"

"No, my lord."

Apollo tipped his head back, flexing his shoulders, stretching his neck. The god commanded him, "Make love to me, my Achaean warrior."

This was an old routine by now. Apollo had once told Sinon he enslaved him because of his pride. Apollo occasionally wanted to feel weak—a difficult problem for a god. Sinon supposed Apollo thought he had solved it, in possessing a proud slave.

He was taller than Apollo, when Apollo was wearing what Sinon thought of as his human form. When the god had been mortal, this was how he had looked: slender and young. What he had learned, watching this god—this man—over the years: Apollo was lonely. For all his power, he had to command someone to make love to him. Sinon could almost feel pity for him. In that, he found some affection for his master.

Sinon touched Apollo's chin, tilted his face up, and

kissed his lips, long and lingering. Apollo melted into his arms.

He had some small power over a god, which when he thought about it was terribly ironic.

Later, Apollo slept curled against Sinon like a child, his head resting against the other's shoulder. Sinon's breath stirred his golden hair. Lightly, he ran a finger along the beardless cheek. The god fit so compactly in his embrace. It was almost enough to make him feel protective. He kissed the top of Apollo's head.

He had begun to drift to sleep when Apollo stirred and murmured, "There's someone in the house. Come in through the closet."

He meant the doorway to Olympus.

A moment later, she appeared at the entrance to Apollo's bedchamber. Looking over Apollo's naked body, Sinon saw her. She regarded them, meeting his gaze. She was armored, a sword girded at her side, her helmet under her arm. He didn't know what to do. He couldn't exactly bow to her from his current position. He didn't like being caught like this, having this woman see him tangled in bed with his male lover. That pride again. His impulse was to bury himself under the covers like a child having a nightmare. If only there were covers.

Smiling, Apollo snuggled closer to him. Without opening his eyes he said, "Athena. Care to join us?"

No reaction marred her hard expression. "Tempting, but no. We haven't got time."

"Maybe later, then?" Apollo said hopefully.

"Zeus is planning something."

"He's always planning something."

"He's *really* planning something this time. It's what we've feared."

At this, Apollo sat up. Gratefully, Sinon shifted out of his way.

"He's doing it at last, is he?"

Athena nodded. Apollo ran his hands through his hair. "That crazy old man."

"What's wrong?" Sinon said quietly. If they had been in Olympus, or in the courtyard, or anywhere but in their postcoital bed, he would not have had the impudence to ask. If they'd been anywhere else but in bed together, Apollo would not have deigned to answer.

He shook his head. "Zeus is going to ruin everything. Well, then. It's time. Once again the children must rise up against the Father."

He stood and recovered his tunic, discarded near the bed. Striding across the room, he went to a chest in the corner, opened it, and pulled out of a set of armor: breastplate, greaves, helmet, shield, sword. All were blindingly golden.

"I assume you have a plan?"

"He's currently away from Olympus, on one of his liaisons. We can occupy his palace and wait for his return."

"Sinon, help me with this." He gestured to the straps on the breastplate. Sinon, infected by Apollo's urgency, didn't bother dressing, but went to the god and helped him fasten on the armor. The divine conversation continued. "That's it? No intrigue, no subterfuge, none of that wiliness that makes us love you so?"

"I thought the direct approach would be best."

"Who is with us?"

"Almost everyone."

"Almost? Athena, this is not a task to be undertaken with half measures."

"I don't trust Hermes. He'd expose us just because to him it'd be funny. Hades will not help us, but he will not hinder us. He'll stay in his palace. Dionysus can't be bothered, says it can't really be that serious."

"None of those is unexpected, I suppose."

"I cannot find Hera."

"No matter. She certainly won't stand by Zeus."

"That's what I thought."

Apollo stepped away from Sinon and looked himself over, tugging here and adjusting there, squaring his shoulders, settling into the fit of the armor.

He tucked his helmet under his arm and said to Sinon, "There. How do I look?"

Sinon and Odysseus had often helped each other with their armor. His throat tightened, and he looked away.

"Magnificent, my lord."

Apollo smiled. The god outshone his own armor. "Thank you. Oh, here—" He took a second sword out of the chest, along with its belt and scabbard, and gave it to Sinon. "Take this."

Sinon held the weapon at arm's length, as if uncertain what to do with it. The last time he'd held one of these, he'd impaled himself on it.

"Why do you give me this?"

"Because you might need it." He crossed the room to Athena, and together they left.

Sinon went after them, following a few paces behind. "Are you going to kill Zeus?" he said, disbelieving.

Athena glanced over her shoulder at him before speaking to Apollo, "Is he always so outspoken?"

"Usually. It amuses me to no end."

"Apollo!" Sinon called. The god turned on him, and Sinon flinched, taking a step back. All at once, Apollo seemed to tower over him. Sinon found his courage and said, "How—how could you do such a thing? He's . . . he's a god. He's *Zeus*."

The god returned a glare that was intense, inhuman, without any of the sun's warmth.

"And I am Phoebus Apollo." Sunlight poured in through an archway leading to a courtyard, limning him in gold, when this conspiracy should have been happening in darkest night.

They were at the closet that held the doorway to Mount Olympus. Apollo pointed. "Watch this door. Stop anyone who tries to come out of it, unless it's me or Athena. Do you understand?"

And what if it was Zeus who came through?

"Yes, my lord."

Apollo opened the screen in front of the closet. He gestured Athena into the passage first; then he followed. The pair disappeared.

Sinon slumped against the wall and slid to the floor, letting the sword lie across his thighs. By the gods. By the gods indeed, what was happening? What could Zeus be planning that would make the rest of Olympus take up arms? The two or three times Sinon had seen him, he'd been overwhelmingly imperious, holding himself apart from the others, a lordly figure. Perhaps simple jealousy prompted a rebellion.

Athena and Apollo had aligned against each other

during Troy. Now they aided each other. The alliances of the gods were transient things. Sinon supposed he ought to have been grateful Apollo had not tired of him after all these years and disposed of him in some horrible manner suitable for the tales of bards.

If only Apollo had tired of him years ago and set him free.

Incongruously, he thought of praying. He ought to pray to someone, as he had when he was a boy, as he'd been taught by his parents. *Thank Zeus,* they said. Or, *Bless us, Apollo.* But there were no gods—he knew that. Only people with more power than they knew what to do with. If he lived for a few centuries, he might learn the tricks of their power, find a little power of his own, become his own god. The god of lies, the god of slaves, the god of lost hopes. He could build shrines and have people worship him.

No. If having all that meant he'd become like them—no. All he'd ever wanted were good friends fighting at his back and a little honor to take home with him when the war was done. A lovely woman to mother children for him, to carry his honor in later years.

He hooked his finger under the chain around his neck and pulled. It dug into his skin, pinching. But it didn't break. It didn't come off.

He heard footsteps approaching, the gentle slap of leather sandals on the tile in the hallway. He hurried to his feet, his blood racing. He held the sword ready.

The footsteps stopped.

No guests were staying at the palace. Another servant would not be so stealthy. Sinon had been quiet;

the intruder shouldn't have heard him. He was just around the corner. Sinon could almost hear breathing. He kept his own mouth closed, drawing quiet breaths through his nose.

He inched to the edge of the wall to steal a glance at who was there. Quickly now, look around and duck back—

What he saw made him hesitate.

An old man stood there. He held a dark cloak wrapped around him. His thick gray hair swept behind his ears. The mouth within the beard frowned.

It was Zeus.

Sinon lurched back, holding the sword before him like a shield, almost falling as he stumbled on his own feet. Putting his arm out, he caught his balance. The pose he struck wasn't graceful—his legs were splayed, his back hunched. He stared as if a hydra had just reared before him.

They regarded each other for a moment, the old man standing calmly, Sinon gripping the sword in a defensive stance. Zeus pushed back the edge of his cloak, revealing his hand. Sinon flinched, as if warding off a blow. Then they froze, once again waiting for the next action.

Gesturing to the doorway, Zeus said, "Have they already gone?"

The hairs on the back of Sinon's neck stiffened. He nodded.

"May I pass through?"

This was Zeus, King of the Gods. He could strike Sinon down with a thunderbolt. The Greek warrior held his sword ready out of sheer habit and principle—it was what one did with a sword. He couldn't stop the god! But the god had asked.

For a choking moment, Sinon wondered what it would be like to be a child, with this man as his father. He could go to him with his hurts, cry on his shoulder, and he would not be mocked. His fears would be smoothed away.

Sinon saw himself being held by this man and comforted. Zeus the Father.

He looked away and shook his head. It was a trick. Zeus was making him feel this way. Just as Apollo made him feel desire and pleasure.

Zeus said, "The one thing we cannot do is make mortals feel anything. We can seduce, cajole, trick, and bribe, but we cannot force. We can enspell, but spells fade. In the end, your emotions are your own."

That made the war within his heart that much worse. The loyalty, the hatred, the despair, the love, the memories—they all belonged to him, and he could blame no one else for them. Sinon bit his cheeks to keep from crying out.

Zeus said, "If you're not held by some oath to try to stop me, please let me pass."

Sinon was Apollo's slave. The chain around his neck made him so. But Apollo had never broken him; he'd never laid oaths upon him or demanded fealty. He'd depended on Sinon's . . . friendship. His honor.

"What's going to happen, my lord? What will you do to him?"

Zeus studied him, and his gaze was like Athena's, heavy and searching, until Sinon felt that his heart as well as his body was naked before him. Sinon's back bowed. He breathed hard, as if he carried a great weight.

"Are you his friend?"

Sinon started to shake his head, then said, "I don't know."

"A slave, then. How long has he had you?"

"I don't know. He took me the morning after Troy fell."

Lips pursed, Zeus nodded. "More than forty years. If my plan works, you'll be free to leave here."

Forty years. He should be an old man. Why didn't he feel the press of age?

A generation had lived and died without him.

He could not keep grief from cracking his voice. "My lord, where would I go?"

Zeus said with kindness, "Wherever you want to. Let me pass, son."

He was still, in some deep part of him, a soldier. He'd been given an order, and he trembled with the thought of breaking it.

But what *exactly* had Apollo said as he left? Stop anyone who tries to come out of the passage. He'd said nothing about keeping someone from entering.

Feeling as weak as a newborn, yet vaguely relieved that he had made a decision that would not require him to try to fight the Father of the Gods, Sinon lowered his sword. He knelt, head bowed. Turning the sword in his hand, he rested its point on the floor.

He remained there, honoring the god.

"Close your eyes, child."

Sinon shut his eyes tightly. He felt a touch on the back of his head, like that of a father ruffling his child's hair.

He didn't remember falling asleep. When he awoke, the sun was rising. He lay on the floor, curled on his side, the sword near to hand. Evidently, he'd collapsed where he knelt and slept through the night.

At once, he sat up.

The sun was rising, meaning that it had set and that night had come to the Sun Palace.

13

Evie went to the Storeroom.

The instinct assailed her as soon as she crossed the threshold.

It's not hers.

"I know, I know," Evie murmured. She was speaking to herself, because the whispering voice was her own.

She opened the drawer that held fruit: dried fruit, jeweled fruit, some pomegranate seeds in a little crystal box—the ones Persephone hadn't eaten. She had to dig in the back of the drawer for the apple of Discord, as if it hid from her. Her fingers skittered off it as it rolled away. She used both hands to trap it and pick it up, then secured it in the pocket of her army jacket, where it lay like a lead weight.

When she turned to go back to the door, the Storeroom had become a mess: boxes pulled into the aisles, flagpoles toppled across her path. Evie had to wrestle through the mess, shoving crates back into place, straightening spears and poleaxes out of the way. The shafts of wood were slippery, and she never imagined she could be so clumsy. She kept knocking things over.

This was taking too long. She slumped against a set of shelves and glared at the would-be museum pieces around her.

"I'm in charge of this place, aren't I?"

Only when your father dies. She didn't want to be in charge of it, not ever, if she had to watch Frank die.

She pushed on. *It shouldn't leave here.*

"What difference does it make? Hera gets the apple, she starts a war that's going to start anyway."

There is no story for this.

The apple belonged to Aphrodite; that was how the story went. Paris had given it to her. She might return for it someday.

"I don't know what Hera will do to Dad. I don't know how else to help him."

At last she cleared enough of her way to reach the threshold. She put her hands on either side of the doorway and waited. The apple seemed heavier than even a sphere of gold ought to be—so heavy, she couldn't drag it another step.

She took a deep breath. She hated this. She'd escaped, she'd gotten away from this town, and now the house itself wanted to lock its hold on her. That was the destiny she'd fought against: she hadn't wanted to grow up to manage the Safeway or be a cop in town, or at best go to Pueblo to work in a bank or in real estate. That wasn't *her* destiny, she was better than that.

Better than her dad, who'd stayed to take care of the Storeroom?

He'd had a family, worked like a dog his whole life

to support them, to send her to college. He'd taken care of his parents, all of it with strength and patience. She'd abandoned all that. She couldn't wait to leave her parents, and soon they'd both be dead.

That was why he had to live, why she had to save him. She couldn't watch over the Storeroom, because she didn't want to spend the rest of her life in Hopes Fort. She didn't have the courage.

"Isn't the whole Storeroom more important than one thing in it?"

No answer came.

"If I have to use this to bring him back, so he can be caretaker again, isn't that okay?"

It was a rationalization. She didn't need the phantom voice of instinct to tell her that.

"If I don't bring this to her, she'll come and take it. She might destroy everything to get it."

Something in that rang true, because the instinct wavered, the sanctity of the Storeroom thinned.

You'll return. You'll stay to take your Father's place.

"Yes," she said with a sigh. Sacrifice this one thing to save the whole. Tracker would have understood.

She stepped through the doorway. Discord's apple lay heavy in her pocket.

Upstairs, Evie knelt on the floor of the kitchen and held Mab's head in her hands. "Guard the Storeroom, all right? Good girl. Good Mab." Evie rubbed Mab's shoulders hard, as if that made up for abandoning her, and Mab looked up with eyes so shining and beseeching, she might have been crying.

Alex had been waiting for her in the kitchen. Silently, he followed her to the car.

They hadn't driven far when he said, "You're planning on just giving it to her? Did you actually bring it with you?"

She had to stop at the turn onto the highway. Ahead, great fissures zigzagged across the pavement, slabs of asphalt thrust up against one another, making the road impassable. The earthquake.

Evie pulled over and climbed out of the car. She hadn't thought the quake was that strong. Not enough to turn a highway into confetti. Hopes Fort must have been right over the epicenter.

"I guess we walk," she said.

"This is the work of the gods," Alex murmured. "Poseidon, the Earth-shaker, could use his power to level entire cities, yet he'd leave neighboring settlements untouched. You lived in Los Angeles. Do you think a quake that did this to a road would have left your house standing?"

The Walker house was over eighty years old and not in the least bit retrofitted for quakes.

She started walking, cutting down the sloped bank off the shoulder and onto the naked field along the highway. Alex followed.

"So it was Hera," she said, tromping over the old furrows cutting the earth.

"Or someone working for her."

"How many people does she have?"

"At least four, including Robin. He's the one from the parking lot the other day. I'm not sure how many others there are."

You, Evie thought. He was the only one who knew anything about her. What did that say about him?

They walked for half an hour, Evie trying not to be self-conscious of Alex at her heels. He was watching, she realized, like a bodyguard: scanning in all directions, glancing over his shoulders in a regular circuit. Looking for danger. She almost felt safer. Except that he made her nervous, and she didn't know what to say to him.

"Do you have a plan?" he said as they reached the first buildings of town, a gas station and a trailer park.

She ignored him, kept walking. Probably another ten minutes to reach the cemetery.

He persisted. "Do you think she'll really just let him go?"

She hadn't thought about it. The main solution burned in her mind, as the apple swung heavily in her pocket. What other choice did she have but to give it to Hera?

"Evie."

She kept walking, hoping he might grow frustrated and leave.

"Evie!" He grabbed her arm.

Instead of stopping, she spun and jerked away, batting at his arm like he was a bug. "Leave me alone!"

She wanted to run, but he kept hold of her sleeve. She could only back away, while he followed like a fisherman playing his line.

"I want to help, but you can't just walk up to her without a plan. You can't trust her—you can't trust any of them."

"What do you suggest?" Her voice was cold.

If he'd let go, she would have run, and he must have known that because he didn't let go.

"Find out if Frank's guarded. Create a distraction

to lure away Hera's people. *Then* we can get him away from her. *Without* giving her the apple."

"That sounds like something out of Homer."

He shrugged. "What can I say? It's a classic."

"Please let me go."

"But—"

Evie couldn't have said where they came from, or where they'd been hiding. Maybe around the last of the mobile homes on the row, or behind a truck parked on the street. They moved so quickly, Evie blinked and they appeared. Merlin took her arm and hurried her back, while Arthur faced Alex.

The warrior closed his left hand around Alex's neck and held his sword low, with the point aimed at his captive's belly.

"Who are you?" Arthur demanded, his voice clear and firm.

A vague smile grew on Alex's face, a kind of mystic realization. "It's you," he said, his voice a breath.

"Who are you?"

Alex glanced back and forth between Evie and Arthur for a moment, as if trying to decide something. Then Evie saw where Arthur's sword was aimed and remembered what Alex wanted more than anything.

"No!" She lunged toward him, but Merlin held her back.

Alex dropped forward and slid onto the point of Excalibur.

Arthur let go of him and tried to pull back, but that only hastened Alex's intent. Without Arthur holding him upright, Alex fell on the sword, impaling himself before Arthur could draw it away.

Evie screamed and Arthur cursed, catching Alex by the shoulders before he could crash to the ground. The warrior eased him down, cradling him on his lap. It was a scene out of Tennyson, if only they'd both been wearing medieval plate armor instead of jeans.

Arthur said roughly, "Idiot! Why did you do that?"

Blood covered Alex's shirt and coat and pooled on the ground beside him. Wincing, he clutched at the blade. Blood smeared his hands.

Shaking, he propped himself on his elbow and lifted himself from Arthur. He hooked his hand on the sword's guard. His voice tight, he said, "Could you help me get this thing out?"

Merlin's grip went slack. Her scream still raw in her throat, Evie crouched beside Alex. Excalibur protruded from under his ribs, looking vaguely ridiculous.

"Please?" Alex said again. "Before it starts to heal like this?"

Arthur gripped the sword with one hand and placed the other on Alex's chest. Holding the other man's wrist, Alex helped by leaning away, while Arthur yanked out the sword in a clean movement. Alex's breath hissed, but a moment later, the creases of pain on his face eased, the tension dissipated, and his hand—which he'd been holding flat over the wound, fell away. He'd stopped bleeding.

She touched his shirt, saw the rip. Pulled it open and tentatively touched the healed, unblemished skin underneath. His hand closed over hers before she could pull away.

"There, you see?" he said, smiling. "I'd die for you. If I could."

She pulled away, lost her balance, and fell on her backside.

"Who are you?" Arthur said.

Still looking at Evie, he answered, "Sinon of Ithaca. Also Alex of nowhere. You know, I really thought Excalibur might kill me."

"You are one of the immortal gods," Merlin said, suspicion darkening his expression.

"No." He started to climb to his feet, Arthur helping him. "That implies I have some power to go along with this. I don't."

Merlin looked unconvinced. "What is your concern with the Walker household? I've seen you with the lady twice now."

"I had hoped to find something there that could break my curse. Failing that—I only want to help the lady."

Merlin and Arthur had placed themselves between Evie and Alex. The pool of blood was growing sticky on the ground at her feet. Arthur still held his sword ready, though Evie didn't know what good he thought it would do. He said, "You aren't handing her over to Hera, then?"

That made sense only if Alex's pleas for her to stay away from Hera were some kind of reverse psychology. He seemed far too desperate for that.

Alex looked stricken. "No, I'm not." His tone was flat, as if he knew he wouldn't be believed.

Merlin said, "Hera is holding her father. We were coming to tell you." He gave Evie a nod.

"Is he all right?" she said.

"Yes, for now. They're at the cemetery."

"I have to get him back—"

"Not by yourself," Merlin said. "You should return home. It isn't your place to face the likes of her."

"Then what am I supposed to do? Sit around and wait?" That was what she'd been doing for the last week—waiting for her father's health to fail, waiting for the world to end in a rain of bombs. Waiting to give up.

Arthur said, "My lady, he's right. You'd be safer."

He was talking to her like she was some character in an epic. Some wilting lady in a tower. "Why do any of you care what happens to me?"

Merlin huffed like it was obvious. "You need help. Also, you are the heir to the Keeper of the Storeroom. Your place is there. It's your destiny."

She didn't *want* a destiny. Not like that. She only wanted daydreams, tucked safely in the pages of her writing. She looked beseechingly at Alex, like she thought he would know better—he'd read *Eagle Eyes;* he knew the extent of her destiny.

"I have to get my father back," she said firmly. It was *his* destiny they wanted to protect.

Arthur drew a handkerchief from his pocket and cleaned the blood off Excalibur's blade. "And you will. With our help."

"We were just talking about that," Alex said. "We need to distract Hera, get her away from Frank. I can go to her and find out who she has guarding your father, and what we need to do to free him."

He must have had his own agenda, his own reasons for wanting to keep the apple from Hera. Which returned Evie to the same question: Could she trust him?

Arthur sheathed the sword in the scabbard on his belt. "I think Merlin and I can overcome them now. There were only three of them in the car."

"Easy odds, I think," the old man said, cracking his knuckles.

"Just like the old days."

"Hold on a minute," Alex said. "You don't know who these people are, what they can do. This is Hera, the goddess."

Merlin regarded him. "Sinon of Ithaca. *Helleni-kouei?*"

Alex looked startled. "Yes."

"Then you're from a land that worshipped her."

"*I* don't worship her. Give me half an hour. I can find out what's happening—I can spy for you."

"And if you betray us, we can kill you?" Arthur said, indicating Alex's stomach, amused.

Alex smirked. "Evie, I only want to help you."

He looked as earnest as Mab would, sitting on the front porch watching her leave for the grocery store: large brown eyes, hopeful and shining. All she knew of him—besides what she'd seen, which she had to admit was just as earnest, just as loyal—was what she'd read in Virgil. That told the story of how he was the consummate actor. He could make anyone believe anything. He convinced the Trojans to break their own walls, to bring in the treacherous horse.

He was either lying or he wasn't.

"She said for me to come alone."

"And you can't let her have the apple."

"All right," she said finally. "Half an hour. But then I'm giving her the apple."

Slowly, he nodded. "Where will you be in the meantime?"

Evie said, "Behind the office at the northwest corner of the cemetery."

"I'll see you soon, then."

"Um—don't you think you should change your shirt?" She pointed at him, where drying blood covered his front.

He looked at himself, shrugged. "I'd forgotten. Never mind." He made a loose-handed salute to Evie, nodded briefly at the others, and ran down the side street along the trailer park.

Staring after him, Arthur crossed his arms. "What a strange man."

Bruce had ten minutes to pack everything he thought he'd need for the foreseeable future—surely only a week or two—into a couple of bags. Some clothes, a first-aid kit, matches, food and bottled water, sleeping bag, winter coat. A desert-island book. Or five. He spent a full minute standing in front of the bookshelves, trying to pick. He had a bunch of files on his laptop, but the battery would last only so long.

It was only for a few weeks.

Then why was his stomach in knots, and why did this feel like it was going to be forever?

Callie, her auburn hair tied up in a disheveled knot, looking domestic in a sweatshirt and jeans, stood by the door, a duffel bag slung over her shoulder. She was tapping her foot, fidgeting, wanting to leave and trying to be patient, for him. Her face was pale. She kept glancing out the open door, to where James's

SUV waited at the curb, its motor running. Bruce almost dropped his bags and ran to hug her right then, if for no other reason than to make her smile.

She was his desert-island book.

He had one more thing to do. He dialed the number for Evie's cell phone. The phone rang and rang, his stomach clenched tighter and tighter, until her voice mail clicked on.

He didn't have time to wait for her to call back, so he left a message.

"Evie. Some of us—me and Callie, James, his roommates—are leaving the city. James has a place in Napa. It's not safe here anymore. So we're running. I don't know when we'll be able to come back. I don't know when I'll be able to get back to work. I just wanted you to know, Evie, working with you on *Eagle Eyes* was great. The best work I've ever done. You helped me do better than I ever thought I could. Thanks. Maybe we can do it again sometime. I'll see you. When this all blows over."

Sighing, he turned off his phone.

Comics took up no space at all. They were flat and inconsequential. He grabbed a few copies of *Eagle Eye Commandos* sitting next to his worktable and shoved them into his bag.

Three hours later, they were speeding north on I-5. Behind them, smoke towered above the burning city.

Hera asked the Wanderer to walk with her along one of the paths in the cemetery. They left the car parked in the middle of the grounds. Robin was in the backseat watching Frank, who'd sat stiff and silent for the last hour. They all watched for the daughter. One way or another, she would come.

Despite his withdrawn nature, the Wanderer was handsome and polished. She could take him anywhere, and his manners would do him credit. He took a pack of cigarettes from the pocket of his jacket and offered it to her. She drew one from the pack, and he took one himself. He lit hers with an antique Zippo, then his own. Smoking was a way to delay, to draw out time. She knew the Wanderer used it as another way to read people: how they held the cigarette, how they exhaled, did they do so nervously, or did the movements calm them. She could let him think he was reading her, learning more about her—confiding in him bound him to her. If he felt he was a partner—or even a paramour—and not simply a soldier, he'd be more loyal to the goal.

"Do you think he could be persuaded to join us?"

"Who, the old man? Walker?" he said.

"Yes. Assuming the daughter fails to cooperate, we might convince him to give us the Storeroom. For a price, of course."

The Wanderer looked at the flat horizon and shook his head. "I don't think he has a price."

"Not even a cure for his illness?"

His lips curled. "His illness frightens him. But he won't try to avoid it."

"What if we threatened his daughter?"

He shrugged. "I don't think you could threaten them both and expect them both to give in. They'll think you're lying to both of them. You need at least one of them to get the prize."

"You can bluff only one player at time?"

"Something like that." He tapped off the ashes. "I think you're better off threatening the daughter. She's younger, more emotional. The older one—he's bound to the Storeroom. He's tied up in the same magic guarding that place. I don't think he could sell out to us even if he wanted to."

Robin—curse him—jumped out from behind a nearby headstone like some kind of carnival prop. He turned to lean against it, as if he'd been there for hours, hinting that he'd heard every word they'd said, whether he did or not. Bluffing with the best of them.

Hera regarded him coolly, without the least bit of surprise. "Aren't you supposed to be guarding our pawn?"

"I can see him from here. I can be at his side in a moment if he tries anything. I thought you should know, the Greek slave is coming."

"Should I leave?" the Wanderer said.

"No." She'd need him to help read the newcomer.

"Should *I* leave?" said Robin from his gravestone.

Her voice honey-sweet, she said, "Would you even if I asked?"

Grinning, Robin didn't move.

The Greek came up the drive that cut down the middle of the cemetery. He looked wretched. Blood covered the lower half of his shirt and most of his lap, as if he'd been stabbed and bled all over himself. He didn't seem hurt.

He glanced at the car parked halfway up the drive, but continued toward her. She waited, dropping the cigarette and stepping it flat. Hands shoved in his coat pockets, he stopped a good distance away, eight or ten feet, not displaying excessive familiarity. Watching his step. He was wary. She wished she could read mortals as well as she could in the old days. Something else, something besides her, was worrying him.

"What happened to you?" she said, regarding his gory clothing with a grimace of distaste.

"I fell."

"Ah. So, are you here because you have information for me? Is Evie Walker on her way?"

His expression was calm, revealing nothing. "What are you going to do to them? When you have the apple, what happens to the Walkers?"

"Why are you concerned with them?"

Here he winced, as if uncertain, and didn't answer. Anyone could see what it meant, even without divine powers.

From his perch on the headstone, Robin said, "The Walkers have many allies. Tell her, Greek."

The Greek gave nothing away—he'd had lots of practice hiding things. One wondered that he ever talked at all.

Robin shrugged off the silence and spoke, grinning. "I saw Merlin at the house. Arthur can't be far behind. *That* Merlin. *That* Arthur."

Hera didn't bother asking why Robin hadn't seen fit to tell her this earlier. The edge in his tone bothered her—the Greek had offended Robin, who of course had taken it personally and would goad him when he could. Hera would have to watch the hobgoblin carefully.

The news he delivered was disconcerting—what did it mean, that more magic than hers was at work here? Britain's greatest heroes—she'd heard rumors of Merlin's power, and if even half of them were true, he'd be an opponent of consequence. Or an ally of great worth. If she could have a word with them, show them that her plan had the greatest chance of restoring order to the world, the influence of her pantheon would increase.

By the gods, as the mortals said, what an exciting time to work, with so much magic returning to the world.

Hera stepped up beside the Greek and wrapped her arm round his, pulling him so that they strolled together down the walk, past rows of weathered granite stone decorated with plastic flowers.

"You were a spy for the Greeks, weren't you?" she said to him. "I trust you haven't lost your touch. Where is the girl now?"

"Maybe I could take you to her. She wouldn't expect that."

"Can't you simply tell me if she's coming?"

He held back, tugging against her like an anchor. "You're not going to hurt her."

Hera gave him a reassuring smile. "Of course not. I'm not a brute." With her urging, she started him walking again, guiding him to the northern edge of the cemetery, where the town lay.

Robin and the Wanderer followed a few paces behind.

"Where did you find Robin?" the Greek said.

"Sulking in a pub in Dublin. I've found my lieutenants in the strangest places. I'm not picky. All I ask for is loyalty. Have you thought about joining me?"

"I served a god once. It didn't suit me."

"You wouldn't be a slave with me," she said with a laugh, putting seduction in her tone.

"Can you get rid of this?" He hooked his fingers around the chain on his neck.

She touched it, running her fingers along the skin underneath as she did. She was disappointed that he didn't flinch. "I don't know. I could have my friend the Marquis have a look at it."

"The Marquis?"

"A scion of the British aristocracy and a student of magic. Formal for my taste. But he has his talents. He found the Storeroom for me."

"Did he? He must be powerful."

"It's not so impressive as it sounds. He didn't find the Storeroom so much as follow the path of one who already knew where it was."

The Greek hesitated a step.

Hera studied him. "How did you find the Storeroom?"

"I looked for it," he said.

She said in a low voice, "I could use someone of wisdom. Of age. That's what my people lack. The experience that comes with the age of an immortal. We gods were thousands of years old by the time we came to Greece. We'd ruled in other lands under different names. But the old ones in all the lands are gone. The pantheons seemed to have a knack for killing themselves off. Everybody had a Ragnarök. You may be pleased to hear that you are one of the oldest people I've encountered in my recent travels."

"That doesn't comfort me, my lady," he said. He glanced over his shoulder at the ones who followed, and his voice changed, becoming colored with false brightness. "I'd like to meet this Marquis of yours."

"He's busy," said Robin, overhearing them. "Spending all his time trying to crack that shell around the Walker house."

"Having trouble with that, is he?" the Greek said.

Robin said, "He insists it'd be easier if he knew who cast the spell in the first place. It certainly wasn't the Walkers."

"I see."

The Wanderer moved forward to speak softly in her ear. "He's hiding something."

The Greek was a game escort, holding her arm politely, if not affectionately. He walked at her pace, which was slow. She could study him at her leisure. He stared ahead, his face still.

"What do you know of that family?" she asked.

"What would you have me know?"

"You have some affection for them. For all I know, you might have been following them from the beginning. What do you know of the magic that protects them?"

His mouth remained closed. Hiding something, indeed.

"It's a simple question, my dear. If you don't know, say so."

"It's very old magic. Older than you."

The man avoided the question like someone with a geis laid on him. "What if I asked very nicely?"

He didn't say a word.

"He knows," said the Wanderer.

Hera said, "At first, I believed that Zeus made the Storeroom. A last act before his martyrdom, to take up all our things of power and put them away. But the Marquis says no, it wasn't him. So who? I don't know how, my Greek, but you knew of Zeus's plan. You were there."

He didn't answer, and she didn't trust him, not a whit. If he meant to join with her, he would say what he knew. He was trying to distract her—wasting time. She glanced over her shoulder at the car, where Frank Walker sat. He was still in place.

Just as it was difficult to bribe an immortal, it was difficult to threaten one. So she didn't threaten *him*.

"If I harmed them both, what would happen to the Storeroom then?"

The Wanderer moved ahead of the Greek, stopping him with a hand on his shoulder. They stood like that for a long moment, the Wanderer holding his gaze. The Greek's eyes widened. His neck strained, like he was trying to look away but couldn't.

Hera watched with interest.

"Prometheus," the Greek said suddenly, his voice tight.

"Ah, of course," Hera said. She should have guessed that herself. "Thank you."

She would have to deal with the Greek later. She couldn't trust him, and she wasn't even sure anymore if she could use him. But she would keep him close until the moment she decided to dispose of him.

"We'll wait for the Walker girl here. You wait by the car. See for yourself that we haven't harmed her father," she said, touching the Greek's chest. "I wouldn't want you to cry a warning to her." He presented her a bow that might have been mocking, if she'd had the time to be insulted. To the Wanderer she said, "Go with him. Guard Mr. Walker."

She gestured to Robin, who followed her to the edge of the cemetery.

Softly she said, "Wait. Hide. You are my reserve."

Robin saluted and disappeared in a flash of magic.

Hera slipped behind the hulking tomb of one of the town's founding fathers.

In the days of Olympus, they'd made a game of shape-shifting themselves and others. When he still had a sense of humor, Zeus placed bets about what outrageous forms he could take on to seduce his latest prize. She'd never had the patience for such games. She still didn't understand the swan.

Zeus had been the King because of the ease with which he imposed his will on others. He didn't command or threaten; rather, his personality expanded. His moods crept out like a fog bank to encompass all those around him, so that he saw his own mood reflected back at him, in the people around him. He was like that even in the oldest of days, before they were gods, when they were little more than confused and naïve children testing small powers and talents they collected like seashells in the sand. Their sibling rivalry turned deadly at times—the stories told about them by Egyptians, Sumerians, and others hardly exaggerated, recounting chopped-up bodies scattered in rivers, swallowed infants, journeys to the land of the dead. But they always managed to put each other back together again, using the tricks and spells of nature that they'd learned.

Zeus rightfully became their King when he killed their father, a bitter old man who wasted his time and power battling the clan of Titans. Instead, Zeus befriended them. Even Hera couldn't argue, though she had been Queen of her own lands before. Zeus's will absorbed them all.

And when he decided that he'd had enough, that he didn't want to rule anymore and he didn't want to hand over his place to a son who might kill him, he wiped them all out. There was too much magic in the world, he said. It was in danger of destroying all of human civilization, not just Troy. A civilization built through the worship of gods, Hera told him. But he couldn't hear that he was wrong, and in his righteous arrogance, he worked a spell of magnificent destruction. He destroyed magic. He murdered those best schooled in its use, the gods and goddesses who had lived for millennia.

In his ennui and guilt, he used his own life as fuel for the spell and took the rest of them with him.

Hera was his sister and his wife. She'd healed his wounds and eased his pains, though he never liked to admit it. They were never associated with love—it wasn't their dominion. But she knew him. She knew she could not stop him. So she defended herself. It took all her power, expended in a brilliant shielding flash, and it almost wasn't enough. The spell left her old, weak, powerless. She almost had to start from scratch, relearning all the magic she'd spent centuries perfecting. But she persevered. She lived. She was almost what she had been.

She couldn't yet transform herself into something magnificent, like a hawk, or large like a bear or a cow. But a little thing, a quiet thing, was all she needed now.

She became a cat, a small gray creature who would not be noticed. Moving four-legged and low to the ground required a shift in thinking, a level of defensive paranoia—danger might come from any direction. But she gained a litheness and ease of movement that made crossing the cemetery, dodging headstones, and leaping the odd flower arrangement a joy.

Sitting primly, she rested under the rear bumper of the sedan and waited.

Evie waited behind the auto garage with Arthur and Merlin, on the opposite side of the cemetery from the caretaker's shack, where Alex said he'd meet them. Ten more minutes. She could see the car where her father was being held. One other person was inside. Alex walked along the parallel road, arm in arm with Hera, accompanied by two of her flunkies.

"He's betraying us," Merlin muttered.

She didn't think he was. This was just what he'd done at Troy—talking his enemy into betraying themselves. Merlin was being paranoid.

"Or he's distracting her," Arthur said. "The car is unguarded now."

"Not for long enough to save Dad."

The afternoon shadows were stretching.

"I'll circle the grounds," Merlin said. "Try to catch a hint of what they're saying."

He smoothed the lapels of his suit and strode off, a man with purpose. Evie watched: he looked both ways, started crossing the street, raised his hand as if calling a cab, then disappeared. A shimmer in the air remained for a moment, like a line of heat rising from the pavement. Evie blinked, and blinked again.

She said, "He could have done that and just walked into the house to take the sword, if he'd wanted to."

Arthur shook his head. He was watching her, rather than the vanished Merlin. "When he turns incorporeal like that, he can't affect the physical world. He couldn't have turned the doorknob. Besides, your house is guarded."

"That's what they tell me."

"Merlin has followed your family's fortunes for many years. You were always the Keepers."

"It seems like everyone knew that but me."

They leaned against the wall like vagrants, out of sight of the cemetery. Waiting was hard, when she knew how close her father was, and what might happen to him before she could help.

She said, "When did you wake up? I mean—when did you know it was time to return?"

He looked to the distance, where her own gaze had lingered a moment before. "It happened slowly, I think. I was injured when I went to sleep. I'm still not sure how long ago that was. When I woke, they—the ladies who healed me and made me young again—told me that much had changed. I lived in the world again for a time, to learn the new ways. I was in a village in Wales. A modern version of the place where I grew up. Then Merlin came. Then I knew my destiny."

He spoke with the simple clarity of a mystic whose worldview was uncluttered, whose path was set in a perfect line. In the midst of all this talk of magic and destiny, she wondered if there was room for a person behind the legend. If Arthur was a person—or an archetype.

"It must be hard. Not having a choice. What if you wanted to stay in the village? Get married, have kids. Be normal."

He smiled wryly and shook his head. "I've learned something: What many of us call destiny is really our own instinct. We know what is right, but we don't want to admit it, especially if what is right will lead to our own death. We call it destiny so we don't have to accept responsibility for making those decisions. Human instinct is stronger than anyone will admit."

"Do you miss them? Guinevere, Lancelot. The others."

"That life—it was another life. It seems like a dream now. I slept so long, everything before waking was a dream. I would prefer to remember it as a dream, I think."

"Hey, look." Evie touched his arm and pointed to the cemetery.

Hera and one of her henchman—the young one whom Alex had called Robin—were leaving, walking to the edge of the grounds and presumably beyond. Another minion, a polished man in a suit and trench coat, walked back to the sedan. Alex, hands shoved in his pockets, walked with him.

Alex and the other man were with her father now.

"I like these odds a little better," Arthur said.

With a hiss of air and shimmer of heat in front of her, Merlin appeared. Evie flinched, startled, as if a television had flashed to life nearby.

"Arthur, I think you can fetch Mr. Walker yourself," he said before her heartbeat had calmed down. "I'll follow the others and delay them if I can."

"Agreed. My lady, wait for us here."

Before she could argue, they were across the road, Arthur moving at a jog, as if to battle.

Alex might have told Hera where to find them, and

told her that Arthur and Merlin were with her. Hera was probably looking for Evie, and she'd set a trap for the others. Or maybe this really was their chance.

In either case, if things went badly, she could still give Hera the apple, use that to bribe her father free. She touched the shaped gold in her pocket, warm against her fingers. For the fairest.

As a cat seated under the bumper, Hera listened to the Greek try to start a conversation with the Wanderer.

He leaned on the car, near the window where Frank Walker sat. The Wanderer stood nearby, his arms crossed.

"What did she promise you to get you to join her?" the Greek said.

"Perhaps I was just curious."

"Thought you could learn a few tricks?"

"No. Not many left to learn at my age."

"You're old?"

"Relatively."

"How old?"

"I met Christ."

Conversationally, the Greek said, "I saw him once, preaching at a village near Tyre."

"He was a good preacher."

"And a hell of a wizard."

"Yes."

There was a pause; then the Greek said, "Your friend in there doesn't look well."

"I'm fine," the old man grumbled through the closed window.

"No," said the Greek. "I think you look ill. Are you sure you don't want to step out and get some air?"

The Wanderer said, "I don't think that's a good idea."

Hera wished she could see. This was turning into quite the little show. Perhaps she'd make herself a sparrow next time.

"No," Frank said, his voice thoughtful. "He's right. It's a little stuffy in here. Do I look pale?"

"A bit," said Alex.

"I might be nauseated."

"Come on, I'm not a fool," the Wanderer said.

"Nor do I take you for one, which is why I think you'll allow this fellow to vomit outside the car rather than inside."

Hera couldn't believe it. The Wanderer was actually going to fall prey to the charade.

The car door opened. Footsteps crunched on gravel as someone climbed out of the car.

Hera emerged from under the bumper, a gray cat racing around the Greek. She padded to a stop in front of the Wanderer, who held Frank Walker by the arm, outside the car. Out of her hiding place, she spotted a hulking warrior running toward the car.

She made herself whole and human and, crossing her arms, regarded the three men. "That will be quite enough," she said.

Evie saw a startling flash of light, and the cat who'd made a dash along the driveway became Hera. She stood only a pace or two away from Alex and her father, who'd been leaving the car.

Alex had a plan. He'd been trying to get her father out of the car. He really had been trying to help.

Arthur shielded his eyes and slid to a stop. Merlin had disappeared. The other man sprang at Alex, who fell back, slamming against the gravel drive, and rolled, slipping out of his attacker's wrestling grasp. Arthur drew his sword and lunged forward as if to run again, but he didn't move. He stood like a statue, balanced on the balls of his feet, frozen. Hera pointed at him. Her power was stronger than the ancient king's will.

They needed Merlin now. If Evie shouted, maybe he'd hear and come running. Unless the others found a way to stop him, too.

Alex's attacker recovered quickly, with enough speed to grab Alex from behind and wrap his arm around his neck. Alex thrashed, struggling to break free. Her father sat in the car, gripping the edge of the door, looking bewildered.

So much for the distraction—they'd missed their chance. Evie had her ransom payment. She could end this.

She knew this corner of the cemetery because she'd visited here every time she'd returned to Hopes Fort over the last five years. She knew the grave markers here without looking at them. Irving and Amelia Walker, her father's great-grandparents. Frank's grandparents, her grandparents. Then Emma Doyle Walker. She walked across the dead grass like she was walking to visit her mother's grave, like she knew where she was going and what she was doing, like this was any other walk. She reached the road leading to where the car was parked before any of them noticed her.

Alex, fighting the grip his opponent held him in, saw her first. He stopped struggling, which made his captor pause to look, and in moments, their attention drew the others.

"Evie, go back!" Arthur said through clenched teeth. His body trembled, fighting against the invisible grip that held it.

Hera stepped forward to meet her. Evie stopped ten paces or so away, before she came too close. Hera followed her lead, maintaining enough distance between them that they had to raise their voices to hear each other.

"Did you bring it?" Hera said. She wore high-heeled boots on the gravel drive, and her balance never wavered. Did she use magic to achieve her beauty and poise, or was she just that elegant?

"Yes." Evie felt scruffy in her coat and jeans. But she had something Hera wanted. She had to remember that.

"Excellent. I'll gladly release your father. I'll even set your knights-errant free, though you disobeyed my instruction to come alone. But I want to see it first."

Evie took the apple from her pocket. She kept a tight grip on it, not knowing what tricks Hera might use, whether she could yank it through the air with her mind, like any number of comic book superheroes.

Hera's gaze softened, an awe-filled smile easing her features. Evie caught sight of Alex in the corner of her eye. He looked like he was going to scream.

"Mr. Walker, step out of the car, please," Hera said.

Her father pulled himself out of the car. He didn't look happy.

"Now, girl, toss me the apple."

"Let Alex and Arthur go first."

Hera nodded at her minion, who let Alex loose. Alex made a jump; whom he could attack or what he could get away with, Evie had no idea. But a man—the young man from the motel parking lot—moved in front of him, his arms crossed. He'd appeared from nowhere. Like magic. Alex froze.

Hera had trapped them all very well.

Next, she made a twisting motion with her hand, and Arthur fell forward, snarling. He raised his sword.

"Arthur! Stay back, please!" Evie said.

Scowling, he lowered his sword.

"Now, please," Hera said, her waiting hand outstretched.

The apple felt firm in Evie's hand. She didn't want to let it go. "What are you going to do with it?"

Hera's smile changed, turning thin and sly. Evie had the feeling she was being made fun of.

"Why, take over the world, of course."

Evie's grip on the apple tightened. She didn't understand how such a little thing could rule the world.

It isn't the tool or thing, but the one who wields it.

Then something happened. Hera misinterpreted her hesitation.

The goddess continued, "I could use your help, Evie. I need as many allies as I can find. While you may not think you have any power, you hold—or will soon hold—the stewardship of a great collection of treasures. You could be my Keeper of Treasures. I would honor you."

She made a gesture that encompassed Alex and Arthur.

"They may have told you that I want to break this world. What else would I do with the apple of Discord but cause strife and turmoil? And they're right. I do want to break this world. The storm of violence has already begun. All the props are in place. But I would break it so that I could make a new one. An ordered one."

Evie had heard such claims before, many times. Every time a separatist group drove a truck bomb into a hospital, whenever terrorists crashed a plane into a building or a suicide bomber stepped into a crowded marketplace, it was in the name of a new world, or a better order that would rise up from the ashes of the old.

Evie stood twenty feet away from the grave marker of Emma Doyle Walker. Fifty-three years old, playing tourist at the Pike Place Market in Seattle when a twenty-year-old misguided activist blew herself up and murdered eighteen people.

"There's a place for you, Evie Walker. We can work together."

Hera didn't use bombs, but she took hostages. She had different tools and she'd been working at it longer, but the rhetoric was surprisingly similar.

Evie had often wondered what she'd say to the woman who killed her mother, if she ever had a chance. More often than not, all Evie wanted was to punch the bitch out. She'd spent the last few years using Tracker and the Eagle Eyes to stop as many terrorists as she could.

She didn't have a gun. She couldn't just walk up and shoot them, as Tracker had. So if Tracker didn't have a gun, and her compatriots and a hostage were still in danger—what would she do? If everything depended on her, and she had the confidence to act, what would she do? Because she'd be damned if she was going to give in to this woman.

She took a step, then another. Hera might have thought Evie was moving toward her. But really she was moving toward the space between Hera and the car, where her father stood. The driver's seat was empty. The key might still be in the ignition. She didn't dare look behind her, where Arthur stood. He could take care of himself. She looked at her father and hoped he knew her well enough to guess what she was doing. She looked at Alex and bit her lip. She needed his help. She needed him to keep Robin away.

Approaching Hera, she hefted the apple, testing its weight, getting ready to throw it. Hera lifted her chin, rounded her shoulders, getting ready to catch.

Evie threw, Hera reached, but the apple never left Evie's hand.

She ran, shoving the apple back in her pocket. In her other pocket, she found the sprig of rowan Alex had given her. She threw this instead. Hera grasped at it, flinching when the leaves hit her face, stumbling—actually losing her poise—when her hands flailed for a target that wasn't there.

She had to trust the others to do their parts and couldn't take a moment to watch for them. She barreled into the sedan's front seat and groped for the ignition.

No key.

She gripped the steering wheel, wondering if she could start the car through sheer willpower. Whenever Jeeves hot-wired a vehicle, Bruce just showed him fiddling with wires on the steering column. Evie didn't have to actually *know* how to do it.

One of the back doors slammed. There was Frank, clicking the lock on.

Her father leaned over the front seat. "No keys?"

"No," she said, a wail creeping into her voice.

"Evie! The window!" On the other side of the car, Arthur held Hera's well-dressed henchman in a headlock with one arm, twisted at such an angle that the man had to struggle to keep his balance. Arthur raised his other arm, like he was getting ready to throw something.

The car had automatic windows that didn't work with the engine off. She scrambled to the passenger-side door, and as she opened it, Arthur tossed. As he did, his prisoner wrenched out of his grasp and ran.

A car key on a rental company keychain landed in her lap.

She couldn't think about how many bad guys were out there or what the others were going through to oppose them. She had her task: Take the key and get her father out of here.

As she slid the key into the ignition, her hand shaking, her mind numb, a hand slapped onto the windshield in front of her. The well-dressed man who'd been with her father, Arthur's former prisoner, pressed his hand flat to the glass and caught her gaze. Caught it, and held it.

. . . *what he'd seen over the years, the centuries, would make a man weep with despair, and he was cursed to see it all, to wander for all time, until the Second Coming of him called Christ the Lord, and that was the real curse because the wizard who named himself so would not return—he'd sacrificed himself and was gone. But the one he'd cursed had found a power of his own: He could take what he had seen and he could show others. The horrors, the despair, plague, massacre, torture, enough to shock the strongest of men, more than enough to chill a modern girl,* and this showed through his eyes, and Evie felt cold, her joints aching, her muscles cramping, her eyes filling with tears.

Then she saw nothing.

"Drive, Evie." Reaching from behind, her father covered her eyes with his hands. By feel, she turned the key, sparking the engine to life. Her muscles were her own again; the man's hold on her was broken. Her father sat back, and she could see to shift into drive. Tires spun on the gravel and the car jolted forward. The man fell away.

She drove, hoping she stayed on the straightaway, uncertain of her bearings. She needed to find the others. Alex was wrestling Robin among the gravestones. Arthur was chasing after that strange man again. Where was Merlin?

The goddess appeared in the middle of the lane, standing in front of the oncoming car, wholly unconcerned.

Evie pushed on the gas as hard as she could.

The car stopped as if she'd slammed into a wall, and the passengers fell forward. Evie's foot leaned on the gas, the engine revved, the tires kicked up a spray of gravel, but the car didn't move.

Hera didn't have to raise a hand. She only stared, lips parted in wonder.

Frank picked himself off the floor, where the sudden stop had thrown him. He put his hand on Evie's shoulder and squeezed.

"What do I do?" she said, bracing herself on the steering wheel. What did destiny think it was doing, trusting the Storeroom to people who had no power to face such magic?

"I don't know."

A feathered thing rocketed from above, toward Hera. The goddess saw it at the last second and flung an arm to shield herself against the falcon that came at her, talons outstretched. She was distracted only a moment, and she struck back with a hand that had grown claws of its own as the falcon veered away. Their battle took them off the road.

Hera's concentration was broken. The sedan leaped forward, free from her grip. They continued on the road out of the cemetery. The falcon—Merlin, a shape-shifting wizard—screeched and veered out of sight. Hera looked after the car, then after the falcon, and seemed uncertain which to attack first.

Evie could only drive and hope.

In the rearview mirror, she saw Alex running after them. No sign of Robin. She slammed the brakes. Her blood rushed painfully in her ears for the few moments it took him to reach the car. When her father opened the door and helped pull him inside, Evie was already moving again.

A thump crashed on the trunk of the car, then sounded on the roof. Evie craned over the dash, trying to look up through the windshield to what had jumped on the car.

Above her, Excalibur glinted in Arthur's outstretched arm.

She hit the button to open her window. His hand gripped the edge of the roof.

"Drive!" he shouted. "Don't look back!"

"Bloody hell!" Alex said with a laugh.

In command of the fiery steed, Evie drove.

The highway was destroyed because of the earthquake. In her mind, she mapped out the way she'd have to take to get home, the dirt roads around the back of town that would get her to the farmland near the house, and from there she'd have to hope for tractor paths.

She still had to get to the other side of town, which meant she still had to drive through town. A block away from Main Street, emergency lights flashed ahead. The police had the way barricaded.

"I'll go around," she said, thinking aloud. Front Street to Third Street, along the neighborhood—

"Stop!" Johnny Brewster ran toward her, flanked by a pair of deputies. He had his gun drawn. Evie braked, swerving sideways as the car slid to a halt.

Arthur knocked on the roof of the car. Alex opened a door and leaned back as the warrior slipped inside and tried to look natural, his sword resting on his lap.

Now *that* wasn't conspicuous.

"What do I do?" she said, glancing at her father in the rearview mirror.

He looked pale, his lips pressed nervously together. "Stop, I suppose. It's Johnny. He won't give us trouble."

But there was a woman following the police, walking calmly, knowingly. She was lithe and predatory.

Evie's stomach churned. She was the one who'd come to the house to tell her her father had been kidnapped.

Johnny didn't lower his gun. Even when Evie met his gaze, when he had to know it was her, his friend and harmless, and that Frank was in the backseat.

Alex said, "You're going to have to drive, Evie." He stared ahead at the oncoming troopers.

"But it's Johnny, we just have to explain—"

"We have to get out of here."

"Evie, get out of the car! Keep your hands up!" Johnny called. The other officers moved around to flank them.

"Dad, that woman with him is working for Hera. I think Alex is right. She might have told them anything."

Her father's car window hummed open. He leaned his head out. Alex held his arm, like he wanted to pull him back, and Evie nearly screamed at him.

"You, too, Frank! Out of the car!"

"What's the problem, Johnny?" Frank said.

"Those men in the car, I need to take them in."

"Why? What have they done?"

"They're wanted. I've got warrants."

Evie shouted out her own window, "Whatever that woman told you, it isn't true. She's lying. They haven't done anything."

Johnny glanced back at the woman. She didn't move; her expression never changed. Three cops held guns trained on the car.

"I could arrest you for harboring terrorists. Both of you! They're *terrorists*, Evie. You don't want to help them!" His jaw clenched. He was close enough that Evie saw sweat on his face.

"I can't do much against guns," Arthur said softly. "Not that many of them, at least."

"I can take as many bullets as you need me to," Alex said.

Arthur muttered something that sounded like, "Good God."

She'd gotten a citation from the President recognizing her patriotism. She couldn't believe she was about to do this.

"Dad, get down," she said, and put the car into gear. She stepped hard on the gas pedal, and the car screeched forward, hit the curb, bounced onto the sidewalk, then off it again as she cranked the wheel around. The officer who'd been standing there lunged out of the way.

Shots rang out. Evie flinched, ducking reflexively while still trying to steer. She hadn't expected them to shoot. These were Hopes Fort cops—how often did they have to shoot in the line of duty? When did they ever have to stop runaway cars?

She squealed around the next corner and was five blocks away before the sirens started after her.

"The cops here are a little slow on the uptake, aren't they?" Alex said.

"That's Hopes Fort," Frank said. "Is everyone okay?"

"I don't think they even hit the car."

Evie drove until the pavement gave way to dirt. One car screeched to a stop at an intersection to avoid hitting them, the only oncoming traffic they encountered. Once again, that was Hopes Fort. But the sirens—two or three sets of them—were getting closer.

A flash ahead caught her attention. One of the cars was approaching from the other direction. They were going to hem her in.

Out of town now, all around them lay barren winter fields, plowed clean, waiting for spring planting.

She hoped the sedan had good tires.

White-knuckled, glancing manically in the rearview mirror, Evie leaned the wheel to the right. The car slid off the road, listing as it rolled onto the shoulder, which sloped to a ditch. Steering a wide arc meant she didn't have to touch the brakes, and she had no faith in her ability to execute a Hollywood turn-on-a-dime at high speed. In moments, she was driving across the field, spewing a cloud of dirt behind her. She checked her mirrors and couldn't see the cop cars through the dust.

An honest-to-God car chase, straight out of an issue of *Eagle Eye Commandos*. Not to mention the larger-than-life heroes surrounding her. She couldn't wait to tell Bruce about this.

Home was about five miles ahead. She'd never considered going anywhere else. No one argued, so she kept going. Home was safe; the others must have thought so, too.

"They don't seem to be following," Arthur said, twisting to look out the back window.

The police cars were still there: One stopped on the road, two others slid down the embankment to the field, where, near as Evie could tell, their tires were spinning. They were shrouded in a huge cloud of dust, which was getting farther and farther away. Hopes Fort police cars: ten years old and in need of new tires. Or maybe they had a little luck on their side. Merlin was still out there, after all.

Something thudded against the right side of the car. Evie looked in her mirrors, out the window, but she couldn't see what had struck them. It almost sounded like she'd hit an animal.

The same noise slammed against the left side, and suddenly a canine head thrust over her father's still-open window. Paws hitched over the glass, it barked, guttural and ferocious, saliva spraying, eyes dark and shining. Alex pulled her father away, and Evie used the master control to shut the window. It slid closed slowly, and the barks still echoed, even after the animal lost its purchase and fell away.

The hits sounded all around them now, animals throwing themselves against the car on all sides.

"Coyotes," Frank said.

Evie drove through the middle of a swarm of them. They came from all sides to intercept her, inexplicably committing suicide in their attempt to jump on the car, to claw through the metal. The prairie was filled with coyotes; they yodeled at each other through the night when she'd lived here. She hadn't imagined so many of them, though. Hundreds of them came at her, a sea of fur.

Her instincts cried for her to stop the car. She hated driving over them, hurting them. But if she stopped, they'd rush the sedan and maybe find a way inside.

"They're Hera's," Arthur said.

"Or one of her followers'." Alex watched out the back window as the sea of coyotes, alive and dead, spilled away.

She thought she'd be driving too fast for them, even over the dirt, and that they couldn't keep up.

But new ones, seeming to spring from the earth itself, replaced the old.

"They can't hurt us," Frank said, but his tone was uncertain.

Alex huffed. "Yeah, until we try to get out of the car."

That problem presented itself quickly as the Walker house appeared, a block on the flat horizon.

"Do I slow down or what?" Evie said.

No one answered, and she swerved, hoping for a solution to present itself in the extra few moments.

"You might as well stop," Alex said. "We'll run out of gas eventually."

"What about the coyotes?"

"One thing at a time."

Bouncing hard, passing from cropland to the dried-up grasses of the prairie, which was untilled and rocky, Evie aimed for the house. Her passengers braced against the front seat. She paralleled the road leading to the house and counted it a small blessing that no police cars were waiting there. The broken highway had helped them on that front.

The car's shocks were shot. She didn't dare slow down, but the vehicle slid and swerved under her, the wheel jerking out of her hand. She clung to it to try to keep it steady, like she was guiding a ship in a storm. She'd never noticed so many ditches and dips in the land, which she had always insisted was maddeningly flat.

One last burst of gas, one last rise to scale, and she roared onto the driveway, cut left toward the house, throwing the men to one side of the seat. She hit the brakes, the car lurched, and they were still. She gasped, and her heart pounded like she'd run the whole way from town herself.

Two dozen or so coyotes swarmed around the car, yipping and leaping to claw at the windows, which were smeared with their saliva and blood.

"Now what?" Her voice quailed.

Arthur, sword in hand, prepared to open the door. "Close it when I'm out," he said to Alex, next to him.

"Are you crazy?" Evie cried.

But he'd already shoved the door open with his feet. Slashing a clear path with Excalibur, he gripped the edge of the roof and hauled himself up. The sound echoed inside the car as he hit the roof and steadied himself. Alex kicked a coyote away and slammed the door shut as soon as he was clear.

As the chalky smell of the dust settled, the coyotes' scent became discernible—a musky animal odor of unwashed fur and hostility. One of them sprang onto the hood of the car. Evie flinched back as it lunged up the windshield, its claws smacking the glass. Excalibur swept down, caught the animal on the shoulder, and cut deep. It squealed and fell, rolling off the hood. Then Arthur was at the back of the car, stabbing a coyote crawling up the trunk.

"It almost makes it all worthwhile," Frank said, his voice hushed. "Getting to see him fight."

The sword flashed again, and another coyote yipped and fell.

Alex shook his head. "This isn't a proper fight. It's slaughter. This wasn't meant to hurt us. It was meant to slow us down, annoy us. She still needs one of you alive, to get into the Storeroom."

A new sound entered the fray, more barking, but deeper, rougher, from a large dog. Queen Mab came racing from the back of the house, eating yards at a time with her great stride.

She barreled into the nearest coyote, slamming her claws on it and closing her jaws around its neck. It yelped, and blood poured into its sandy fur. In a moment it lay still. Three others sprang at the wolfhound.

"She'll be killed," Evie said, her breath catching. "They'll kill her."

But Mab wouldn't be left out of the fight. Her purpose was to defend the house.

Mab writhed and caught a coyote by the throat, even as another scraped its claws down her back. She didn't seem to notice, wanting only to kill her enemies. Arthur's sword swung again, another coyote fell, and Evie hoped that Arthur could kill enough of them to be able to help Mab before the coyotes finished her.

It would be far too close. For every throat Mab ripped out, two more coyotes rose up to sink their fangs into her legs and flanks. Arthur stood on the hood now, slashing to keep them away from her, hollering at them to get away.

A bright light flashed, like lightning, though the sky held no storm clouds. Arthur fell to his knees, shielding his eyes with his left arm, and the coyotes yipped and cowered away.

A voice rumbled a word that Evie couldn't make out, but it rattled her bones. She covered her ears to make it stop. They all covered their ears, even Arthur. He kept Excalibur in hand, though he hunched over on the hood of the car, distracted. Vulnerable.

Evie thought the worst until the coyotes, the dozen or so that were left, gathered themselves and ran, bundles of wounded fur and muscle racing from the driveway onto the prairie.

A falcon hovered over the newly cleared driveway. Then another flash of light blazed, and the falcon disappeared.

Merlin stood before them, his sleeves rolled up, the top button of his shirt undone.

At once, they all left the car. Claw marks scored the paint all over it. Arthur jumped off the roof and met his friend and mentor, clasping his arms.

"A simple scouting mission, you said," Merlin grumbled.

Evie and her father went to Mab, who was panting hard and trying to pick herself up. The hound was more red than gray, bleeding from gouges taken out of her neck, shoulders, back, flanks, and belly. She flattened her ears, peered up at them, wagged her tail a couple of times, and didn't make a sound.

Cradling Mab's head, Evie heard herself making nonsensical comforting noises, telling Mab what a good girl she was. She was a foolish dog, really—she didn't have to fling herself into the fight like that. She should have stayed safe. But she was a dog with a mission, and who was Evie to criticize?

Her father took longer to lower himself to the ground, on obviously complaining limbs. He hissed with pain before adding his own voice to Mab's praises. "That's a girl, it's okay, girl."

Alex knelt beside her. "How is she?"

First aid didn't seem remotely useful. Evie said, "I don't know."

"Well, her tail's still wagging, so it can't be too bad, eh?"

Mab's watery gaze seemed to ask him if he were joking.

"Can you do something for her?" Frank rubbed Mab's head, almost absently.

"I've been a soldier for over three thousand years. I ought to be able to dress a few wounds. Let's see if we can get her into the house."

"I've got her." Arthur had joined them. He got to one knee and scooped the hound up in his arms. Mab's immense body nearly obscured him, but he hefted the weight with seemingly little effort. He moved slowly and carefully. Mab yelped once, but didn't struggle.

Slowly, with Frank leading the way and Alex walking near Arthur, they went into the house.

Merlin hung back, scanning the prairie around the house. Evie waited for him.

"They're out there," he said. "A gathering storm. They'll lay siege to the place."

Movement caught her gaze. She looked out to what had drawn his attention. A few coyotes remained, loping around the edge of the property. They didn't approach or make any threatening moves; rather, they seemed to be patrolling, marking a circuit around the house, watching for anything that might approach, or try to leave.

"What do we do?" she asked.

"Wait. Plan. Pray, if you're so inclined."

And whom did one pray to, when deities appeared and kidnapped your father? They went to the house. Merlin backed up to the porch, keeping his gaze outward, still searching the surrounding fields.

The others had placed Mab on a bath towel on the kitchen table. Alex presided over the impromptu operating table. His tools were a bottle of peroxide, a box of gauze, and a thread and needle.

"She's going to be fine," he told Evie after she'd locked the door. "So long as she doesn't enthusiastically rip the stitches out as soon as I'm done. But you wouldn't do that, would you, girl?"

Mab gamely attempted a tail wag. Her expression was humanly woeful.

He continued conversationally, "And I suppose you've had your rabies shots? Never mind."

Her father leaned against the wall, his arms crossed over his stomach.

"Dad, are you okay?"

"You didn't have to come after me like that," he said, his voice low.

Her tone was matter-of-fact: "Yes, I did."

"She didn't act alone, Mr. Walker," Arthur said.

Her father closed his eyes. "I know. Thank you. Thank you all. Alex, let me get you a clean shirt. That one's a little messed up."

The front of Alex's shirt was scarlet. The rest of them had escaped relatively unscathed, but he looked like he'd seen battle. "Thanks. That'd be nice."

Frank started to turn, then stumbled, slumping against the wall.

Evie reached his side in a heartbeat. Arthur was there as well, lunging across the kitchen. Alex, needle in hand, could only watch.

He brushed them away. "It's the stress catching up with me, that's all."

"Dad!" Recriminations were laden in the word. Tension edged her voice.

Not waiting for explanations, Arthur stepped in and pulled Frank's arm over his shoulders. "Come along, friend."

"Bed," he said with a sigh.

"That's right."

Evie followed them, wondering why her father would accept help from a mythical stranger and not from her. Though she supposed you didn't argue when King Arthur insisted on carrying you to bed.

As a final insult, her father indicated for Arthur to pause outside the bedroom door. "Evie, stay here."

Arthur took him inside and closed the door.

Back to the wall, she slid to the floor, pressed her face to her knees, and covered her head with her hands.

Some long minutes later, the door opened and closed again. Arthur emerged, a white T-shirt in hand, which he put over the back of a chair near Alex.

Arthur then moved to sit on the floor beside her. "He took something for the pain. He's resting now."

She sniffed loudly and wiped her face, attempting to hide that she'd been crying. She looked away from him, not wanting him to see. Her voice caught, though, and betrayed her. "I try to help him, but there's nothing I can do."

"No," he said. "There isn't."

He touched her shoulder, and she took the invitation to lean against him while he held her, his chin resting on her head.

At least she wasn't alone anymore. How bad could things be if Arthur of legend was fighting for her? He didn't seem much like a legend just now. He was a solid, human presence, warm and protective. She rested in his arms, grateful for the moment to catch her breath.

A throat-clearing sounded nearby. Alex, looking sheepish.

"I was wondering if I could get help carrying Her Majesty to the sofa? The dog," he explained, gesturing with a thumb over his shoulder when Arthur looked quizzically at him.

Evie stood quickly, flushing, embarrassed that she was flushing because she had nothing to flush about. Except that Alex was staring at her like she did.

Arthur carried Mab to the sofa. The dog filled all of it but a corner where Evie sat and stroked her head. The fur there was silky, flat against her skull. She hoped to calm the dog into sleeping, giving her wounds a chance to heal. It hurt to see proud Mab so weak.

Alex stood behind the sofa and watched over them. Arthur had moved away, to look out a window.

Merlin watched Alex closely. "Three thousand years, you said. That would make you older than I am."

"Likely," Alex said without facing the wizard.

"How? How does one live so long and survive being run through by Excalibur? You *must* be one of the old gods. Like her."

Alex looked at each of them, Evie last. His hands clenched on the back of the sofa. For a moment, she thought he was going to leave, turn and storm out as he'd done whenever she'd asked too many questions. But Merlin was difficult to refuse.

When he finally spoke, he spoke to her. "I fought

beside Odysseus in the Trojan War. The day after we entered the city"—he didn't have to tell that part of the story—"I was taken prisoner by Apollo, who was unhappy with the turn of events. He enslaved me and intended to keep me for all eternity, enspelling me, to make me ageless and impervious to harm. Things didn't quite work out, but I was stuck."

"Apollo the god?" Merlin said.

"He wasn't a god." Alex straightened and paced along the back of the sofa, his gaze downcast. "*Hera* isn't a god. None of them were. They were just people with too much power who used it for their own gains. You, Merlin—you matched her in a fight. You have as much power as any of them. You could have been a god, but instead you chose to serve. That has been one of the worst frustrations of my long life—living among the prayers, the shrines, the temples, the saints and knowing all the while that the gods we worship are just people."

Arthur had found a cloth dish towel from the kitchen and was cleaning Excalibur. The movements were slow, methodical. He said, "There is the one God. The true God."

Alex suppressed a chuckle and shook his head. "They died. The gods I worshipped as a boy are all dead. Zeus sacrificed himself to destroy the ancient pantheon and change the world. That's what it takes to change the world, you know: a person of great power sacrificing himself, trading his own life for the transformation. So he did, and in a few years, the footprints of the many gods faded. When the gods stopped answering prayers in so personal a manner as the myths tell, the myths changed, the many gods became one. A god who was an idea rather than a person was born. He became all gods."

"Then what of Christ his Son?" Arthur said, true to his own legend.

"Do you know I saw him once?" Alex, brash and insensitive, continued. "He could have been the greatest wizard since Zeus himself. The power of Zeus, the charisma of Apollo—he could have been a god. But a lot of magic had left the world by that time. It's my theory that he learned somehow of what Zeus had done—the sacrifice of self for power. It's a story in so many cultures: the hero gives his life to restore his land, and is reborn as the king. That was what he was trying to do, I think. He succeeded, in a sense: I think he'd have been surprised to learn how far his name has spread. And how it is used. But he gave his life for that fame. His followers wait for his coming that never happens. And meanwhile, thousands of minor wizards work their magic in his name and call them miracles."

"You are a mad blasphemer," Arthur said.

"Thank you, my lord."

Evie kept petting Mab's head. The dog was breathing deeply, sleeping. "Hera lived," she said. "And magic is coming back into the world. What do we do?"

Merlin turned from the window. "Miss Walker, do you believe that Hera will start a war if she gets what she wants?"

The apple still nested in her pocket, pressed against her hip. Long ago, Discord created the apple for the express purpose of sowing strife. Its power had not diminished. Hera would know how to use that power. Such a little thing, rolled onto the floor of the U.N. General Assembly. Metaphorically, of course. She would offer one or another country weapons, money, political dominance—and see them fight for the prize. She could offer one supremacy in space, another free trade, a third a telecommunications empire. Watch them take her bribes and do her bidding.

"She can manipulate the one that's already starting," she said, not certain how she knew, or where her growing confidence came from. Except that her father was dying. He succumbed, and she knew more than she should.

"Then we take our stand against her. Someone must oppose her."

Arthur gazed at Merlin with a shadowed look in his eyes. Past battles, lost wars—who knew what memories played in his mind's eye?

"Is that why we're here, Merlin? To build a new kingdom from the ashes, as we did before?"

"You are here because someone must oppose her. Who better than you?"

Alex crossed his arms. "How? Oppose her how? Do you know where she is? What her next plan is?"

Merlin scowled. "She'll come here, of course. We'll wait for her."

"We'd be fighting a purely defensive battle if we stay here. We can't win."

Arthur sided with Merlin. "I'd like nothing better than to take the fight to her, but I have no forces and no knowledge of her position. Here, our position is at least mildly defensible."

"The house is protected," Evie said. "No one gets in unless invited. No one gets into the Storeroom except the guardian and his heir."

The men looked at her, but her gaze was distant. She couldn't pay attention to them. She recognized the Storeroom, the power it had carried for centuries, as her family immigrated from place to place, carrying its contents with them—somehow they carried everything as they traveled. The knowledge of how they did it eluded her still. She could ask her father. He'd know.

"Then we're safe for now," Alex said. His brow was creased, watching her with uncertainty. Like he didn't know her. "Perhaps we should get some rest. So that we're ready when she comes back. She *will* come back."

Evie closed her eyes, wanting to forget. Give the knowledge back to her father. "Yes."

Arthur glanced out the window, his gaze searching the distant horizon. "We'll keep a watch in shifts. Sinon's right. You should try to sleep."

That was astute, the *try* to sleep. Evie felt exhausted to her very bones, but she hated the idea of falling asleep. Even with Arthur standing watch.

"Feel like taking a walk?" Arthur said to Merlin.

"Another scouting mission?" the old man grumbled.

Arthur grinned. "I thought we'd make sure there aren't any more of those dogs prowling around."

Merlin made a distracted motion of assent, and the two strode to the kitchen door.

Before they went outside, Evie hurriedly stood and called to him. "Arthur. Thank you. Thank you for staying."

He nodded and gave her a smile—a vivid smile that would inspire his people to follow him into battle. They couldn't lose, not with Arthur leading them.

Then he and Merlin were gone, the door closed.

Alex unbuttoned and peeled off his shirt, stuffing it into the trash under the sink. He washed his hands and arms to the elbows. The water ran pink off him. Evie'd guessed right, he was well built under his coat. He had sculpted muscles on his arms, shoulders, and chest, flexing with his movements. They weren't excessive, but they promised an efficient strength.

"You're falling in love with him," he said, his tone too flat to be mocking, as he stared at the running water.

She started to be angry. She wanted to be angry at his presumption. But the emotion faded.

Instead she made half a laugh and shook her head. "Of course I am. Aren't you? But no, not really, I think. He's too heroic. Larger than life, untouchable. Like Superman. He scares the shit out of me. I'm not good enough to fall in love with that. Not brave enough. Or beautiful enough."

"Don't sell yourself short." He stalked over to the chair at the kitchen table and pulled on the clean T-shirt.

She should say something here, she thought. If this were a story she was writing, the character would have to say something. She didn't know *what*, so if it were a story, she'd have to walk away from it or put in some little stars to remind her to go back to it and fill it in. She liked writing because she could always go back and change things, or think of something better to say. Wittier. She had no wit.

She looked away, to the table where her work was

still scattered. Uselessly, now. The comics, her laptop, the stories they contained, seemed so far away. Her phone lay on the table among the debris. The screen showed a missed message. She picked up the phone— she had reception again—played back the lone message, and listened. It was Bruce, who didn't leave messages, but always waited for her to call back.

"Evie. Some of us—me and Callie, James, his roommates—are leaving the city. James has a place in Napa. It's not safe here anymore. So we're running. I don't know when we'll be able to come back. I don't know when I'll be able to get back to work. I just wanted you to know, Evie, working with you on *Eagle Eyes* was great. The best work I've ever done. You helped me do better than I ever thought I could. Thanks. Maybe we can do it again sometime. I'll see you. When this all blows over." The *when* sounded despairing.

Useless. It had all been useless.

She played the message again. Bruce sounded tired. She wondered how much work he'd been able to finish before fleeing. She hoped he and Callie and the others had made it out of the city.

"Evie, you've gone white."

Shaking her head, she set down the phone. Sleep, rest—wasn't that what she was supposed to be doing? She sank into the armchair, pulled up her knees. Her stomach was in knots. She'd never rest again.

"Evie?" Alex moved closer. He looked like he might be about to hover. She didn't want him any closer. He might try to comfort her, and she might start crying.

She said, "How did you know to come here? How did you find this place?"

He set his hand on the back of the sofa. "I tracked you down."

"But how?"

Shrugging, he glanced away. "Old-fashioned detective work. I knew your family at the beginning. When you were first given stewardship of the artifacts."

The mind boggled. "When was that?"

"Three thousand years or so. I lost track of the family for a while. They migrated a lot. Every time there was a war, one of them took the Storeroom and left. To protect it, probably. Some of the leads were almost impossible to trace. But I had plenty of time."

That was what she should do: collect the Storeroom and run to escape the war. But when war was everywhere, where could she go?

She admired his dedication in spite of herself. "You must be disappointed. You did all that work for nothing."

"On the contrary," he said, his smile softening. "I got to meet you."

She blushed and didn't know what to say. Witless, again.

"I have to tell you," he said. "I might have given her the key to the house's magic. I—I have another curse, you see. Apollo made this chain so that I must always tell the truth. I've found some fairly contorted ways of speaking *around* the truth. But sometimes I have no choice. I'm afraid I'm a terrible spy. Not like the old days."

That was what happened when one tried being a double agent. She knew that from subplots of the comic book. As for the key to the house's magic, and why Alex would know what that was—she didn't understand. Still, some knowledge eluded her.

"Everything you've said is true?"

"That's right. Or true to me, at least."

He said he couldn't lie, and that he'd die for her if he could. What could she say to argue with that?

"Why are you telling me all this?"

"Because I want to."

She ought to ask Alex to tell stories about her family. All of them, back through the centuries. She didn't know anything about her family.

"I'm going to try to rest." She smiled thinly, touched his arm as she passed him, and went to her room, shrugging off her jacket, the weight of gold still pulling at its pocket.

"This is taking too long," Robin said as he paced back and forth near the Marquis. Through a windbreak of cottonwoods, they could see the Walker house in the distance. The intrepid heroes had successfully defeated the Curandera's coyotes. She had collected the animals from miles of prairie and turned them to her will, but they were only animals in the end. They could harass, but they didn't know how to break into the house.

This had *all* taken too long. They should have been able to overcome the mortals in the cemetery. Hera should have been able to make the girl hand over the apple. The whole affair with the elder Walker had proceeded clumsily. And now he was set babysitting the self-important magician.

He'd stopped caring about any of that.

The Marquis had cleared the weeds and brush from a space until only flat dirt remained. On the tablet of dirt he traced a series of figures in powdered chalk. A square, and in the square was inscribed a circle, and within the circle a star, with Greek letters at the points. Incense burned in a brazier. Red candles flared and flickered in the wind.

"Time is master of us all," said the nobleman. "Please be quiet."

"Can you really break through the magic guarding the house?"

The Marquis's lips tightened and he managed a brief glare at Robin, who was pleased at the reaction. "Prometheus built these enchantments and his magic is very old. But now that I know their maker, I've learned the nature of his spells."

He sprinkled a new powder on the brazier, which flared green. He held his hand over the star and seemed to meditate for a time. Impatient, Robin watched. This seemed like such a cumbersome way to practice magic. Artificial, structured, dependent on too many patterns, rituals, tools. Robin didn't understand; magic had come easily to him. He'd been born in the wild and raised to its rhythms, had always felt the world's power in his blood. He was part of that power, immortal, forever young. He had only to think, to wish, to be, and his magic came to him. He pitied the Marquis, who studied magic as a science and surely didn't feel the power in his blood. Surely he would never be a god.

"It didn't take this long to find the path here."

"Yes, it did," said the Marquis, unperturbed. "You were simply more patient then."

Robin was five times as old as this whelp. How dare he be so smug. "I don't think you can do it."

"You certainly aren't making the task easier. This is a different sort of problem, Master Robin. Finding the place was like following a blazing arrow pointing the way. It had already been found, and I had only to mark the path. This is more like storming a castle."

"Why couldn't Hera do this herself?" That was always the rub, wasn't it? Did you want to serve a greater power that needed *your* help? A truly great power wouldn't need anyone's help. *He* didn't need anyone's help.

The Marquis said, "The risk. If I do it wrong, the house might kill me. Now, if you'll pardon me."

Robin stared at him, curious for the first time all day. Now, this could get interesting. . . .

The magician left the ritual markings and walked in a wide circle that swept around the property. Robin followed. The man had created another space, with similar markings, candles, and incense, exactly opposite the first. When they reached the other ritual site, Robin felt a tightness close in, a hum of power that hadn't been there before. The Marquis had closed a circle of magic around the Walker house.

"Remember, Hera only wants the protection gone. She wants the magic *in* the Storeroom maintained."

The Marquis sighed. "Will you let me do my job?"

Robin couldn't interpret the gestures he made, or guess why he did what he did, but he couldn't deny the power, the shape of it, the tremor closing in on the house. It raised the hair on the back of his neck. He wondered what would happen if he kicked a little dirt over one of those symbols. The Marquis didn't even see him do it.

There was a presence, a force inside the house, and the Marquis was opposing it. Robin watched the house, expecting it to collapse, or burst into flames, or shoot lightning at them.

Then the feeling went away.

Expressionless, the Marquis let his arms hang loose at his sides. He said, "It's done."

Then the Marquis dropped to his knees. He didn't make a sound, just worked his mouth for a moment or two as if trying to draw breath. His arms hung as if paralyzed, and the realization seemed to pass across his face that while he had succeeded, something had gone wrong. Then he fell, facedown into the dirt, and lay still, dead, after what must have seemed too short a life after all.

Robin clicked his tongue. "So much magic requires sacrifice. Hera will surely mourn you." He kicked a bit of dirt on the Marquis's nice coat.

Time to fly, Robin thought, smiling. Nothing had frustrated him like this in centuries. He wanted to break something. It was invigorating. He raced away, light as air.

Alex had become . . . overwhelming. If it were any other time and place, if her father weren't dying and the world weren't ending . . .

And why should that make any difference?

She curled up in bed, pretending that she might actually be able to sleep. Alex had said he was going to sleep in the armchair. She'd left him alone in the front room. She should go back, to keep an eye on him. Keep him company.

She should stop thinking about him at all.

A distant roll of thunder sounded, rattling the windowpanes. A winter thunderstorm. Rare, but not impossible. There might even be snow. A white Christmas. The holiday was still a couple days off. She'd forgotten. Evie pulled the pillow over her head and hugged it there. She was supposed to be pretending to sleep.

An ache caught her gut, a feeling of such profound dread, she almost vomited. She pressed her hand to her stomach. She'd felt this when she got the call about her mother's death.

She sat up. Someone had died. Her father—

Mab started barking, loud enough to shake the house, when she should have been resting. A door opened, squeaking. Her father's door. She heard him say, "Mab, hush!"

She stifled a sob. He was okay.

A man jumped onto the bed.

Before she could scream, he straddled her and shoved her back, pinning her with his legs and body, and locked his hand over her mouth. Glaring up at him, she struggled, but he only held tighter. Despite his slight form, he was strong.

"Evie Walker. Evie, Evie." His nose was an inch from her face, his breath caressing her. The young man bared his teeth when he smiled, vicious. He was Hera's henchman, Robin.

"Do you know what's happened?" he breathed into her ear. "You're no longer safe. These walls will not protect you. I turned myself to dust and crept in through a crack in the floorboards. What do you think of that?"

Her mind raced, even as her body tried to thrash. She heard his words, but couldn't make meaning of them. Scream, scream for help. But she couldn't.

He said, "Hera is coming. She can have the apple. I want you."

After hundreds of years, the island of Ithaca grew barren and difficult, and the family's prosperity was divided between too many sons. Niko hadn't wanted his share of land, the wealth that lay in olive groves and flocks of sheep. He took the main of his inheritance: the contents of the Storeroom, packed away into an underground cellar. The artifacts were what he truly inherited from his mother, who had inherited them from her father, and so on, eldest child to eldest child, for generations.

When the Storeroom came to Niko, he stood on the cusp of migration. He had to leave, or be drafted into the army. Under Alexander, Macedonia was swallowing the world. While he didn't like to be called a coward, he felt in his bones he had a different calling, a stronger calling, one that meant he had to flee.

The room was just large enough for him to turn around in. He surveyed the items, packed into shelves and nooks carved into the earthen walls. Swords, shields, helmets, lyres, winged sandals, golden fleece, woolen cloaks. One by one, he placed them in a leather satchel. The bag never grew heavier, never bulged, no matter how much he put in it. The bag itself was magic—the bag was the Storeroom, made small.

Niko knew the stories. Even if his family had no magical legacy, he'd know what many of these items were. Here was the ball of twine Ariadne gave to Theseus, to lead him out of the labyrinth. Two quivers of arrows, one silver and one gold, had belonged to the twins Artemis and Apollo. And here, a golden apple bearing an ancient inscription. The characters had long ago faded from knowledge. Niko couldn't read them, but he knew the story, and he knew what it said: "For the Fairest."

Gingerly, he set it into the bag with everything else.

The Storeroom didn't used to have this much, a vague familiar memory told him. But magic was going out of the world. Here it lay, inert, the stories finished and done with. The age of heroes had ended. It made Niko sad.

All his possessions contained in a bag over his shoulder, he sailed west, to a peninsula of warring chieftains that seemed unlikely to unite and develop aspirations of empire-building anytime soon.

14

❧

Night had come to the Sun Palace.

The room was the same. A chair sat against the wall. An arch opened onto a porch. Beyond that was the garden, where a bird called from one of the trees. The fountains were silent.

Picking up the sword, Sinon stood. The screen was still pulled back from the doorway he'd been guarding. But the doorway—through it was a small room, only a few feet square, meant for storage.

The closet was just a closet. The doorway to Olympus was gone.

Sword in hand, he stalked through rooms and hallways, expecting an ambush. The place was so still, his own footsteps made him wince. He went to the garden.

The path led out past the hedge. Beyond this was an open field. Sinon could see the horizon. The path trailed away from the palace.

The sun rose and set twice more. Apart from a few bowls of fruit, jars of wine, and the odd pastry left here and there on discarded platters, there was no food. The wine pitchers were empty. The god had always summoned their meals, from where Sinon didn't know. Some of the trees in the garden bore fruit. But Sinon would have to leave if he didn't want to starve.

He wondered if he could starve. He still wore Apollo's chain around his neck.

On the third day, Sinon lay on his pallet. The sun had risen to noon, and he was still trying to find the will to climb out of bed. Once he did that, he would have to find the will to leave the palace and take that path to the horizon. Facing that would mean facing that he was afraid of it. Afraid of the world that had grown older without him.

A man walked through the room, from one door to the next, without noticing Sinon lying there. Startled, Sinon took up the sword—he slept with it—and rose to follow the intruder.

The stranger was plain, with brown hair tied into a tail, of average build, but vibrant. He moved with purpose. A leather satchel hung over one shoulder, but he didn't seem to mind the weight. He went to Apollo's bedchamber. There, he found the god's lyre resting in its corner, and started to put it in the bag.

"You, stop there," Sinon said, pointing with the sword.

The man looked over his shoulder, but didn't seem disturbed. The lyre disappeared into his bag. He then went to a table by the wall and looked in a box sitting there, where Apollo kept his golden circlet. Seeing the circlet in place, he closed the box and put it in the bag.

"I said stop!"

The man let his arms hang at his sides. "If you're going to try to run me through, get on with it."

The intruder was unarmed, or seemed to be. Sinon didn't feel quite right just charging him and slashing his head off. But he'd lived among the gods long enough to know there was probably a trick to this. Apollo was testing him.

Sinon approached him slowly. "First put down the bag. Then tell me who you are."

He didn't put down the bag. He said, "I am Prometheus."

Sinon stared. Whoever he was, he could have attacked Sinon then and he wouldn't have thought to defend himself. He repeated flatly, "Prometheus."

Prometheus, who brought fire and knowledge to humanity, who was at the heart of all the stories of creation, one of the Titans, who were older than the gods even. Wiser than the gods. His brother was earth-bearing Atlas, and yet he looked so *normal*.

Sinon laughed nervously. "The Prometheus of the stories isn't a thief."

The man grinned. "You're wrong. The Prometheus of the stories stole fire and gave it to humankind." Next, he went to the chest where Apollo kept his armor and weapons. From it he drew a quiver of arrows and slipped them into the bag as well.

The bag was no more full or bulging than it had been before.

Sinon couldn't stand being treated as inconsequential, like he was harmless. Especially by someone claiming to be *Prometheus,* of all the outrageous lies.

Taking his sword firmly in an attacking grip, he charged the stranger. In three strides he crossed the room, moving swiftly, for all that he hadn't done this in so long. He arced the sword low and drove up, to catch the intruder in the gut.

Then the intruder was gone. He stepped to the side faster than a blink and put his hand around Sinon's throat. He shoved against Sinon with the force of a thunderstorm. His throat collapsed, he couldn't breathe. Sinon's body swung on the fulcrum of that grip, and he crashed headfirst on the floor. Bone cracked; skull crushed.

Sinon lay for a moment, blinded by stars that flashed in his vision, nauseated because he could feel the bone knitting back together, could feel his throat re-forming. He lay still, swathed in pain. Then he gasped, able to breathe through a newly healed windpipe.

He sat up slowly, dizzily. He touched the back of his head, which was slick with blood. He cursed softly. He should be dead. If only.

"What are you?" The man who claimed to be Prometheus walked a slow circle around him, a pace away. "You're not a god or a demigod. In fact, you smell mortal. So what are you?"

Sinon was feeling better by the moment. Less broken. Grunting, he picked himself off the floor, regarding with some disgust the blood on his hand. He should have just let the man loot the Sun Palace.

"Apollo's idea of a joke," he said.

"You don't look amused."

"Do you have any idea what his sense of humor is like?"

The man chuckled. "I do. I've known him since he was a child."

"You're really Prometheus." Of *course* he was, if he

could stand there so calmly after tossing a man onto the floor like a sack of grain.

He bowed his head. "And you are—?"

"I—I'm Sinon of Ithaca." How long had it been since he named himself so? The name didn't seem to fit anymore.

"Good to meet you, Sinon of Ithaca."

"Might I ask—what are you doing? Why are you taking his things?"

Prometheus smiled. "If you'd asked so politely in the first place, I would have told you."

Suppressing a smile of his own, Sinon looked away. He supposed there was a lesson in that.

Prometheus said, "Let's talk. Is there food here?"

Sinon picked a bowl of apples and figs from the garden, and the two sat on the bench by the pond where Apollo had tricked him with the nereid. As they shared the fruit, Prometheus asked him for his story, and Sinon told him, starting with the night that Troy fell and ending with Zeus asking to pass through the doorway to Olympus.

The last few days made more sense when he spoke of it aloud. He hadn't wanted to understand before. Now, he was able to ask, "What's happened? What did Zeus do?"

Prometheus's smile thinned sadly. "He destroyed Olympus."

Sinon winced, unbelieving. Of all the wonders he had seen and heard, this was the least believable. "He *what*? What about Apollo?"

"Gone. They're all gone. Zeus brought them all to Olympus—then he destroyed it. And himself."

"I don't believe you." Gone. Might as well say the

sun was gone. Or that twilight had come to the Sun Palace.

"You will."

He felt tears start. He pressed his hand to his eyes to stop them. Why should he cry? Why should he mourn them, for all the grief they'd brought him? He certainly wasn't mourning Apollo.

Prometheus was wrong. Sinon couldn't believe him, couldn't imagine a world without the gods. The gods *were* the world: the sun, the moon, the oceans, thunder and storms, life and death.

"Why would he do such a thing?" he said, trying to keep his voice from choking.

"After Troy, Zeus felt that the gods had grown too powerful. And too petty. He wanted to return fate to humanity. Let mortals decide their own destinies again."

"But the gods have always held our destinies in their hands. The gods created men!"

"No. The gods created the stories to secure their own power over men. Now, without their awe to back them, the stories will fade. He came to me with the plan. I've always been the one protecting mortals from the likes of them. I thought the solution severe. But I didn't argue. Troy—Troy was a debacle."

"I know."

Prometheus nodded. "Of course. The consequences of Troy will continue for ages, I fear. So, Zeus had his plan, and he asked me to clean up when he was finished. I'm collecting their things—the ones that are magic. Hermes' sandals, Artemis's arrows, Poseidon's trident. We wouldn't want someone to get hold of them and cause trouble."

He nodded at Sinon's hand. "I'll need that sword."

"Why?"

"It belonged to Apollo. It's magic."

He looked at it. It looked like a sword. It felt normal. "Magic, how?"

Prometheus shrugged. "Perhaps it's capable of slaying an immortal."

Sinon quashed a moment of dizziness. *I could have stopped Zeus. . . .* As he'd stopped Prometheus. Zeus had known his very thoughts. He couldn't have stopped him.

He offered the weapon to Prometheus, grip first. Prometheus put the sword in the bag, with all the other treasures of the gods.

A world without the gods. He swallowed back a lump in his throat.

"Can you take this as well?" He hooked a finger on the chain around his neck.

Prometheus touched it, drew it through his hands, all the way around as he studied it. Sinon had studied it—it had no clasp, no seam.

When Prometheus shook his head, Sinon's heart sank.

"The magic in this isn't tied to Apollo. It's fed by the power of your own body, your own life. It in turn preserves you. It's a sustaining circle. As long as you live, the links cannot be broken. As long as the links remain unbroken, you will live."

There would be no consolation at all for him.

"Before he left here, Zeus said I would be free. He was wrong."

"I think the cruelest thing a mortal can learn is that the Father of the Gods isn't perfect."

He rose to take his leave, distracting Sinon from

his contemplation of the pool of water. Mosquitoes darted along the surface. They never had before.

He said, "What will happen to me?"

Prometheus stopped, turned. "I don't know. Your fate is in your own hands now. You won't die. You can't be killed. You're like a god now."

"Except that I have no power."

"That's why Zeus didn't kill you, too."

"And what about you? You have the power of a god. Will you set yourself up as the divine king now?"

"I've always worked against the gods. That was why Zeus trusted me." He slung the sack over his shoulder, preparing to depart. "Thank you for the fruit."

Sinon didn't want to be left alone. He stood with Prometheus, put his hand out, but didn't go so far as to touch him in his effort to stop him. "Where—where are you going? What will you do next?" As if he could innocently follow along.

"I need to find someone who can be trusted as a caretaker for a collection of magically potent artifacts. Someone immune to the forces of magic, at least a little. It would help if this person had a good head on his shoulders."

"Odysseus," Sinon said without thinking.

Prometheus's eyes lit. "Ah, of course. He has a son, doesn't he? A family to carry on as custodians when he's gone—"

Damn, Sinon thought. Never bring your friends to the attention of the gods. "Why can't you be the caretaker?"

"Because it needs to be someone here, and I'm not staying."

"Why not just destroy them all?"

"And release all that power back into the world? No. It needs to be tucked away, safe and inert, to leave men in peace."

"Don't you think that family has had enough trouble from the gods?"

Prometheus grinned. "Families like that can't avoid trouble from the gods. So—would you like to come with me when I travel to Ithaca?"

That was an idea. Perhaps he should try going home.

15

Robin gave every indication of being able to take Evie. Somehow, he clamped her arms to her sides, immobilizing her, yet could still pat her down, searching her pockets for the apple. He did more than search: he groped, stroked, tucked his hand down the waistband of her jeans, and his fingers suddenly seemed longer, reaching for her, brushing the skin of her hips.

She could barely suck breath through her nose. His grip suffocated her, but she drew as much air as she could, arced her head back, and screamed. Her throat tore with the noise that came out muffled, like distant thunder.

He moved his hand, pressed his mouth over hers, and laughed as he kissed her, swallowing her scream. "Hush, my dear, and you'll learn what the love of an immortal is."

She bit him.

She didn't think she succeeded in catching anything between her teeth; she could only snap, like a dog behind a fence. Nevertheless, he hissed and drew back, only for a second, and she had just enough air left to cry out. When he leaned his forearm against her throat, pressing down, she choked against the pressure as loudly as she could, hoping that someone in the house heard.

Even though Robin was killing her, she felt a great sense of relief when a pounding started on the bedroom door, punctuated by barking from the living room. Robin looked back at the door, pointed, and something happened—the pounding faded, becoming muffled as if the door were barred now.

She turned her head to slither out from under him, writhing, trying to escape.

When the thumping against the door stopped, so did she. Too tired, too out of breath, her muscles failed. She lay half on her side, her back twisted painfully.

And Robin was still there, his mouth against her neck. "Now, where was I? Ah, I was searching for rare fruit. Let's find out what that Greek bloke sees in you."

When one of her characters found themselves in an impossible situation, Evie had time to think of clever ways for them to escape. Her characters were always so clever, instantly clever, without even thinking about it, because their author had the luxury of revision. Now, in an impossible situation, Evie couldn't make her brain work to be clever. No time for revisions if she failed here.

"If you don't have it here, I'll just have to look for it when I'm finished," he said. "If you had listened to me the first time we met, we could have had such a lovely time together. We could have been friends."

She'd left her jacket hanging on the doorknob of the bedroom. If she told him it was there, maybe he'd leave her alone.

Evie and Robin flinched together as the bedroom door splintered inward. Like a cat, Robin sprang away, his back to the wall, facing the door. A second blow tore through the plywood, then a third, then Alex, gripping an axe, pushed through, murder in his eyes. He cut himself, climbing through the broken plywood of the door, and held the axe ready.

His gaze scanned the room and focused on Robin. Alex swung the axe over his head and charged. Wide-eyed, Robin backed away on tense limbs. He appeared to be terrified, but at the moment Alex brought the weapon down to strike, Robin disappeared. Alex slammed the axe into the top of an antique dresser, wedging it half into the wood.

A wisp of smoke and rush of wind whipped through the broken door, to the main part of the house.

Snarling, Alex needed several attempts, jerking back with his whole body, to rip the axe out of the dresser. He paused only a moment before storming after Robin.

"Are you all right?"

She nodded, quickly and birdlike. He leaped through the chopped-up door.

My hero, she thought vaguely before scrambling off the bed and following.

Alex stalked to the kitchen, hefting the axe and looking like something out of a horror film. Robin wasn't there. Alex searched the room, every corner in which the imp could hide.

Near the sofa, Mab half sat, half sprawled, and barked to wake the dead. Frank was on the floor with her, arms around her body, holding her back. Some of her stitched cuts had started bleeding again. His arms were shaking. The only reason Mab didn't break free was because the dog was weak as well.

And there Robin appeared, behind Alex, holding a butcher knife from the Walkers' own supply.

"Alex!" Evie screamed, too late.

Expertly, Robin drove the blade up, through the soft part of Alex's lower back, under the ribs, through the vital organs. Alex arched his back and growled; Robin twisted the blade.

Alex wrenched away and stumbled back. Evie's heart ached. She wanted to run to him, like the heroine in a bodice ripper. For a moment, she forgot what he was. It was easy to forget.

Never taking his eyes off Robin, Alex reached back and pulled out the knife. He swept the axe around one-handed, hacking at Robin. Robin jumped, writhed in midair—inhumanly, like he was made of smoke, defying gravity—and disappeared again, and Alex cut through nothing.

Blood covered the back of his shirt, bright red against the white fabric. His hand was red with it. Still, his face creased with intensity, he searched for Robin.

"Not entirely mortal, are you?" said Robin's voice, disembodied. It had no focus, but diffused through the whole room, without source. "Let's see how mortal you are."

Alex stood his ground, waiting for Robin to show himself. He seemed calm, like a soldier waiting for battle, the faintest smile on his lips.

Abruptly, he fell back, flinging out his arms for balance. His knees buckled, as if something had struck them from behind. Robin appeared, light flashing into form, a reflection taking shape. He crouched on Alex's chest and punched him, knocking his head back. Alex grappled for the axe, which had dropped a few feet away. Robin looked like a slender young man, almost a boy, but he had supernatural strength. Alex couldn't upset him from his perch.

Taking careful steps, desperate not to attract attention, Evie stepped to the kitchen. She skirted along the wall until her feet left the hardwood and touched tile. She had to find a weapon, preferably one that required minimal skill.

Alex managed to unbalance Robin, twisting violently and slipping out from under him. There was a crack, like a bone breaking or a shoulder popping out of joint. It had to have come from Alex, but he didn't look like he was in pain.

Robin was too fast. Before Alex could find the axe or establish his position, Robin was on him again, legs wrapped around his middle. He laughed, pulling Alex's hair while Alex reached, futilely clutching at him. Next Robin grabbed the chain around Alex's neck. He twisted it, tightening it until it pinched deep into Alex's skin, cutting off blood and air. Alex's face flushed, turning darker and darker red, and it seemed as if Robin could pull the chain clean through his neck, decapitating him.

Alex surely wouldn't survive that.

Evie grabbed the cast-iron skillet off the stove top.

It was almost too heavy, but if she moved it fast enough, her wrist hardly felt the weight. Two-handed, she swung it like a baseball bat, aiming the flat bottom to connect with Robin's head.

It crunched on impact. There should have been some resistance, some recoil, but her arms hardly felt a jolt as they finished out the arc. Robin followed the arc, spinning sideways, falling limp on the floor, jerking to a stop.

Evie stood ready, skillet in hand. But Robin didn't move. At this angle, his head seemed flattened, and a trickle of blood leaked from his ear.

Alex lay on his side, his hands hooked around the chain, holding it away from his neck. His breathing wheezed, as if the air passed through a damaged windpipe. Evie's own breath felt harsh in her lungs; she might start hyperventilating. She dropped the skillet and tried to breathe slower.

She knelt beside Alex and touched his shoulder, helping him roll onto his back. He had to be all right, after all he'd been through. He opened his eyes, and she sprawled on top of him and kissed him. After a moment's hesitation, his lips moved against hers and his arms wrapped around her, one hand lacing into her hair to hold her in place.

Uncertain, she broke away and lay her face against his neck. Eyes closed, she breathed his scent—sweaty, a touch of blood where some of the links of the chain had broken skin. She wished she could rest here for a long time, warm and protected. The next few minutes were going to be difficult and confusing.

Alex was difficult and confusing. "I'm sorry," she said finally.

"For what?" he whispered, wheezing as he chuckled with his damaged throat.

"For doubting."

"Oh my dear, never mind."

A wet canine nose interrupted. Mab arrived and

pushed toward Evie's face, licking and nosing until Evie moved, thereby proving she wasn't dead.

"Oof." Alex, innocent victim of Mab's affections, halfheartedly pushed the dog's head away. "I should kill the beast, but I spent all that effort sewing her up."

Evie sat up and reassured the wolfhound, scratching her ears and looking into her sad eyes.

Her father made his way toward them, leaning on the wall for support. His hand wrapped around his middle, and his face was ashen, his jaw clenched in pain.

"Are you all right?" His voice was soft, difficult to hear. She wanted to laugh that he'd ask her that question. He looked like he was about to collapse.

Slowly, Alex sat up. He touched her hand, gripped it where it rested on her knee, and watched Frank's slow progress. He passed them, went to Robin's prone form, and with one hand on the wall, he knelt and touched Robin's neck.

She didn't want to hear the word. She hadn't meant to kill anyone. She didn't think she could kill anyone. She never expected to have to.

"Dead?" Alex said. Her father nodded.

Evie felt for remorse, but it was a distant, tired thing. Weakly, she said, "I didn't hit him that hard."

Nodding at the skillet, Alex said, "Cold iron. Magnificent. Even better than rowan."

"Dad?"

Her father had slumped against the wall. Mab whined and stepped toward him, nuzzling him. He winced and held her away. Evie went to help him up, but he pushed her away as well.

"How did he get in?" Alex said. "I thought the house was protected."

Her father said, "It's gone. I woke up. I felt it go."

"Me, too," Evie said. She listened, uncertain what she expected to hear, unclear what she expected to find when she stretched her mind like she would reach with her hand. She visualized the shape of the house, and knew that there should have been a second skin around it, a force to keep people like Hera away.

Instead, harsh wind knocked against the window-panes, and the thunder came closer. The Storeroom was unprotected. *The end, the end.* But it still spoke to her. The core of it remained. She was still the heir.

"Where are Arthur and Merlin?" Alex said.

Evie and Alex stood together, helping each other up. He let go of her hand as he raced to the kitchen door, opened it and stopped on the threshold. Evie crowded behind him, looking out.

Full-bodied black thunderheads roiled above, mov-ing faster than the wind that buffeted the house, some of them swirling in the wrong direction. This was the kind of storm that wreaked havoc on the Great Plains in the middle of summer, spilling lightning and torna-does on fragile, unsuspecting towns. Gouts of dust rolled across the plain and smacked into the house, with the rattling sound of hail.

The thunderhead spun its circle above the Walker house.

In a flash of lightning, a figure appeared on the porch. He'd run up the steps, a shadow in the wind. Startled, Evie flinched back, and Alex stepped in front of her, his arm spread protectively. But it was Arthur.

He carried Excalibur, which shone bright silver, even in the darkness. Blood streaked the blade.

"I've been fighting off more animals round back. Are tigers native to this part of the world?"

Weakly, Evie shook her head.

"Are you well?"

"Evie killed the hobgoblin," Alex said, grinning happily at her.

Arthur nodded and made a pleased-sounding grunt. "Well done."

Evie decided they were both so cheerful because they were in their element, surrounded by danger, doing battle.

Merlin came over the edge of the roof. He rolled off, dropped, seemed to hang in the air for a moment, then landed on his feet. He brushed off his shirt and trousers as he rushed to the porch. Even his short gray hair tossed in the fierce wind.

"They have some sort of witch with them," Merlin said, raising his voice to be heard. "The storm is hers. She's well protected. I can't get to her." He frowned thoughtfully. "I've always had a bit of a weak spot with enchantresses."

"I can't fight the winds, Merlin. You must do something."

Her father arrived at the doorway. Evie stepped aside to give him room. His skin was pale, drained. His face lined with pain. He seemed to move in slow motion.

"Evie, go to the basement."

The old tornado drill. "What about you?"

"I'm going to give it to her." He turned his hand, revealing what he'd been holding tucked against his stomach. The golden apple. He must have taken it from her jacket in the bedroom, picked out from the wreckage of the door where it had been hanging.

Alex's hand clenched on her shoulder. But Evie didn't move.

"You can't do that," she pleaded weakly. "It'll give her everything—"

"No, it won't. Evie—she can't have the Storeroom. It holds objects more powerful than the apple. Our duty is to protect them. Even if we have to make sacrifices."

"But to sacrifice the world?"

He smiled with unfathomable wisdom and knowledge. "It's happened before. But the world always comes back, Evie."

He turned to walk out into the storm.

She grabbed his arm. "You can't go out there!"

"Why not?" he said. "Because it'll kill me?"

He'd been dying all along, and this was better. Wasn't it? Wouldn't Homer have thought so?

"There are stronger forces than Discord. They must survive. Go into the Storeroom. Find the box." Then he looked at Alex. "Go with her. Help her."

"Yes, sir," Alex said, his voice tight.

Merlin said to Frank, "I can send them to a safe place. It's why we're here—to protect the seeds, to help grow a new world after the chaos."

Her father nodded. "Good. But wait—wait until Evie tells you to."

"But I won't leave!"

They all focused on Frank, who stood like a pillar, untroubled by the wind buffeting him.

Hushed, Alex said, "Sometimes a person can change the world by sacrificing his life."

Arthur saluted Frank with his sword. "I will give them the time they need."

"But you—" She looked between Arthur and Merlin. "This isn't your story, you shouldn't be here. You shouldn't have to, to—" Die here, sacrifice themselves—

"Don't worry about us," Arthur said, laughing. "We've been through much worse than this."

"Haven't you been paying attention?" Merlin said. "Our story is just beginning!"

"Dad—"

"When she gets the apple, she'll be distracted. She won't be thinking of the rest of the Storeroom. You'll have an extra few minutes."

"But, Dad—"

He touched her face, a fleeting brush of fingers along her cheek. Her skin tingled with it. "I didn't get to say good-bye to your mother. This is better. Good-bye, Evie."

He started down the steps. Alex held her back, gripping her arms, and she leaned against him, toward her father.

Mab pushed out the doorway, moving stiffly, her wounds bleeding. On the first step she nudged Frank, gazed up at him, and wagged her tail.

Evie paused. She whispered, "Go with him. Take care of him."

Her father looked down at the dog and laced his fingers in the fur on her neck. She was exactly the right height for him to lean on her. He met Evie's gaze once more, then turned away. They walked down the steps, onto the driveway.

From the wind, mist, and darkness, a trio of figures approached to meet him and the dog at his side. One of them was tall and poised, like a goddess. The others, a man and woman, her lieutenants, emulated her carriage. A space of calm formed around them. The wind didn't gust there.

"Come on, Evie," Alex said into her ear. "Come on!" He gripped her around the middle and hauled back, stumbling with her into the kitchen. Merlin followed, and Arthur protected their retreat.

Into the house, through the kitchen, down the stairs. A window shattered as a piece of debris struck it. Dad was still out there. Hera wouldn't care if he lived or died.

She'd felt very little when she found the Marquis's body. His death hadn't entirely surprised her. She'd been prepared to make sacrifices. He'd succeeded, and that was something. The house was free now. Maybe she would name a bird after him.

In the space of quiet she'd created, Hera watched the old man and the dog approach. No, he wasn't an old man. He was solidly middle aged, but old before his time. Dying. Even the dog seemed to be on its last leg, limping, bleeding from a dozen hastily stitched cuts.

For the first half of her life, she hadn't bothered even to think about what that must be like—dying. Then, she almost had, when Zeus pulled his trick. She didn't much like the feeling. She'd vowed to avoid the possibility in the future.

Frank Walker entered the stormless space without blinking. He held the apple in his hand.

It pulsed with power in her eyes. She'd seen that power the first time it rolled into her sight, at the wedding. Not everyone had seen it, even among the gods and goddesses of Olympus. Aphrodite had, and of course, Athena. The three of them exchanged glances across the banquet hall, each challenging the other: *It will be mine.*

If she were to be charitable, she'd admit that Aphrodite had won it fairly. She'd rightly seen into Paris's heart, seen him for the idiot he was, and played to his basest desires. With what Hera and Athena had offered him, he could have acquired any woman in the world, including Helen. But the boy hadn't been able to see past his libido.

She and Athena both should have known better. Aphrodite had bested them.

But now, finally, the apple would be hers.

"Mr. Walker," she said amiably, ignoring her minions and the chaos billowing around her. "I was just coming to make your daughter another offer. I took the wrong approach last time—I understand that now. She doesn't want power. She doesn't want to be part of a new pantheon. She wants to save her mother, but since she can't do that—she wants revenge. Am I right?"

"Can you give that to her?" he said.

"I can do away with the system that caused her pain. It's as close as she'll ever find. This age is over. Nothing can stop that now, you know that."

Walker smiled sadly and shook his head. Hera quelled a spark of rage. She hadn't seen such a look of condescension on a man since Zeus.

"What do you think this is going to do, really? You think you can use it to wipe the slate clean. But the so-called chaos that's already out there, that you want to take advantage of, the wars and terror—that isn't chaos. It isn't discord. It's orchestrated. The gods of this age, the ones who made this world, pushed it into fear and chaos to stay in power, they made the world this way. They're the ones who must be broken. *This* breaks the power of the gods." He gestured with the golden apple.

Troy had been the beginning of the end. Troy had happened when they overstepped their bounds—when they manipulated the fates of men for the sake of a trinket. When men destroyed civilizations for the sake of status. The gods of this age—oh, yes. Discord already ran loose in the world. This artifact was meant to overpower those who sowed chaos. Use the values of the age to turn the tables.

His role as the Keeper of the Storeroom had given him understanding. How did a mortal gain such wisdom? His family had been living with this power in their cellar for over three thousand years. She wondered: Who had been the first? Who from the age of heroes had founded this line?

She nodded to him with the respect he'd earned.

He pulled something else out of his pocket: a cell phone. He offered her both, one in each hand.

"You need energy. You need a life to do this thing. Take mine."

The sacrifice had to be willing. He was. And she was sure she had the skill to guide such power.

"Are you sure?"

"I have a condition. A request. This is for my daughter. To keep her safe. Build a world that will keep her safe."

"I will. To the best of my ability, I will."

He reached out with the apple. She covered it with one hand, touching both its gold surface and his cool flesh, creating a link. After three thousand years of waiting, she felt the object's power—the hum of an oncoming storm.

With her other hand, she took the phone. It was already on. Deftly, she dialed with her thumb, checked the screen briefly, then met Frank Walker's gaze.

This would be myth. This would be turned into metaphor and told in stories. The two of them would be the founders of a new age.

She didn't turn away as the phone rang against her ear. Then, there was an answer.

"Hello, yes," she said. "I'd like to order a delivery."

In a secret room in a distant city, the power brokers worked their spells. The lobbyist from one country, the general from another, the president of a corporation that did business with them all. They moved their pieces across the board and manipulated the world to their best advantage.

Then came a knock on the door.

A lackey answered it. There was a man in the uniform of a delivery service. He offered them a square box, small enough to fit in a hand, wrapped in plain paper, unmarked but for an address which read:

FOR THE GREATEST.

Evie found the flashlight and went to the Storeroom. The box, he'd said. Which box? She didn't have a clue. The room was a jumble of antiques and knick-knacks, forgotten museum pieces. Lore and treasures. Her mother's writing was still on the shelf, as if it held some magic other than memories.

Alex had stopped at the threshold. He was almost laughing, hysterical, when he said, "I still can't go in there."

She shook her head, clearing it of a sudden certainty that Alex belonged here if she wanted him to be here. The power of this place was *hers*.

"Alex." She went to him and reached out her hand. "Sinon. I think you belong here. You fell out of time, didn't you? Like everything else here. An artifact of legend, forgotten by the myths."

He wore a strange, distant smile. "Forgotten, eh? Dante wrote a place for me in hell. Shakespeare used my name. I became a metaphor for treachery. But—if I could change the past, I wouldn't. Not a minute of it," he said with a frantic edge. "The past brought me here."

When he wouldn't take her hand, she took his, so they were connected across the threshold. "They all thought you died, and you didn't. You belong here."

"*Moros maruma moo emetrei. . . .*"

She narrowed her eyes, inquiring.

"It's something Cassandra said. Fate has measured out my thread . . . to a frayed end. I'd forgotten." He squeezed her hand.

She pulled him into the Storeroom.

He looked at her; then he looked around. "Gods, this place is unreal."

Merlin waited outside the Storeroom. Arthur was at the top of the stairs. He scurried down a few more steps when the sound of wood and metal groaned above them, crashing with the noise of destruction.

"The house is collapsing!" Arthur called.

"We should hurry," Alex said.

"But I don't know what to do." She looked around. There was something she was supposed to save. Something more important than the end of the world itself.

On top of a crate, she found a neatly folded leather bag. The bag was part of this. It had been here from the beginning.

She was on the verge of knowing.

Alex stared at the lyre on the shelves. His hand paused an inch or two from touching it. He clenched a fist and drew away. "It reminds me of someone," he said when he caught her watching him.

Next he turned to the rack of weapons. He pointed, his hand shaking a little. "I might need a sword," he said softly. "Could I have this one?"

It wasn't the best sword on the rack, dull and bronze-looking, ancient and stubby compared with some of the more impressive broadswords around it. She expected the odd voice to resist. But it didn't argue.

"Sure," she said. "Take it."

His face lit with wonder. "Apollo gave me this sword."

The room had never mentioned that. When he came to the door wanting something, she could have given him this.

But it wouldn't have killed him, and that was what he wanted.

Then the voice flared, screaming. She screamed to match it and fell, her knees striking the concrete, her hands at her temples.

And she knew that her father was dead. In that moment, she knew everything else as well. Everything she needed.

Alex was at her side, holding her. Heart pounding, she said, "Help me find it. We've got to find it. A box. A small box." She showed dimensions with her hands.

She shoved aside a stack of folded banners and a pile of reptilian scales the size of her hands. She listened to the voice whispering *you're getting close.*

"My lady, you'd best hurry," Merlin called from the next room.

Plank by plank, the ceiling flew away, screeching with the agony of destruction. Spaces of open sky showed through swirling dust and debris. The walls, the roof, were gone. Smelling of brimstone, howling air pulled at her, lifting her. Around her, scraps of cloth and paper, splinters and shrapnel, flew upward. Her ears popped, wind thundering around her. Alex held the waistband of her jeans with one hand and the sword with the other. He anchored her, or she might have flown away as well. Together, they crouched on the floor, protecting each other.

There, shoved far back under a bottom shelf, was a box, small enough to sit on a girl's lap. It was made of simple wood, bound with bronze hinges. A latch secured the lid.

Stretching, she was able to reach it. She clawed it from its resting place and hugged it to her chest. She still had the sack draped over one arm, but no time to put anything else in it.

"She's coming!" Arthur cried.

The wind's ferocity never dimmed, even though Hera had what she wanted. But she wanted Discord and destruction, and she was getting it. Shelves toppled, boxes lifted from their places. The contents of the Storeroom were being sucked into the funnel of a tornado, which seemed to roar with a human voice.

"Now, Merlin! Now!" Evie cried.

"Come on!" Merlin said from the other side of the doorway.

Alex wrapped his arm around her middle and hauled her to her feet. They ran. Merlin pointed at them as they passed through what remained of the doorway.

"Blessings on you both," he said, a wild look in his eyes, his hair blown in a halo around his face. "We'll see you on the other side!"

Then the doorway disappeared, showing a rectangle of light instead. They went through it, to searing light and a room with no air. She hoped Alex was holding her, because she couldn't feel him anymore. She tried to scream, but could not breathe. But she held the box, and the voice that told her what it was, told her that her father had died for it. All he knew, she now knew. And there was no time.

James drove. They'd gotten out just in time. Behind them, the interstate was being closed down, all traffic stopped. Homeland Security had raised the alert status to red, severe. The government expected an attack at any moment. They weren't even sure from whom. China, India, Russia—did it matter?

Along with six people, the SUV was crammed with supplies like tents, sleeping bags, tools, and bags of groceries: canned food, bottled water, toilet paper. Bruce had known some of his friends occasionally displayed far-out survivalist tendencies—they planned stuff like this for fun during gaming sessions. Now, he was grateful. He wouldn't have thought of toilet paper.

Callie lay against him, her head pillowed on his shoulder, crying silently. Numbly, he held her. The radio blared a static-laden news report on NPR:

"—been an exchange of nuclear armaments on the Asian continent, no word yet on what targets—"

The weather had chosen to reflect the current mood of world politics. Black thunderclouds barred all sunlight; the world was dark. James gripped the steering wheel, struggling to hold the vehicle on its course against a terrible wind. It howled and battered debris against the windows.

"Holy shit! Look at that!" Tony, James's roommate, pressed his face to the window and craned his neck, looking up. "Do you see it? Do you see it?"

Bruce looked out his own window and tried to see. He had to look almost straight up, as straight up as he could, to directly over the car.

Funnel clouds. A dozen winding, fingerlike swirls of twisting clouds snaked down from the storm, stretching ahead of them to the horizon.

They couldn't do anything but keep driving. There was no escaping this.

"So where are they, man?" Tony said.

Bruce glared at him. "Who?"

"The Four Horsemen."

It wasn't funny.

A flash filled the sky. They all shut their eyes, or turned away to avoid the flare. Lightning. In a storm like this, it had to be lightning.

If a nuclear bomb struck, would they even know it?

The radio cut out with a high-pitched whine.

If the world ended, would anything come after? Would they be able to look back and know what had happened?

Bruce closed his eyes and pressed his face to Callie's. "I love you."

A second flash came, white hot, and he never saw the end of it.

Hera entered the Walker house. The game was in motion, the power was in play, but there were a few loose ends left here. She would leave no loose ends.

Part of her entourage flanked her: the Curandera at her right hand, the Wanderer at her left. She still had to see about the girl. She owed it to Frank Walker to make sure she was safe.

Such a prosaic little house to serve as a repository for such great treasures. It was a common trick, hide something beautiful in something plain, disguise the desirable with the humble. It had worked, for a time. Now, though, the house's roof had blown off, and debris buzzed in a whirlwind around them. The storm was ripping the house apart to its foundations. Hera and her lieutenants moved in a sphere of calm, protected and untroubled.

The Wanderer moved a few steps away. "Look, there," he said, gesturing Hera closer.

On his side, half his face bloody and caved in, lay Robin Goodfellow. Beardless, boyish, and innocent—even dead, he looked like everything he was not. She'd told him not to attack the house on his own. She'd asked him to wait, and he'd said he would, with that mischievous glint in his eye that indicated he didn't care if she thought he was lying. He'd always had his own agenda, and she never cared, as long as it didn't interfere with hers.

It didn't, even now.

"Come," she said, and drew the others away from him.

The Storeroom was in the basement. In her space of calm, she went down the stairs, as the world howled around her.

At the base of the stairs, Arthur and Merlin stood guarding the doorway to the Storeroom.

They weren't guarding much. The ceiling spun up and away, piece by piece, floorboards and wiring ripping and disappearing into the storm, pipes and ducts exposed like bones. Arthur held his sword, the legendary Excalibur, in both hands, and stood with his feet apart and well braced, his blond hair flying around his face. He grinned up at her, maniacal. Beside him, Merlin gazed with chilling calm, standing as if they were in a park on a summer day. He had enough power to be a god. She wouldn't even have to train him, as she would the others.

What would she have to bribe them with, to bring them to her side?

"Arthur!"

Merlin tugged the warrior's arm. Arthur laughed, spun, ducked through the doorway into the Storeroom—and disappeared.

The wizard offered a brief salute to Hera and followed him. A light sparked around the doorway and was still, and the door was just a door, leading to a room in the process of being ravaged by a tornado.

She saw no sign at all of Evie Walker and the Greek.

She finished the walk from the stairs to the door of the Storeroom. The ceiling was gone now; the walls were following, and the contents of the room—shelves of artifacts, boxes and bags, spears and swords, cabinets of gowns, crowns, golden balls, ancient horns, lyres, flutes, and bones—spun up and away, caught in the whirlwind, and disappeared. All that magic, flying back into the world, scattering, and the cycle would begin again, the stories would begin again.

She raised her hands and laughed as notebook paper covered in writing fluttered around her.

Family, loyalty, duty. The stories his father told named these as the greatest attributes a man could have. All honor came from the way one behaved toward one's family, friends, and comrades in arms. Abstract virtues were all well and good, but they could be twisted to serve unworthy ends or unscrupulous people. One marked the greatness of a man not by the crown upon his head, but by his actions.

Telemachus didn't know his father until he was full grown. He didn't hear these stories until he was a man with children of his own, and Odysseus told them to his grandchildren. But Telemachus knew the lessons because he had grown up with a symbol of them more powerful than any story Odysseus told: his mother, Penelope, at her loom. Her loyalty to Odysseus never wavered. Watching her, Telemachus learned of family, loyalty, and duty.

Telemachus never thought of having adventures of his own. His father's adventures were so famous, how could the son ever match them? He would be content to stay at home and have the quiet life his father had missed.

He forgot, though, that Odysseus hadn't asked for his adventures, and one day a stranger came to his door.

16

Sinon had thought Prometheus would open an enchanted doorway, and they would step through to the land of Ithaca in an instant. But he didn't. They took a boat.

As Sinon stepped onto the shore of the island of Ithaca, he wrapped the edge of his cloak over his shoulder against the chill autumn breeze coming off the water.

"How long has it been since you've been back?" the man—man?—beside him asked.

"I set sail with Odysseus. Ten years before the fall of Troy." That was how he marked time now. Before the fall of Troy, and after.

"Has it changed much?"

"I don't know."

It hadn't changed, at least at first glance. Time played tricks, and he was a young man again, waiting to go to war. He expected to recognize faces in the village. He thought he did, almost. But he looked again, and saw that there were more houses, in different places. The fishing huts he had expected to see farther up the beach were gone. A stone wall separated the beach from the town. That hadn't been there before. Many people worked and traveled on the path leading from the dock, all of them strangers. The island had prospered. And why not, when Odysseus had led them all these years?

"Are you coming?"

He shouldn't. What would he say when he got there? "Yes."

He still knew the way to Odysseus's manor. He led Prometheus there.

It, too, seemed the same: a stucco wall surrounded the house, but the wooden gate stood wide open, welcoming visitors. Chickens scratched in the dirt, children played with dogs, women worked in the yard spinning wool and hanging wash to dry. Odysseus had lands with tenants, servants and wealth. He was as much a king as Agamemnon had ever been, though unlike Agamemnon, Odysseus had never cared for crowns or displays of power.

Sinon stood at the gate for a long time, hugging himself under his cloak. Prometheus waited for him, and Sinon was about to give in to his second thoughts and turn around, when a boy almost grown, fifteen or sixteen years old, came around the corner and leaned on the wall. He had dark shoulder-length hair and a proud tilt to his chin.

"Sirs, are you needing shelter?"

I know that face, Sinon thought. He glanced away to hide his look of wonder.

Prometheus had to speak for them. "I was told in the village that this house is famous for its hospitality."

The boy beamed, his smile lighting his face. "It is! That is, if the guests are polite. This is the house of Odysseus, my grandfather. Have you heard of Odysseus?"

"Of course I have. His tales are famous from one end of the Mediterranean to the other."

"I'll go get my father. Come in!" The boy stepped between them, took them by their elbows, and pulled them into the yard. Then he ran off behind the house.

"Friendly lad," Prometheus said with a grin.

Sinon studied the house and its yard, the work going on, every face that eyed him curiously and gave him a smile. This was the life he might have had. A wife and children. A farm. Laughter.

He couldn't go back.

A moment later, the boy returned, running ahead of a slim man of middle age. He had gray in his dark hair and beard, but his expression was bright, his body strong, and his long stride almost kept up with the boy's enthusiasm.

"Father, here are the strangers!" the boy said proudly, as if he had found treasure.

The older man smiled and came forward. "Give me your arms, strangers, and rest with us awhile. I am Telemachus. This is my youngest son, Polymedes."

Prometheus offered his hand, and the men gripped each other's wrists. Telemachus repeated the gesture with Sinon.

Sinon said, "Son of Odysseus. I am honored to meet you." He had his father's eyes. *Gods, Odysseus must be so proud of him.* "I am—Call me Phaetus."

"And I am Inachus," said Prometheus.

"Welcome. Come in and take rest."

The boy Polymedes ran ahead, and Sinon asked, "How many children do you have?"

"Ten, may the gods help me." He laughed.

Telemachus guided them inside and brought food and drink while they sat at a table near the hearth. The household gathered for the evening meal, and everyone treated them as honored guests. Prometheus sat at Telemachus's right hand, Sinon sat beside Prometheus, and they listened to the stories of the day: of cats that caught mice, of a child learning to walk, of a fisherman's son courting a daughter of the household.

Sinon knew what he looked like—a strapping warrior of perhaps thirty years of age, a little worn by travel, but at his prime. Certainly not old enough to have seen Troy fall. Telemachus would think himself a good twenty or thirty years older. Sinon tried to remember that, and when his host asked questions about where he came from and what he did with himself, he tried to make appropriate answers—answers that weren't lies and yet hid the truth. *I've worked as a sailor. We fought off pirates once.* Prometheus spoke little, watching the proceedings with a pleased smile.

Before the meal was served, Polymedes and a maiden a year or two older than he entered, between them guiding an ancient man stooped with age, his hair thinned to wisps. Before thinking, Sinon stood, leaning on the table to steady himself. He had prepared himself for this sight. Nonetheless, he wasn't ready for it.

Telemachus leaned over to whisper to Prometheus and Sinon.

"The storytellers call him Many-Minded. I must warn you: Age has taken most of those minds from him. My mother's death last year nearly destroyed him. But I still honor him as head of this household. At least in spirit." He moved to take his son's place by the old man's side and helped guide him to the head of the table.

Odysseus, his skin gray and loose on his bones, swatted them away. "Leave me, leave me. I'm not crippled, curse the lot of you." His voice cracked, and he kept shaking his head. His eyes were clouded.

Sinon thought he might weep.

The girl said, "Grandfather, remember your manners. We have guests this evening."

"Curse them, too!"

She looked quickly at Sinon and Prometheus. "He doesn't mean it, sirs. Please don't mind him."

"I know," Sinon said gently.

They ate. Sinon stole glances at the old man. Halfway through the meal, Sinon caught him staring back. Their gazes met, and Sinon almost dropped his knife.

He's pretending, Sinon thought. *He* knows.

At the end of the meal, the two grandchildren guided him away. When they passed by Sinon, the old man fell. Everyone in the room jumped. Sinon reached to catch him, but Odysseus stopped his own fall by grabbing Sinon's arm. His knobbed, arthritic hands dug into his skin.

Odysseus stared hard at him. Sinon wanted to hug the old man tight enough to break bones. But his grandchildren righted him quickly and led him out of the hall.

"Are you all right?" Prometheus whispered, his brow lined with concern.

Sinon nodded. "I'm just a bit shaken. Being here again, seeing him again, is so strange."

"You'll never get used to your friends growing old without you."

Telemachus touched Sinon's shoulder. "Let me show you your rooms."

At the end of the hall, Prometheus stopped them and spoke in a low voice. "Telemachus, I would speak with you privately, if you're willing. I need help, and I think you're the man for it."

And so Prometheus would charge Telemachus with guarding the treasures of the gods, would enchant this family, this household, and they could never have the peace Odysseus had earned for them. Would Prometheus give Telemachus the chance to refuse? Would Telemachus refuse? Sinon doubted it.

Prometheus turned to follow Telemachus down the passage, to the room where they would have their conversation.

In the middle of the night, Sinon went searching for Odysseus. He had marked which part of the house he'd been taken to. He listened at the doorways of bedchambers and entered the one where he heard no snoring.

Odysseus's bed was empty, the coverlet pushed aside. The old man sat by the window, leaning on a cane, looking out at the moonlit ocean.

Sinon cleared his throat. Odysseus didn't react, so Sinon said, "Will His Lordship indulge a visitor so late?"

Odysseus looked at him sideways and shook his

head. "I know now that I am truly mad, because I see a ghost. A ghost has come into my house. I see the ghosts of all my dead warriors behind your face, Sinon."

Sinon entered the room and leaned on the wall by the window. What could he tell this man? What insanity had brought him here, to see his hero in such a state? *I had to tell him.* Explain what had happened to him, why he hadn't sailed home from Troy.

He hadn't had a chance to tell anyone good-bye.

"You're pretending, aren't you? You're not as senile as you're letting on. It's your way of letting go, of letting them take over the running of the household without feeling your authority hanging over them."

Odysseus snorted. "I don't know what you're talking about. I'm mad. Demented. Everyone says it. So should you."

That was a message. *Don't tell them my secret. Don't say it aloud, even in private. Don't even think it.*

"I defer to your wisdom, old friend."

"Your face," the old man said. "It's just like it was. Oh—" His eyes widened, a new realization overcoming him. "It isn't you. You—you're Athena in disguise. My lady, you've made yourself look like Sinon—why? What message do you have for me?"

"I'm not—Odysseus, my lord, I really am—" He looked away, tears pricking his eyes. He should not have come. He should not have disturbed an old man with ghosts.

He straightened. He tried to make his gaze and manner as imperious as Athena's. "Rest easy, my friend.

I only wished to look upon you and see that you are well."

"I am well. But tired. Very tired, and haunted by too many ghosts."

Sinon squeezed the old man's shoulder, then returned to his room, where he lay awake all night, staring at the ceiling.

The next morning, Telemachus's mood seemed subdued. Or Sinon may only have imagined that it was. His family acted no differently, as they would have if anything had been wrong. Prometheus was the same, but he no longer carried his leather satchel. So Telemachus had accepted the task of guarding the artifacts. Sinon wondered what the immortal had told him to convince him to say yes. Perhaps the man felt some sort of overwhelming sense of duty.

The family breakfasted. Odysseus didn't join them. After, Telemachus saw them off at the gate of the manor. He offered them a few days' provisions. They accepted, as befitted the laws of hospitality. When Sinon blessed Telemachus and his house, he did so without calling on the gods, so the words would be true. Outside Olympus, no one had noticed the destruction of the gods. And what did that say?

Prometheus commented on this, as they walked the road to the village. "You didn't name any gods to bless him."

"Of course not."

"It sounded strange, don't you think?"

He hadn't called upon the gods in a long time. It didn't sound strange at all. He shook his head.

"What will you do now?" Prometheus asked.

Before coming here, Sinon had thought he might settle down, farm, find a wife, as he'd been destined to do at his birth. But he couldn't do that now.

He could see the ocean from here. "Maybe I can hire onto a boat. See if I remember how to sail. Travel to the ends of the earth. How does that sound?"

"It sounds marvelous," Prometheus said. "I commend that plan."

Which, surprisingly, made Sinon feel a little better. "What will you do?"

"I think I'll travel as well." He didn't look across the water, though, but up, neck craned back, squinting into the sun. "To the sky, the stars. There are other worlds than this one. I'd like to see them."

He would go to live among the constellations, the myths and legends preserved in the night sky. A fitting end to his story. In the coming nights, Sinon would look for a new collection of stars.

"Will you ever return?"

"I doubt it. I don't think humankind needs my help anymore. Or wants it, really."

They reached a fork in the road, one branch leading to the village and the other leading to the hills, where shepherds took their sheep and goats to graze. Prometheus offered his hand, and Sinon gripped his wrist, as if they were two friends on the road, and nothing more.

"I leave you here. Live well, Sinon of Ithaca," Prometheus said, then departed along the path that led to the hills.

Sinon watched him for a moment, thought of running after him, to beg him to take him along—*there's nothing left on earth for me now.* But Prometheus's departure seemed much like a dismissal. If the immortal had wanted a companion, he would have offered to take Sinon along.

Sinon went to the village and the ocean, hired onto a ship setting sail for Egypt, and left Ithaca forever.

17

❧

Evie awoke cradled in Alex's lap. She curled around the box, covering it with her body. He draped one arm across her back, and with the other hand he stroked her head, running his fingers through her hair. He was singing softly, absently, the notes faltering. The words were lilting—Greek.

He sat propped against a slab of gray rock.

She stirred. He drew his hands away; she missed them. She could have stayed cradled with him forever, and with him, that really meant something.

Their rock was one of many set in a wide circle. They were old, lichen covered, weathered. Lintels joined some, and broken slabs lay about. Farther out, lower marker stones were scattered on a plain of green grass, the color deep and striking against the slate of the stones, and the rolling gray clouds of the overcast sky. The breeze was warm, summerlike. It should have been—it used to be—December. It should have been cold.

Merlin had sent them to Stonehenge—but it wasn't, because the plain overlooked an ocean. A cliff sloped down to a rocky beach where waves rushed and crashed. The air smelled of salt and seaweed. There were no roads, no gift shop, no barriers to keep out the graffiti artists. They were cast into a desolate world. A desolate time.

"What is this?"

"I think it's Stonehenge. Or it used to be Stonehenge. Or it will be—" He shook his head. "I don't know. I used to be able to recognize it when the gods played with time."

She started to sit up, then changed her mind. The moment was so peaceful, she should be able to rest. Like Tess of the d'Urbervilles, who slept at Stonehenge before they came to hang her.

"It's all gone," she said, her face pressed against Alex's thigh. Irrationally, she thought of her laptop on the coffee table. She laughed, and pinched her nose to keep the sound from turning into a sob. "I'll never find out what happens to Tracker."

"Don't you know?"

"Not really. I keep writing to see what happens next."

"Then tell me. Tell me now what happens to her."

She did, the last pages of storyline, Tracker's trek across Siberia, her loneliness, confusion, the desperation as she signaled for the helicopter, betting her life that whoever she called would help her and not kill her, and that moment when she saw the American flag, the symbol she'd devoted her life to, and didn't know if it meant she was saved or damned. And she didn't know what happened next. She hadn't decided if the men in the helicopter were good guys or bad guys. It was such a little tragedy.

"I can't decide if the end should be happy or sad," she said. "By all rights, Talon should step out of the helicopter and save her. That should be his uniform she sees. But it seems too easy. She spent the whole book learning how to save herself."

"I think it should have a happy ending. She learned to save herself, yes. But she can still get help now and then," he said. "I'd like your story to have a happy ending."

Me, too, she thought. "I hope Arthur and Merlin are okay." She didn't think she'd ever see them again. She and Alex had been yanked out of the old world and brought to a new one. She hoped they arrived here, too, and were just somewhere else. And Bruce, and everybody, and the world could get back to normal.

"I imagine they are," he said absently. His touch against her scalp was hypnotic, and she let it lull her.

He said, "Was it worth it? Was that what you were meant to save?"

"Yes." It had to be. It had to be enough. She stroked the edge of the box. It called to her; it was hers to keep and protect.

"What is it?"

She sat up, but stayed close to him, tucked under his arm. "Pandora's box."

His whole body tensed, a panicked flinch. "And that's supposed to save us?"

"Shh." Her father had been right. About everything, and the instinct spoke true after all. This was everything. They had saved it all. She unhooked the latch and opened the box.

Alex jerked, trying to reach around her to slam the lid shut, but she shifted, blocking him.

"It's okay. You know the stories—it has only one thing left inside. The only thing worth saving." Inside, resting on a piece of raw wool padding, was a small gem glowing with pure white light. No larger than a thumbnail, yet it filled her whole vision. "It's hope."

She closed the lid and latched it. The clouds swept across the sky, part of a storm, but the storm was passing. Low rumbles of thunder were distant.

"Wait here." Alex eased away, preparing to stand. The back of his T-shirt was still covered with blood, where Robin had stabbed him. The blood shone wetly—was still damp. So not too much time could have passed.

When he saw her staring at the mess, he grumbled, and pulled the shirt off, showing his tanned, muscular body that had been fighting for three thousand years.

He still had the sword he'd claimed in the Storeroom. Holding it ready, he moved a dozen paces away and looked intently up the coast.

A figure approached, a woman in a black evening gown, a chiffon scarf dancing behind her in the wind. She should have had trouble walking across the soft earth in high heels, but she came with smooth, untroubled steps, her chin lifted, her arms easy at her sides.

Alex waited in a ready stance, standing guard. There, at last, Evie saw it: the Greek warrior who must have stood on the beach before Troy, his body sculpted, the muscles of his arms tensed, holding his sword at the ready, gripped easily in his hand. His face was calm.

The woman stopped, her gaze resting on Evie, who clutched Pandora's box, then on Alex.

"You live," she said, smiling. "It took me forever to find you. Relatively speaking."

"But it's only been a few—," Evie began, but Hera silenced her with a look that clearly made a comment regarding Evie's ignorance.

"I've vowed to protect her," Alex said, indicating Evie over his shoulder. "If you come any closer, I will strike you."

"Me? You worshipped me at your hearth fire when you were a boy. Your mother held your hand to help you light the offering. And you would strike me?"

"I've learned so much since then. We're no different, you and I."

She reached, like she was going to touch his cheek. He recoiled, leveling the sword's point as a barrier between them.

"Oh, we are different. You are still afraid, and I am not."

She slashed with her hand, an arc of motion across his middle. He parried, but she cut him without touching him, without coming close to his sword. The skin parted. Blood welled and dripped. He grunted and stepped back, holding his belly with one hand, keeping the sword leveled with the other. Then he straightened, ran his hand along the wound—and he was whole. The cut healed. Gripping the sword two-handed, he lunged, driving the point at her.

As easily as she might have touched the wind, she pushed his arm aside, stepped out of the way, and threw him. He flew back, smashing into one of the standing stones. A bloody wound flowered on his temple.

He looked up, glaring. His breath came hard, hissing through clenched teeth. He scrambled to put himself back between Evie and Hera.

Evie watched, awe-filled and trembling. She—her family—weren't supposed to be part of the stories. They were keepers of the stories. But that world was gone now, wasn't it? Magic was real, all the sparking, hand-waving, spell-weaving magic of the stories was real.

Hera raised her hand, and with the motion Alex levitated. Hovering a foot off the ground, he struggled in an invisible grip, cutting with his sword, kicking with his feet. She flattened her hand, and he slammed back against the stone and stayed there. His arms wrenched back, wrists against the stone, riveted as if held by chains. He grimaced with the pressure and dropped the sword.

They'd escaped. They'd earned a happy ending—as happy as the situation allowed. But Hera had found them. It wasn't fair.

Evie hesitated, part of her wanting to run away, take what was left of the Storeroom and try to escape, to protect it.

But she couldn't leave Alex.

"Let him go," she said. Fear made her voice soft. "Leave him alone."

He decided he wanted to die when he heard of the Great Alexander's death. There'd never again be anyone worth following, worth dying for. He fought in the army that had conquered every corner of the world his people knew at that time. He gladly followed the general who reminded him so much of the heroes of his youth, the legends who occupied so many songs and stories. He'd thought perhaps another age of legends was upon them. But history had replaced mythology, Herodotus instead of Homer, and Alexander died. Sinon took his name as a memorial and began to look for a way to die himself. Because it was the only work he knew, he fought as a mercenary in a hundred armies over the next thousand years. He never found another hero to follow.

But he would follow Evie.

After all this time, Sinon—Alex—found he was afraid. He didn't want to die after all. Evie stood nearby. She seemed waiflike in her jeans and sweater, her brown hair tangled in the breeze, her skin pale, chilled. He wanted to tell her to run. But where could she go? Hera would find her. He had to protect her.

Fine job of that he was doing, pinned to a slab of rock. He hadn't dealt with the gods on their terms in a long time. He'd forgotten what they were like—children, pulling the wings off flies. How could the fly fight back?

Hera turned her hand, and he slid to the ground, his back scraping on the stone. His feet touched earth again, but he remained immobilized. Step by easy step she approached, and he realized she could kill him. All that remained was to see how she did it.

"Leave him alone," Evie said. She tensed, like she might dash forward and take Hera on herself. Alex started to tell her to stop, but Hera turned to her first.

"Wait," she said, holding out a manicured hand. "I wish to speak with him, that's all. I've no wish to harm you."

"Like you harmed my father."

Hera gave Evie a long-suffering glance, then paid her no more attention than if she had disappeared.

The goddess turned the full charm of her smile on Alex.

"I know what you want, more than anything else."

Wool and fog, that was the old trick to keep them from knowing what he thought. It didn't work this time, because all his thoughts turned to Evie. Apollo would have laughed at him.

Hera touched his neck, sending gooseflesh rising on his skin. He couldn't flinch away.

Die. He wanted to die more than anything.

No, before that, what had he wanted? On the shores of Troy, during the years of the war, what had they wanted, what had Odysseus spoken of with the light of a distant hearth fire in his eyes? A home, a family. Impossible now.

Hera laid her fingers on the chain around his neck.

"How much a part of you is this? Will you crumble to dust without it? If I take it away, will you die, or will it leave you as you were when Apollo captured you? Say the word, Sinon of Ithaca, and I will remove it. I have that power now."

It was a part of him. Its power sustained him. Without it . . . He looked sideways, at Evie, caught her gaze.

If he died now, he wouldn't have to watch her grow old and die without him.

"Why would you do this?" he said harshly. He didn't trust her. He hated being trapped. He had thought he was done with the gods.

"Curiosity. I want to see what happens."

That was an answer he'd expect from one of the lords of Olympus. His jaw was tense, his whole body painfully tense. "All right. Take it off."

His skin tingled when she brushed her hand along

the chain. She stroked the bronze links, lifted the chain, ran her fingers underneath it, a sensual motion. He closed his eyes.

Apollo, Zeus, Athena, Demeter, Hera, may all the gods protect me and have mercy on me.

She stepped away, and he felt so light that he thought he was floating. His shoulders were light, his neck, all of it, like air. He felt like he was going to fall.

He touched his neck. It was bare. He opened his eyes. Hera stood before him, the broken chain in her outstretched hand.

He felt his own body, his chest and arms, his face. He was still here. He was alive. The next sword he took in the gut would kill him.

Hera held his hand and placed the chain in it, closing his fingers around it. "Sometimes you do get what you want. You just have to wait longer for it than you expect."

He marveled at the chain. It was dull, and trembled slightly with the shaking of his hand. Then it slipped from his fingers, and he fell to his knees.

"Zeus couldn't do this for me," he said, gasping. His life, it was over— No. His life could now continue.

"It probably didn't occur to him to try," she said wryly. She turned to Evie. "And now for you."

"If you harm her—," Alex said, as if he could still make threats after the goddess had defeated him.

Hera ignored him. Evie could only brace for whatever came next.

The goddess reached behind her back, turned her hand, and pulled an object out of the air. She offered it to Evie. "I'm finished with it. It's done its work. Now I'd like you to keep it safe."

It was the apple, sitting innocuously in her hand.

Evie's mouth opened, caught on a disbelieving laugh. "You killed my father for this, and now you're just giving it back?"

Hera said, "After all is said and done, I discover that you are still the Keeper of the Storeroom. As I said, I have no more use for this, now that I have the world the way I want it. I certainly don't want it lying around to cause trouble. You must keep it."

Yes, said the instinct, the voice that had spoken to her ancestors in an unbroken line across centuries. *Keep it safe. Take a bit of Discord out of the world.*

She raised her hand, and Hera set the apple into it. It felt massive, heavy as lead. Evie's hand dropped to her side.

Hera started to walk away.

"Wait," Evie said. "What now? What world is this? What happens next?"

Pausing to turn to her, to take Alex in with her glance as well, she shrugged. "You'll have to figure that out for yourselves. A few survivors of the old world are scattered here and there. Seedlings, if you will. You could find them, start a village together, learn to herd goats or some such. I expect that's what Arthur and Merlin are off doing."

"Where are they?" Evie asked, hopeful. They had to be here, if she could find them . . . nothing would change.

Hera frowned. "Staying well out of my way. But you—if you say a prayer to me now and then, I may listen."

Hera, poised and untroubled, walked away, over the hill, and was gone.

"Unbelievable," Alex muttered, following with a curt laugh. "That beats everything."

Evie went to him. He still knelt, his face creased with what seemed like anguish, or ecstasy.

"Are you all right?" she said.

He looked at her and laughed. "I don't know. I don't know anything anymore. But I think I am."

She sat in front of him. His sword was within reach. "You can die now."

"I know. But I don't want to. The moment she appeared, I didn't want to. When she said she knew what I wanted, she knew better than I did—because I was thinking of you."

They didn't have much. A sword, a box of hope, a leather sack. A broken chain. Each other. A happy ending, of sorts. Discord's apple sitting in her hand, golden and warm. She tucked it inside the sack, where it lay inert and harmless.

She picked up the chain, which seemed frail and innocuous now.

"I'd like to bury that somewhere," Alex said.

She shook her head. "No, you shouldn't do that." Above, clouds raced and tumbled, leaving behind a clean scent of rain. She breathed deeply. "It should go in the new Storeroom."

Sing to me, Muse, of the Lady and Lord who thus came to a desert
After the storms razed and ravaged their home, after fleeing the goddess

*Hera of Wrath, bent on vengeance most grave. On
the Plains of the great stones*
*Peace gave them rest, the storms broke, the skies
calmed; thus was born a new world.*
*Lady of Guardians took as her husband the Long-
Lived Achaean.*

Turn the page for a preview of

After the Golden Age

C A R R I E   V A U G H N

Available in April 2011
from Tom Doherty Associates

TOR® A TOR HARDCOVER   ISBN 978-0-7653-2555-6

I

Celia took the late bus home, riding along with other young workaholic professionals, the odd student, and late-shift retail clerks. A quiet, working bunch, cogs and wheels that kept Commerce City running.

Only a block away from the office, the person in the seat behind her leaned forward and spoke in her ear:

"Get off at the next stop."

She hadn't noticed him before. He was ordinary; in his thirties, he had a rugged, stubbled face, and wore jeans and a button-up shirt. He looked like he belonged. With a lift of his brow, he glared at her over the back of the plastic seat and raised the handgun from his lap. Without moving his gaze, he pushed the stop call button by the window.

Damn, not again.

Her heart pounded hard—with anger. Not fear, she reminded herself. Her fists clenched, her face a mask, she stood. She could hardly move her legs, wanting only to turn and throttle the bastard for interrupting her evening.

He stood with her, following a step behind as she moved forward toward the door. He could stop her before she called to the driver for help. And what could the driver do, but stand aside as her kidnapper waved the gun at him?

She was still two miles from home. She could try to run—in pumps and a dress suit. Right. Really, she only had to run far enough away to duck into a corner and call 9-1-1. Or her parents.

9-1-1. That was what she'd do.

She didn't dig in the pocket of her attaché for her phone. Did nothing that would give away her plan. She stepped off the bus, onto the sidewalk. Her kidnapper disembarked right behind her.

"Turn right. Walk five steps."

She turned right. Her muscles tensed, ready—

The bus pulled away. She prepared to launch herself into a run.

A sedan stopped at the curb. Two men jumped out of the back, and the kidnapper from the bus grabbed her arm. The three surrounded her and spirited her into the car, which rolled away in seconds.

They'd planned this, hadn't they?

In the backseat, one of the men tied her hands in front of her with nylon cord. The other pressed a gun to her ribs.

The one from the bus sat on the passenger side of the front seat and looked back at her.

"You're Warren and Suzanne West's daughter."

Not like this was news.

"What will the Olympiad do to keep you safe?"

"You'll have to ask them," she said.

"I will." He grinned, a self-satisfied, cat-with-the-canary grin that she recognized from a half-dozen two-bit hoodlums who thought they'd done something clever, that they'd figured out how to corner the Olympiad. As if no one else had tried this before.

"What are you going to do with me?" She said it perfunctorily. It was a way to make conversation. Maybe distract him.

His grin widened. "We're going to send your parents a message. With the Destructor out of the picture, the city's wide open for a new gang to move in. The Olympiad is going to stay out of our way, or you get hurt."

He really was stupid enough to tell her his plan. Amateurs.

Wasn't much she could do until he'd sent the message and the Olympiad learned what had happened. She'd leave the hard work to them. She always did.

Then, of course, they blindfolded her so she couldn't keep track of their route. By the time they stopped, she had no idea where they were. Someplace west, by the docks maybe. The air smelled of concrete and industry.

A stooge on each arm pulled her out of the car and guided her down a corridor. They must have parked inside a building. Her feet stepped on tile, and the walls felt close. Finally, they pushed her into a hard wooden chair and tied her wrists to its arms.

The blindfold came off. Before her, a video camera was mounted on a tripod.

The man from the bus stood next to the camera. She smirked at him, and his frown deepened. He probably expected her to be frightened, crying and begging him to let her go. Giving him that power of fear over her.

She had already been as frightened as she was ever likely to be in her life. This guy was nothing.

"Read this." He lifted a piece of paper with large writing.

She just wanted to go home. Have some hot cocoa and cookies. Supper had been microwave ramen and her stomach was growling. The blindfold had messed up her short red hair, making it itch, and she couldn't reach up to scratch it. Irrationally, she thought of her parents, and her anger began to turn toward them. If it wasn't for them and what they were . . .

Thinking like that had gotten her in trouble before. She focused on her captor. This was *his* fault.

She skimmed over the text, groaned. They couldn't even be a little creative. "Are you kidding?"

"Just read it."

In a frustrated monotone, she did as she was told.

"I'm Celia West, and I'm being held in an undisclosed location. If the Olympiad has not responded to their demands in six hours, my captors cannot guarantee my safety—"

"Wait. Stop."

She glared an inquiry.

"Couldn't you sound . . . you know . . . scared or something?"

"Sorry. But you know I've done this before. This isn't exactly new to me."

"*We're* different."

"They all say that."

"Shut up. Finish reading."

She raised her brow. He waved her on.

She said, "If you really want to scare everyone you'd cut off one of my fingers and send it to them. Of course, then you'd *really* piss them off. That whole nonlethal force thing might not apply then."

He stepped forward, fists clenched, like he might actually hit her. "Unless you really want me to do something like that, just stick to the script. I know what I'm doing."

"Whatever you say." She read out the usual list of demands: the Olympiad was to leave Commerce City and not interfere with the actions of the Baxter Gang— "Baxter Gang?" she added in a disbelieving aside, then shook her head and continued. They'd let her go when the Baxter Gang had the run of the city. They'd send another video in six hours to show just how mean they could be, etcetera.

The plan must have sounded so good on paper.

She made a point of not looking at the men with guns who seemed to fill the room. In truth there were only five. Even so, if she did anything more aggressive than mock the man she assumed was Baxter, they just might shoot her.

There was a time when even that wouldn't have bothered her. She remembered. She drew on that now. Don't reveal anything to them. No weakness.

She didn't want to die. What an oddly pleasing thought.

Finally, she reached the end of the script and Baxter shut off the recorder. He popped the memory card out of the camera, gave her a final glare, and left the room. The men with the guns remained.

All she could do was wait.

How it usually worked: the kidnappers sent the video to the police. The police delivered it to the Olympiad. The kidnappers expected Warren and Suzanne West to be despondent over the imminent danger toward their only child and to cave in to their every demand.

What the kidnappers never understood was that Celia West was expendable.

She'd understood that early on. When it came to choosing between her own safety or the safety of Commerce City, the city always won. She understood it, and usually even believed it herself.

She thought she might try to sleep. She'd been losing lots, with the late nights at the office. Leaning back in the chair, she breathed deeply, closed her eyes, and tried to relax. Unfortunately, relaxing in a hard-backed chair you were tied to was difficult at best. Though she imagined her falling asleep in the midst of her own kidnapping would annoy Baxter, which made her want to do it even more. But she was sweating inside her jacket and wanted to fidget.

All the breathing and attempts at relaxation did was keep her heart from racing, which was enough. She could meet the gazes of the gun-toting stooges in the room and not give in to blind panic.

Eventually, Baxter returned to the room. He eyed her warily, but didn't approach, didn't speak. He broke his minions into shifts, sending one of them for fast food. The food returned a half hour later, and they sat around a table to eat. Her stomach rumbled at the smell of cheap hamburgers. She hadn't eaten, and she needed to use a restroom.

Just breathe. She'd had to wait longer than this before. Her watch said that only three hours had passed. It was just now midnight. She had a couple more hours at least. More dramatic that way.

She might say a dozen things to aggravate Baxter.

She figured she could annoy him enough to get him to come over and hit her. That was the bored, self-destructive teenager of yore talking. And a little bit of revenge. If she ended up with a big black eye, things would go so much more badly for him later on.

Then, the waiting ended.

—*Celia, are you there?*—

It was odd, an inner whisper that felt like a thought, but which came from outside. Rather like how a psychotic must feel, listening to the voices. This one was understated, with a British accent. She'd felt Dr. Mentis's telepathic reach before. She couldn't respond in kind, not with such articulate, well-formed thoughts. Instead, she filled her mind with a *yes,* knowing he'd read it there. Along with a little bit of, *It's about time.*

—*I'm going to put the room to sleep. I'm afraid I can't pick and choose. You'll feel a little dizzy, then pass out. I wanted to warn you.*—

She kept herself from nodding. Mustn't let the erstwhile archvillains of Commerce City know anything was happening.

The guard by the door blacked out first. He shook his head, as if trying to stay awake, swayed a little, and pitched over sideways, dropping his gun. Startled, his compatriots looked over.

"Bill? Hey, Bill!"

Two at the table keeled over next. Then one standing by his chair. Baxter stood and stared at them, looking from one to another with growing urgency. Her vision was swimming. Squinting to focus, she braced, waiting, wanting it to be over.

Baxter looked at her, his eyes widening. "You. What's happening? You know, I know you know—"

He stepped forward, arm outstretched. Then he blinked, stopped, gave a shudder—

She thought she smelled sage.

—*Sleep*—

"Celia?"

The world was black and lurching. If she opened her eyes, she'd find herself on the deck of a sailing ship.

"Celia, time to wake up." A cool hand pressed her cheek.

She opened her eyes, and the light stabbed to life a headache that ran from her temples to the back of her neck.

"Ow," she said and covered her face with her hands.

"There you are. Good morning."

She was lying on the floor. Dr. Arthur Mentis knelt beside her, his brown trench coat spread around him, his smile wry. The cavalry, finally. Now she could relax.

He put an arm around her shoulders and helped her sit up. The headache shifted and pounded in another direction. She had to hold her head. On the bright side, members of the Baxter Gang were all writhing around on the floor, groaning, while the police picked them up and dragged them away.

"Sorry about the headache," he said. "It'll go away in a couple of hours."

"That's okay," she said softly, to not jostle herself. "I think I used to be better at this hostage thing."

"Are you joking? That ransom video was a riot. Even Warren laughed."

She raised her brow, disbelieving.

"Will you be all right for the next few minutes?" he said.

"Yeah."

He gave her shoulder a comforting squeeze and left her propped against the wall while he helped with cleanup. As the police collected and removed the gang members, Mentis looked each of them in the eyes, reading their minds, learning what he could from them. They wouldn't even know what was happening.

The wall around the door was scorched, streaked black with soot, and the door itself had disappeared. Spark must have had to blast it open. The room smelled toasted with that particular flavor Celia had always associated with Spark's flames: baking chocolate. Celia was surprised to find the scent comforting.

Her mother entered the room a moment later.

Suzanne West—Spark—was beautiful, marvelously svelte in her form-fitted skin suit, black with flame-colored accents. Her red hair swept thick and luxurious down her back. She moved with energy and purpose.

She paused, looked around, and found Celia. "Celia!"

This was just like old times, nearly. Suzanne crouched beside her, gripped Celia's shoulders, and pursed her face like she might cry.

Celia sighed and put her arms around her mother. Suzanne hugged back tightly. "Hi, Mom."

"Oh, Celia, are you all right?"

"Headache. But yeah. Did you guys find my bag? I had notes from work in it."

"I don't know. We'll look. I was so worried—did they hurt you? Are you okay?"

"I'm fine." She tried to stand, but the headache made her vision splotchy. The floor was nice and stable.

"Don't try to move; paramedics are on the way."

"I don't need paramedics. I just want to go home."

Suzanne sighed with frustration. "I really wish you'd come live at the plaza. It's so much safer—"

Celia shook her head. "No way. Uh-uh."

"This sort of thing wouldn't happen—"

"Mom, they picked me off the bus on the way home from work. I can't not leave home."

"What were you doing riding the bus?"

"I don't have a car."

"Celia, if you need a car we can—"

Headache or no, she wasn't sitting still to listen to this. Bracing against the wall, she got her feet under her and managed to push herself up. Suzanne reached for her, but Celia shrugged away. "I'm *fine*."

She hated being like this. She felt sixteen years old, all over again.

"Why won't you let us help you?"

The question wasn't about this, the rescue from the kidnapping, the arm to get her off the floor. It was the big question.

Celia focused on the wall, which didn't make her dizzy. "I haven't taken a cent from you in years; I'm not going to start now."

"If it'll keep you from getting assaulted like this—"

"Well, I wouldn't get assaulted like this if I weren't your daughter, would I?"

If she'd said that to her father, he would have lost his temper, broken a chair or punched through the wall with a glance, and stalked out of the room. Her mother, on the other hand . . . Suzanne's lips pursed, and her eyes reddened like she was about to cry. Instantly Celia felt guilty, but she couldn't take it back, and she couldn't apologize, because it was true.

"Everything all right?" Mentis had returned. He stood, hands in the pockets of his trench coat, and looked between the two of them inquiringly. He was in his thirties, with brown hair grown slightly shaggy and a pale, searching face. The Olympiad had been active for over ten years already when he joined, as a student at the university medical school. Despite his younger age, he still carried around with him this maddening, ancient air of wisdom.

Celia and her mother stared at one another. Mentis, the telepath, must have seen a frothing mass of pent-up frustrations and unspoken thoughts. They couldn't hide from him like they could from each other.

Nevertheless, Celia said, "Fine. I'd just like to go home and sleep off this hangover."

"Right," Mentis said. He held out her attaché case, unopened and none the worse for wear. "I think this is yours. We found it in Baxter's car."

"Thanks."

He turned to Suzanne. "We should move on. Captain and the Bullet have cleaned up the bank robberies, but two branches of the gang are still at large."

Celia paused. "What's happening?"

"This was more than a simple kidnapping," Mentis said. "It was a distraction. Baxter's people launched attacks all over the city. He wanted to see how much he could get away with while we were busy rescuing you."

If Baxter could have held her indefinitely, moving from place to place, keeping one step ahead of the Olympiad, he might have run them ragged.

They'd taken the time to rescue her.

"Detective? Could you see that Miss West arrives home safely?" Mentis called to a young man in a suit and overcoat standing near the doorway. One of the detectives on the case, he held a notepad and pencil, jotting notes as Baxter's men were escorted out. The cop looked at Mentis and nodded.

She suppressed a vague feeling of abandonment, that she could have died, and now Mentis and her mother were just leaving her alone. But she remembered: the city was more important. And Celia was always saying she could take care of herself, wasn't she?

—*You'll be fine. I have faith in you.*—Mentis's smile was wry, and Celia nodded in acknowledgment.

"Thanks," she said. "For coming after me. Tell Dad I said hi."

Suzanne crossed her arms. "You could call once in a while."

He could call me. "Maybe I will." She managed a smile for her mother and a last wave at Mentis before leaving.

The cop escorted her out of the building. "I'm Detective Paulson. Mark Paulson." Endearingly, he offered his hand, and she shook it.

"Celia West."

"Yeah, I know."

A few awkward, silent minutes brought them to the curb and a swarm of police cars, lights flashing a fireworks display on the street. A half-dozen men were occupied, keeping reporters and news cameras behind a line of caution tape. A couple of hero groupies were there as well—the creator of a low-end gossip website dedicated to the city's heroes, another guy holding up a big poster declaring: CAPTAIN OLYMPUS: OUR ALIEN SAVIOR. There were always a few lurking around every time something like this happened. Instinctively, Celia looked away and hunched her shoulders, trying to duck into her collar.

Paulson brought her to an unmarked sedan. They might actually get away without the reporters noticing. Opening the passenger side door, he helped her in.

While he situated himself and started the car, she said, "Paulson. Any relation to Mayor Paulson?"

He developed a funny little half smile. "I'm his son."

That was where she'd seen that jawline before. And the flop of dark hair. The mayor's hair had gone handsomely salt and pepper in his middle age. Mark's still shone.

"Ah," she said, grinning. "Then you know all about it. I shouldn't pry—but he wanted you to go into politics, didn't he?"

"Not quite. He wanted me to be a lawyer, then go into politics. I got the law degree. Then, well . . ." He shrugged, his glance taking in the car and the flashing lights behind them. "Then I decided I wanted to be on the front lines rather than the rear guard. Make sure no one gets off on a technicality because they weren't read their rights."

"Cool," she said.

"What about you? I mean, your parents—" He let out an awestruck sigh. And who wouldn't, after meeting Spark? "They want you to go into . . . the family business, I guess it is?"

"Oh, they certainly did. Nature had different ideas, though. I'm the offspring of Commerce City's two greatest superhumans, and the most exciting thing I ever did was win a silver medal in a high-school swim meet." Good thing she could look back on it now and laugh.

She still had that medal sitting on her dresser.

"It must have been amazing, growing up with them."

"Yeah, you could say that." The strength of her sarcasm invited no further questions.

Finally, they arrived at her apartment building. Detective Paulson insisted on walking her to her front door, as if one of the splintered Baxter Gang members would leap out of the shadows and snatch her up. She had to admit, twice in a night would be embarrassing.

"Thanks for taking me home," she said, once her door was unlocked. "I know you've got better things to do."

"Not at all," he said. "Maybe I could do it again sometime."

Though he turned away before she could read the expression on his face, she thought he was smiling. She watched him until he turned the corner.

Closing the door behind her, she shook her head. She'd imagined it. Her head was still foggy.

Later, she sat in bed, drinking a cup of chamomile tea and watching the news. All the city's "independent law-enforcement agents" were out in force, quelling the riot of criminal activity. Typhoon created floods to incapacitate a group of bank robbers. Breezeway swept them off their feet with gusts of air. Even the telekinetic Mind-masher and his on-again, off-again lover, Earth Mother, were out and about. Block Buster Senior and Junior were as usual directing their brute-force mode of combat toward a trio of vandals holed up in an abandoned convenience store. The two super-humans were taking the building apart, concrete block by concrete block, until it formed an impromptu jail. Block Buster Senior used to be just Block Buster until a couple of years ago, when Junior showed up. Anyone could tell he wasn't much more than a kid under the mask and skin-suit uniform. Lots of people speculated if the two were actually father and son as their names suggested, or if they instead had a mentor/apprentice relationship. Whatever their story, Celia thought they took a little too much joy in inflicting property damage.

And if they *were* father and son—how had Junior managed to inherit his father's power? Why him and not her?

Most of the coverage focused on the beloved Olympiad, who'd been protecting Commerce City for twenty-five years now. One of the stations had exclusive footage of Captain Olympus and the Bullet, the fourth member of the Olympiad, tearing open the warehouse that housed the Baxter Gang's main headquarters.

The camera could only follow the Bullet's progress by tracking a whirlwind that traveled from one end of the building to the other, tossing masked gunmen aside in a storm of dust and debris. Guns flew from their hands and spiraled upward, shattering with the force of movement. It was all the Bullet, Robbie Denton, moving faster than the eye could see, disrupting one enemy attack after another in mere seconds.

Captain Olympus—the Golden Thunderbolt, most powerful man in the world—wore black and gold, and tore down walls with his will. He stood before his target, braced, arms outstretched, and created a hammer of force that crumpled half the building.

Celia's hands started shaking. The warehouse district was across town. He wasn't anywhere near here. The news reporter on the scene raved on and on about the spectacular scene, the malevolence of the criminals, the courage of the Olympiad.

She found the remote and turned off the TV.